HIGHEST PRAISE FOR JOVE HOMESPUN ROMANCES:

"In all of the Homespuns I've read and reviewed I've been very taken with the loving rendering of colorful small-town people doing small-town things and bringing 5 STAR and GOLD 5 STAR rankings to the readers. This series should be selling off the bookshelves within hours! Never have I given a series an overall review, but I feel this one, thus far, deserves it! Continue the excellent choices in authors and editors! It's working for this reviewer!" —*Heartland Critiques*

We at Jove Books are thrilled by the enthusiastic critical acclaim that the Homespun Romances are receiving. We would like to thank you, the readers and fans of this wonderful series, for making it the success that it is. It is our pleasure to bring you the highest quality of romance writing in these breathtaking tales of love and family in the heartland of America.

And now, sit back and enjoy this delightful new Homespun Romance . . .

LOVING HONOR
by Christina Cordaire

Also by Christina Cordaire . . . her acclaimed Homespun Romance *Forgiving Hearts*:

"Warm and wonderful . . . a valuable lesson of forgiveness and the power of love." —*Romantic Times*

"A beautiful slice of Americana that captures the ecstasy of healing souls, the glory of redemption, and the beauty and purity of love . . . brilliantly and realistically done."
—*Affaire de Coeur*

"Consider this a must on your reading list." —*Rendezvous*

Titles by Christina Cordaire

HEART'S DECEPTION
DARING ILLUSION
LOVE'S TRIUMPH
PRIDE'S FOLLY
FORGIVING HEARTS
BELOVED STRANGER
LOVING HONOR

LOVING HONOR

CHRISTINA CORDAIRE

Margaret Reed Crosby Memorial Library

PEARL RIVER LIBRARY SYSTEM
900 GOODYEAR BOULEVARD
PICAYUNE, MS 39466

JOVE BOOKS, NEW YORK

If you purchased this book without a cover, you should be aware that this book is stolen property. It was reported as "unsold and destroyed" to the publisher, and neither the author nor the publisher has received any payment for this "stripped book."

LOVING HONOR

A Jove Book / published by arrangement with
the author

PRINTING HISTORY
Jove edition / August 1995

All rights reserved.
Copyright © 1995 by Christina Strong.
This book may not be reproduced in whole
or in part, by mimeograph or any other means,
without permission. For information address:
The Berkley Publishing Group, 200 Madison Avenue,
New York, New York 10016.

ISBN: 0-515-11684-X

A JOVE BOOK®
Jove Books are published by The Berkley Publishing Group,
200 Madison Avenue, New York, New York 10016.
JOVE and the "J" design are trademarks
belonging to Jove Publications, Inc.

PRINTED IN THE UNITED STATES OF AMERICA

10 9 8 7 6 5 4 3 2 1

To my darling daughter for all her help and to all my wonderful friends—to Mark who discovered I wrote for pleasure and introduced me to Sandy who took me to VRW where a new world opened for me; to my critique group and Mary B. who with Wendy Haley kept pushing me to write a historical; and most of all to Gail, dear friend and editor, who believes in me—my heartfelt thanks!

LOVING HONOR

Chapter 1

Reese stared out the window at the Texas desert, his stomach in a tight knot. More than anything else in life he wanted this assignment.

Because of him his best friend was dead. It was his right to avenge him.

He felt the muscle in his jaw jump and sharply called himself to order. He would *make* the colonel choose him, but appearing before him as a dark, avenging angel wasn't the way.

"Captain Rivers, the colonel will see you now."

Spinning away from the window, a hard-eyed Captain Reese Rivers of the U.S. Army marched through the door held for him by the corporal.

"Well, Rivers?"

"You're sending a man to investigate the payroll ambush at English Bend, I want to be that man."

"Forget it, Rivers. I'm not sending one of my best fighting men."

"I want to go."

The colonel sat back in his chair and considered the man in front of him carefully. "Are you sure revenge isn't your motive?"

Rivers shrugged casually, his stomach tightening another notch. "It's as good a motive as any." He kept his expression cool.

"Jacob Garner led that patrol. He was a friend of yours, wasn't he?" He watched the captain's face closely.

Reese made his decision. "My best friend, sir." Unconsciously he stood straighter.

The colonel let him wait. Finally he asked quietly, "And you think you'd do a better job than a man who was more . . . detached?"

"I *know* I'd do a better job than any man alive." This time he couldn't stop the muscle that jumped along his jaw, but he managed to keep his voice calm.

The colonel saw the fierce light that flared momentarily in Rivers's eyes. After a brief battle with his common sense, he burst out, "Oh, what the hell. You won't be any damn good to me here if I don't let you go." He aimed and shook a forefinger at the man on the other side of the desk. "I'll give you two months. Then I want you back whether or not you're successful." He glared at his subordinate from under bushy, gray brows. "Two months. And don't mess up the trail so bad that the man I send to replace you can't unearth the men responsible."

"You won't have to send another man. I'll get them, sir. You can count on it." Rivers saluted smartly and stalked to the door. As he closed it behind him, the raw-boned man at the desk heard a hasty, "And thank you, sir!"

He stuffed his cigar back into his mouth and muttered in the direction of the door, "You're welcome, you young hellcat."

Wearily he pulled the never-ending stack of papers back toward him. "See that you get your carcass back here in one piece." He lifted his gaze to the rough surface of the door Rivers had just closed. His sigh sounded more like a rumbling growl. "And God pity the men you're after."

Hundreds of miles away in Richmond, Virginia, Amanda Harcourt stood frowning at the trunks that half filled her bedroom. "This is ridiculous, Polly. We can't take this much. We have too far to travel."

"All the more reason to pack everything you might need, my lady."

"Oh, Polly. How many times must I tell you that titles are not used in the United nor the Confederate states."

"Oh, really, *miss*? Seems like I heard of a German baron or two around. Not to mention our own English—"

"Polly!" Amanda was used to the insolence, but tired of the discussion. Her maid, even though she felt it a distinct blow to her own importance to do so, would yield to her employer's wishes. Amanda just wished she would comply less grudgingly.

She moved to peer into the nearest trunk. "I shall not be needing ball gowns." She smiled to think of how many of her ball gowns she had offered to Confederate brides. Few had been accepted, though, as tradition required that dresses as well as veils be handed down for generations. Those few occasions when Amanda's gowns had been worn by blushing belles to meet their handsome gray-clad husbands-to-be at the altar had given her a great deal of pleasure. "Nor any of these, Polly." She pointed to a splendid array of satins and taffetas that spilled like a fabric rainbow out of a second trunk, dresses too fine to be worn in the war-deprived city.

"Truly, Polly. I am going to Texas to care for my niece. I shall need practical clothes to wear on Coronet. Keep in mind that Coronet is a ranch, not a London park. Now please stop worrying about my consequence and pack so that I may be comfortable." She tried to keep the irritation out of her voice.

"Ah, my lady . . . miss, I know you're that upset about your poor sister-in-law. Such a terrible loss." She patted Amanda's shoulder with the comforting familiarity of a long-employed servant. "Forgive me for adding to your troubles with my clumsy packing. I'll put my mind to it in earnest now. You just go along and see to other things."

Amanda spoke around the lump in her throat, "Yes, quite right. I shall go check with Manderley about our travel arrangements."

She used the excuse to flee the room and on her way down the stairs stopped on the landing to stem her tears. Already she missed her cheerful sister-in-law dreadfully. She had only to close her eyes, and Faith's merry face was clear in her memory.

The petite girl had won David's heart the instant he had seen her. She'd been little more than a girl, the pampered daughter of a duke, but she had known what she wanted, and had captivated David with her first smile. And she had won his youngest sister's heart, her own, very shortly thereafter.

Tears fell freely as Amanda bowed her head there at the window on the landing. How she missed her. Amanda achingly remembered the wonderful times Faith had always troubled to make for her. Now she was going to have an opportunity to repay some of her kindness. Now she was going to try to make wonderful times for Faith's daughter. But, oh, how very hard it was going to be, knowing that Faith was not there to share those good times with them.

She lifted her head and gazed solemnly at her reflection in the window's glass. She must get a firm hold on herself. How could she ever console her brother if she lost control of her own emotions like this at the smallest expression of sympathy?

Amanda was hot and tired. The humidity in this Texas port was high, it felt even worse than in Richmond.

She felt as if she could actually sense in her hair particles of the coal dust that had flown in great clouds from the twin stacks of the steamer.

Not wanting to present a travel-worn picture, she

straightened her spine and made sure her expression was one of calm anticipation. Inside, she was so eager to see her brother's face, to be sure that he was truly all right, it was all she could do not to hang out over the rail.

"Oh, Polly. How do I look?"

"You look lovely, Lady Amanda." Polly wasted no time on the obvious. Her voice took on a note of complaint. "I hope none of this confounded grit got into our trunks, my la . . . miss." Polly swatted at the fine layer of black soot on the shoulder of her own sturdy gray cloak. "Ah, look now. Just see how it leaves a terrible black smudge."

She scowled and pursed her lips. "Thank heaven I didn't brush at yours, miss! I'd have ruined that lovely blue cape, and think what a pity that would be, matching your eyes like it does." She sighed. "Shaking it off is going to be the only way. Filthy stuff! Glad enough I am that we didn't have sparks land on us and burn holes in us like that poor Mrs. Kandry did."

Amanda listened with only half an ear. Anxiously scanning the crowds on the wharf, she searched for her brother.

Her eyes passed over and then returned, in spite of her eagerness to locate David, to the tall figure of a rather unkempt man who stood slightly away from the crowd. Broad shouldered and lean, he was completely at ease. There was no hint that he shared the eager anticipation of the rest of those waiting. He was the only person on shore not looking at the steamer as it was made fast. Instead, he seemed to be searching for someone on the wharf.

Her mind on the rugged man in rough clothing, she answered her maid absently, "I'm sorry to hear that about Mrs. Kandry, Polly." She wrenched her attention from the man in the crowd below with an effort. "At least we are fortunate the new steamers are able to keep to their schedules. You must admit there is no pleasure in being becalmed for days, as we were the last time we sailed from England."

What had drawn her eye to him? His posture, perhaps? He had a military bearing, she noticed. That was oddly at variance with his careless appearance.

Even as she mentally voiced the thought, however, the subject of it slouched against the wall. As his lithe frame adjusted easily to the support of the wall, she discarded the idea that he was a soldier.

He seemed to be scanning the crowd around him, just as she was. No doubt that was what had set him apart. While everyone else down there was eager to find the person they had come to meet, he seemed entirely uninterested in the steamer and its passengers.

She drew a quick breath as, seeming to sense her gaze, he lifted his head and stared straight at her. Smiling slightly, he lifted one booted foot to rest on a keg in front of him, and moved his shoulders sinuously. He reminded her of some great cat, watching for prey. But he was only settling his shoulders more comfortably against the wall, for all the world as if he were making ready for a long and leisurely perusal of her own person.

Quickly Amanda averted her face, one eyebrow lifting scornfully. What a lout, to stare at a lady in such an obvious manner. She was both offended and strangely disappointed, as if somehow she knew him and had expected better of him.

She was rewarded for turning away from him with a glimpse of her brother's blond head. He was just below her, almost at the very edge of the wharf.

David held his hat in his hand, and when she looked his way, he waved it to attract her notice. A grin flashed white in his sun-bronzed face.

Amanda felt tensions she hadn't even been aware she'd had drain from her. "David." She mouthed his name, certain he'd be unable to hear if she called it, and blew him a kiss. She felt herself relax. She was safe again with her cherished brother. And, she admitted, she was relieved to be able to see that he was safe, too.

Now she could begin her self-imposed task of seeing to him and to her niece, Laura. Now she could start repaying Faith, in a very small way, for the great happiness she had brought to her brother. She returned his delighted smile and felt better than she had in days.

From his place against the building, Reese saw the beautiful blonde's shoulders relax. The stocky woman with her, obviously her servant, was grinning from ear to ear, as well. It looked to him like a family reunion of some sort.

For a moment, he let himself appreciate the picture the slender young woman made standing against the sky at the rail of the ship. Even though he refused to let one influence his life, he still appreciated beautiful women.

Sternly he returned his attention to the matter at hand. He'd come to find Jacob's killer. Nothing was going to distract him. He intended to avenge the death of his best friend.

He followed the beautiful woman's gaze to the tall, slender man at whom she was so radiantly smiling. Automatically he marked the man's position there below her.

Suddenly the hair at the back of his neck prickled. Something about the man and those around him sounded an alarm in his mind.

He yanked the brim of his hat lower. As the first passengers crowded down the gangplank, he pushed himself away from the wall, and threaded cautiously into the crowd.

His eyes casually assessed everyone. He was looking them over, searching for a group of soldiers, even as the alarm in his head clamored that he'd found them.

He'd been informed that the lone survivor had indicated the attack on the payroll detail had been a military one, so Reese had known he sought soldiers, not common bandits.

That had narrowed his search considerably. If Jacob's murderers had been bandits, he might have had a task impossible to accomplish in the time his colonel had given him. Military men were another matter entirely.

The fact that Texas men of a Southern persuasion didn't wear their uniforms here—not with Union garrisons all over the Confederate state—hadn't hidden the difference between military men and civilians. That difference always stood out. He'd spotted it easily.

He'd been pretty sure that all he had to do was find a number of disciplined men that seemed to hang together. It had turned out to be easier than he'd expected.

As the crowd on the wharf thinned, a group of six men remained. One of them, the man at whom the beauty had smiled, stood easily erect at the front of the little group. A second stood just behind him and a little to his left, and the other four casually in two pairs to the rear.

Reese grinned to himself. They lacked only their uniforms—cavalry unless he missed his guess, judging by their long legs and slim hips.

Could it really be this easy? He had to stifle an exultant laugh. He'd only been searching for three days.

He followed the direction of the leader's gaze. The man was smiling up at the girl on the deck. Reese saw she'd sensibly elected to wait until the rush down the gangplank was over. With her maid, she stood confidently at the rail, smiling fondly back at the tall blond man on the wharf.

Same color hair, same eyes. Probably related, then, instead of man and wife. Reese ignored the little flare of satisfaction that came with his deduction. He frowned. This was no time to get interested in a woman. He moved closer to the group on the wharf.

From the fast-emptying deck, Amanda caught the rough man's movement out of the corner of her eye. Even at this distance, she could see that his dark brows were drawn down in a frown.

Then her attention returned to Polly, who moved toward the gangplank like a battering ram to clear a path for her.

"Come along, milady. Come along." Amanda suppressed a chuckle to see people spring out of her maid's way, and followed her through to the opening in the rail.

Because David was waiting for her at the foot of the gangplank, it was all Amanda could do not to use its incline as an excuse to run the last few feet and fling herself into his arms. Instead, exercising the control trained into her, she walked sedately up to him and presented her cheek for his brotherly salute.

The warmth in her eyes and voice gave the lie to her cool control. "Oh, David, I am so *glad* to see you."

Stepping back, her hands in his, she surveyed him carefully. He endured her scrutiny, smiling broadly.

How worn he looked, she thought. There were new lines in his face, and his eyes held the deep shadow of a sorrow too great to be borne.

Fervently she hoped her presence would erase some of the strain from his face. She saw an almost fresh scar across the right side of his forehead, and her heart skipped a beat. She'd seen enough of such wounds in the hospital in Richmond to recognize it as the angry path of a bullet. Another inch and . . . She couldn't bear to finish her thought.

David chuckled. "Hallo, Amanda." Then he crushed her in a bear hug. Stepping back he said quietly, "How glad *I* am that you have come."

Quick tears burned in her eyes. She loved him so, this quiet older brother of hers.

Because David and she were so close, she knew how much his beloved wife, Faith, had meant to him. Together Faith and David had had all that the world offered. Now that he'd lost her Amanda could only guess at the pain he must feel.

But he still had Laura. Thank God Laura had not succumbed to the awful illness that had taken her mother.

The man immediately behind David stepped forward, interrupting their reunion, cutting off the silent flow of communication between brother and sister. "I hope you remember me, Miss Amanda."

She turned away from David reluctantly, a cool smile on her lips. "Of course, Mr. Webster. It has not been that long since you accompanied my brother to our home in Richmond. It is nice to see you again." She tried not to mind the interruption. The man was only being polite, after all.

Reese Rivers was close enough to hear the exchange. The name of the Confederate capital filled in another piece of his puzzle. Confederate as well as military. That about cinched it. These men would need careful investigating.

The girl's accent threw him for a split second. Then he remembered the Confederates had many sympathizers in England.

Indeed, for a while, President Lincoln had feared England might even enter the war as the South's ally. They might have, too, except for Lee's illness and the errors in judgment it had brought on at Gettysburg.

He fought down the temptation to feel as if his job were all but done. The cool part of his mind that demanded he act in careful justice must rule. He would have to be absolutely sure that these were the men he was after. Only then could he yield to the savage side of him that would avenge Jacob's death.

Somehow he had to find a way to attach himself to the group. He drew back from the men and the two women who had come off the steamer. He didn't want to be noticed before he had decided on a course of action.

As David and his party moved away, Amanda looked around. "Where is Laura?" Her voice was suddenly anxious. Anxiety filled her eyes as well. "She is not ill, is she?" She tried not to snatch at her brother's sleeve.

David responded quickly to the concern in his sister's voice. "No, my dear, she is bursting with health." He smiled. "In fact, that's why she's not here to greet you." His smile widened to a grin. "Her exuberance made her unable to wait any longer than the first ten minutes or so that we were here, and she went to visit a friend."

He laughed, love for his only child lighting his face. "We'll pick her up on the way out of town."

Amanda saw that his laughter had become tinged with sorrow, and even as she returned his smile, her heart went out to him. How long, she wondered, would it take to get over a loss such as the one David had sustained? Surely even a long lifetime would not be enough.

Lost in her sympathy for her brother, she didn't notice that the man who had attracted her notice earlier was discreetly following them.

Chapter 2

They did indeed add Laura to their small caravan as they left the town—quite spectacularly. Amanda watched apprehensively as the child came, charging fearlessly, braids flying.

She galloped her pony out of her friend's front yard, waving frantically to her aunt and father with one hand. Over her shoulder she screeched, "It was fun, Mary! See you soon," and flapped her other hand in the direction of her friend. All the while her heels drummed against her pony's sides.

The pony seemed used to such behavior. He came pounding on, reins lying knotted on his neck, with only an occasional flick of an ear backward to check on his rider. Soon Laura's friend and her house were obscured by the cloud of yellow dust kicked up by his flying hooves.

Amanda sat smiling and a little shocked, waiting for her niece. One thing she could do for Faith was readily apparent. She could teach her daughter to ride with a little more dignity.

Then Laura was there beside her, pulling her pony up to match the more sedate pace of the buckboard. Before anyone knew what she was doing, the ten-year-old girl stepped from her stirrup to the low wooden side of the buckboard and flung herself into it, leaving her pony to trail behind them.

Laughing and out of breath, she knelt in the bed of the long wagon and threw her arms around Amanda from behind. She ignored completely Polly's, "Gracious Lord, child! You'll kill yourself!"

Amanda twisted around in her seat and caught the girl to her, filled with joy at seeing her again, at finding her safe. With a self-mocking laugh, she realized she was half-afraid that if she let her go, her brother's daughter would succeed in her endeavor to do away with herself. Obviously it was going to take her a little while to adjust to Laura's harum-scarum ways.

"Laura, dearest." She held her away at arm's length. "I hope you will have a little more regard for your aunt's peace of mind in the future. You have quite frightened me out of my wits."

Laura sat back on her heels, grinning at her aunt in appreciation of the great compliment her words had been. She could easily see her Aunt Amanda was far from being scared out of her wits. She asked, "Papa, is it all right if I come onto the seat with you two?"

David told her to come up, and she scrambled, all long legs and youthful clumsiness, onto the bench between Amanda and her father. She planted a hasty kiss on her father's cheek, then spun the other way to say, "Golly, Aunt Amanda. I'm so glad you're here."

"Hmmm. So am I." She tried to look sternly at Laura. "It looks as if I am just in time to save you from becoming a wild Indian."

"But you won't, will you, Auntie?" Laura hugged her fiercely. "I want you to be a wild Indian with me so we can ride all over and I can show you all the things there are to see."

"Your Aunt Amanda is a lady, Laura." Her father's voice was grave. "I am sure she will be happy to help you to be a lady, too."

Amanda looked into the child's eager face, wishing she

could deny ever having been raised to be ladylike in the face of her brother's dreadful pronouncement. "Yes," she said, and leaned down to whisper to Laura. "But we don't have to be ladies *all* the time."

Laura beamed at her. "That's wonderful," she whispered. "What fun we shall have. Oh, I am so truly glad you have come."

The light in the child's face dimmed. Her expression changed and became wistful. "It has been rather . . . lonely"—she gulped and her eyes filled with tears—"lately."

Amanda's heart pained her. There was nothing she could say that would make the girl's loss easier to bear. No word of comfort ever breathed could have the power to console a child for the loss of a mother.

Because she was bereft of speech, she could only hug Laura tightly to her side. After a moment, she bent her head down to rest lightly on top of the child's.

From the ridge that paralleled the trail along which they were traveling, a lone horseman watched. His stern face softened for just an instant as he saw the woman embrace the child.

Then he remembered his friend and his own implacable purpose for trailing this little caravan, and his face became as hard and set as a mask carved in stone.

David's right-hand man, Webster, rode up beside Amanda. "If you'll excuse my absence, Miss Amanda, I'll ride ahead and see if Cookie has gotten things ready for your luncheon."

Amanda looked at him in bewilderment. When he grinned, she nodded permission, and turned to David for an explanation as Webster galloped off ahead. "Luncheon?"

David chuckled. "We thought you'd last longer if we got you up out of this springless buckboard for a while and got a hot meal down you."

Amanda smiled. "How very thoughtful."

Laura said, "We can take a walk, too. That's the best way to get your backside over being numb."

While Amanda stared at her niece torn between shock and laughter, Polly cried, "Well, I never!" and David gasped, "Laura!"

Laura blushed fiercely, but declared stoutly, "Well, it's true!"

Before her brother could mount an attack, Amanda threw herself into the breech. "A walk certainly does sound lovely." She gave the child's hand a squeeze, and said, "Oh, David. What is that little blue flower there along the base of that hill?"

"Well done, sister mine." David grinned good-natured surrender, and told her, "That's a Texas bluebell. This part of the state seems to be full of them. Pleasant little flower." He was smiling down at his daughter as he spoke.

Laura was quick to cement her reprieve. "I apologize for being indelicate, Papa."

From behind them, Polly made a soft, approving sound.

"Look! Smoke! That means somebody's got a fire up ahead. I'll bet that's lunch. I'm starved." Laura stood up to see better.

Amanda pulled her back down to the seat. "I thought we were agreed that you would cease placing undue stress on my nerves, niece."

"Oh. Sorry." She managed to keep her expression contrite, but she couldn't help sniffing the light breeze to see if she could determine what Cookie was fixing for them.

Amanda smiled fondly at her brother over Laura's head. It was good to be coming back to the ranch. It was the place she loved above all others. Even above Kennerley, her birthplace and ancestral home.

Here at the ranch she was her own person. She was free of the constraints and responsibilities of her noble name and of English society's expectations. Here she could be just plain Miss Amanda Harcourt. No one who had not been born to be called your ladyship could ever understand how she reveled in that.

She took a deep breath of freedom. With it came the scent of the mesquite cook fire and something delicious being prepared over it. Turning her head she looked full into her brother's eyes and smiled.

David understood.

Her precious brother loved this wild land, too. Their grandfather had sent them to look after family interests during this war between brothers that echoed the earlier rebellion—the War for American Independence. When he'd sent her to the Richmond town house and him to the ranch, David had embraced the cause of Southern freedom.

Because he had embraced the cause Texas espoused, he'd served in the Confederate States Army. Gallantly, he had fought in a company of Texas cavalry. Wounded, he had come home to English Bend to receive the gravest wound of all. He had come home to find his beloved wife, Faith, dying.

Still he stayed here, not only in obedience to his grandfather, but also under Confederate orders to stay here on the ranch for a while, though Amanda was not told what they were. He was pleased to remain, for, like Amanda, he relished his freedom, glad to stretch it out to escape for that much longer the strictures, pomp, and ceremony that awaited him at home in England.

Only there was no escape for David. Unlike her, Amanda knew, David must eventually return permanently to England. David was inescapably heir to their grandfather's earldom since their father was dead.

She shook her mind clear of her thoughts as David drew the team to a halt. Laura clambered down like a little monkey.

Webster walked over quickly to help Amanda down. Placing strong hands around her waist, he swung her easily to the ground. "This will make a nice break for you, I hope." He smiled easily down at her, admiration plain in his eyes. His hands lingered on her waist for longer than was acceptable as he told her, "We're more than halfway to the ranch."

"Thank you," she said, acknowledging his assistance. She sought for another bit of conversation, but could come up with nothing. It would hardly do to tell him she knew where she was, and that they were, in fact, a little *less* than halfway to the big house that served Coronet Ranch as headquarters.

She looked at Webster from the corner of her eye as he escorted her toward the cook fire. Tall and handsome as he was, he'd always struck her as a man who was perhaps a bit too sure of himself around the ladies. Nothing unusual in that, of course. Most handsome Southerners had a way with women, and Webster's cool blond looks were sure to turn feminine heads.

Amanda, however, had no intention of letting him, or any other man, turn hers. She hoped he didn't decide to practice his charm on her. That would make things tedious.

She was here to help David. She was certainly not interested in forming an attachment for a man in this country. She couldn't help it, she had the typical Englishwoman's preference for the quiet manner of Englishmen. Americans had always struck her as . . . flamboyant, somehow.

She threw a rueful glance to where Laura had skipped up to the cook. Even her precious niece, the product of two very proper English people, was somewhat rambunctious and larger than life.

It must be something about the country itself—something new and raw and almost brawling about it as it stretched and grew and suffered growing pains—that turned out people who refused to be compliant copies of a pattern-card model.

Individuals. That was it. They were all such individuals—except perhaps for the "society" in some of the larger cities. There, at least, people made an effort to conform.

But not out here. Out here, they were all—she borrowed a word from the cattlemen of the area—mavericks. Her niece was not the least among them.

She sighed as she smiled. It looked as if her self-appointed task were turning into rather a handful of a job.

"Aunt Amanda! Look. There are some bluebells."

Amanda looked over to where Laura pointed. Beyond the cooking fire, at the base of the low cliff that formed the back of the shallow canyon, grew a profusion of the lovely blue flowers.

"Com'on. Let's go pick some." Laura took off in a flash, got halfway to the base of the hill, turned, and ran back for her aunt.

Amanda took her eagerly offered hand. Beginning her task of making more of a lady of Laura, she sedately refused to be drawn along willy-nilly toward the patch of blue.

Laura sighed and settled down to a walk. She cut her eyes at her companion. "I hope this isn't a portend of the way you're going to approach our future adventures."

Amanda threw back her head and laughed, delighted. "Portent," she corrected automatically, even as her laughter died. When her bonnet's brim had lifted with the movement of her head, the rim of the cliff behind the hill to her right had come into view.

On it stood a tall, dark horse. She could only see the horse and its rider as a silhouette against the bright Texas sky, but she knew instantly that the rider was the rough-looking man she had noticed at the wharf.

She knew him by the way he carried his head. Somehow, unerringly, she knew him by the way he sat his horse, even though she had never seen him mounted before.

She felt her cheeks flame. Was she annoyed to be spied

on? Or was she annoyed that in her heart she knew so readily who the man was?

She lowered her face immediately, pretending not to have noticed him. Her whole body was astonishingly aware of his presence there above her.

She moved carefully into the mass of bluebells, for the first time in her life conscious of each separate action necessary to move with grace. Never had she felt at such a disadvantage as she was now.

How vexing! Anger toward the unknown on the clifftop rose in her.

Laura looked at her oddly. "Are you okay, Auntie?"

Amanda realized she had compressed her lips and was all but gritting her teeth. She shook off her strange reaction.

It was a free country, after all. The man could ride anywhere he chose. Wasn't that what she herself most valued here in this vast land?

"Yes, dear." Even as she reassured Laura, she chided herself for her foolishness.

She had been stared at all her life in England, stared at by crowds of people because she was the granddaughter of an Earl as well as because she was beautiful. Why should the steady regard of one lone man cause her this tumult?

Fearing this unaccustomed confusion might betray her into an awkward step, to steady herself she lightly touched a shaded ledge of rock that jutted out near the flowers.

There was a whir. A spurt of dust and rock erupted from the ledge. Powdered rock peppered her. An instant later, she heard the sound of a gunshot.

David and the knot of men gathered at the fire waiting for Cookie to relinquish cups of coffee spun as one man toward the two standing among the bluebells.

Webster shouted, "That bastard's shooting at the women!" His gun leapt to his hand and he snapped two shots toward the rim of the cliff.

David threw down his cup and sprinted toward his daughter and sister.

One of the other men drew and aimed up at the man who had fired at his boss's women, but held his fire. The man on the rock above was already sliding bonelessly from his saddle.

A sharp whinny rang out into the startled silence. The intruder's horse lowered its head to nuzzle its fallen rider.

Amanda held Laura in a death grip, her own back turned protectively to the source of the gunfire.

David arrived in a rush. "Are you all right? Oh, God, Laura, Amanda. Tell me you're all right!"

"We're fine, dear." Amanda, amazed at her own calm voice, pushed Laura away from her to look at her anxiously. "You are all right, aren't you, dearest?"

She had to be. They both had to be. Amanda knew David could not bear another blow just now.

And she knew with a stunning blaze of clarity that *she* could not bear the thought that the man on the cliff wished to harm then. Not when, even at a distance, her very heart had recognized him. . . . She was startled to stillness by that realization, appalled.

Everyone around her had exploded into action.

David's men had thrown themselves back into their saddles and were punishing their horses up the steep grade to reach the perpetrator of the outrage, cursing as they spurred.

The horses leapt and scrambled, grunting with the effort to scale the sharply rising surface.

Amanda watched as they reached the big, black horse waiting beside the fallen man. With a gasp she saw the way they yanked the half-conscious man to his feet and shook him.

One of the men drew back his fist to smash their prisoner in the face.

David shouted, "No!" in a voice that had rallied these

same men on many a battlefield, and the man reluctantly lowered his hand.

Amanda swayed with the force of an enormous surge of relief. Fear for the wounded man filled her, taking her breath.

"Bring him down." David commanded harshly. "And find an easier way."

As the men and horses disappeared from the rim of the low cliff, David reached out and swept Laura into one arm and Amanda into the other. Together they walked away from the forgotten bluebells.

With them held to his side as if he would never let them go, David took them back to the campfire.

Chapter 3

Dust rose in a heavy cloud, marking the path David's men had chosen down a gentler slope from the top of the cliff. The roiling cloud of yellow dust was clearly visible for minutes before the men rode into view.

As Amanda watched, they appeared, galloping toward her from around a rocky outcropping. Webster in the lead, they bore with them the limp figure of the man who had fired the shot at Laura and her.

In obeying David's order they may have found a way down from the cliff that was easier for the horses, but the man they had taken prisoner fared little better for it. Thrown carelessly across the saddle of his horse, he jounced, face down and arms hanging limp, with every stride.

As they came closer, Laura said in an awed whisper, "He's bleeding."

Then the men were there, swirling to a halt beside the campfire. Webster seized the unconscious man by the back of his shirt and hauled him off his horse.

He tumbled loosely to the ground and lay there, unmoving.

With a snakelike swing of his head, the stranger's big, black horse snapped at Webster, his huge teeth narrowly missing the man's hastily withdrawn hand.

Webster went for his gun.

David snapped, "Webster!"

With a mighty effort, his second-in-command slammed his pistol back into the holster.

The horse backed away flicking his ears and snorting. His eyes rolled, showing the whites.

David ordered quietly, "Mason, see to this horse."

The man called Mason stepped forward and caught up the trailing reins. He stood quietly a moment, waiting for the horse to transfer its attention to him. Then he said in a low voice, "Easy, boy. Come on, now."

Mason didn't pull at him, he waited for the big stallion to decide to obey. After a moment's hesitation, the great beast dropped his head and reluctantly permitted himself to be led away.

Webster, free of the threat of the big black, reached down and grabbed the injured man's shirtfront. Before David could stop him, he'd slapped the man hard. His hand connected with the unconscious man's face twice, back and forth.

The man's eyes opened, and for a moment, Amanda saw in them pain and bewilderment. Then he focused on Webster's snarling face, and his own became shuttered.

"What the hell did you think you were doing, shooting at the women?" Webster's teeth grated.

"Snake," the wounded man managed. Contempt blazed from his eyes like blue flame. "Shot at a snake, you stupid son-of-a—"

"Watch your mouth!" Webster drew back a fist.

David clamped Webster's wrist in an iron grip. "That will do, Web!"

With a sound like a growl, Webster stepped away from the bleeding man.

The wounded man rested on an elbow. He was groggy, but he refused to fall back and lie helpless in the dirt before these men.

The group waited in silence as one of their number

walked back to the flowers. He was going to check the rocky ledge Amanda had placed her hand on.

"David. He's bleeding. Shouldn't you try to stop the blood?"

David ignored his sister, watching as his man reached the patch of bluebells and searched the rock ledge just above them.

"Oh, for heaven's sake!" Amanda wanted to hit somebody. Instead, she lifted her skirt and tore a strip off the hem of her petticoat.

Examining it quickly, she discarded it as not clean enough. It came as no surprise. It had dragged through the dust of the canyon here, and before that it had trailed across the tar and dirt of the dock.

She tore off another strip higher. As she folded it into a pad, she caught Webster looking with interest at the part of her skirt she had lifted. She shot him a venomous look, deliberately hiked her skirt up again and tore another, narrower strip from her petticoat with which to bind in place the pad she'd made.

Her assaulted emotions were not in such turmoil that she failed to realize that she was furious. She hoped Webster thought that the stolen glimpse of her ankles was ample reward for his having betrayed his gross lack of good manners.

Kneeling beside the wounded man, she began to tug at his blood-soaked shirt. She wanted to get his shirttail loose from his pants so that she could lift it to see his wound. She was so close to him, she could hear his teeth grate as he clenched them.

Amanda knew she wasn't squeamish. She'd discovered that about herself when she'd volunteered to help at the hospitals in Richmond. Knowing she was adding to this man's pain even as she tried to help him made her stomach churn, though.

"Amanda!" David was beside her instantly. "What are you doing?"

"I should think that would be obvious." Looking at him as if she could strike him, she told him, "I am doing what *any* decent person would do. I am coming to the aid of a wounded fellow human being."

The man in question looked as if he found the situation amusing. Her eyes widened when they met his mocking gaze. His attitude startled Amanda.

David looked momentarily stricken at his sister's reprimand, then his face closed. "You are right, of course." He took the pad she had made and looked up at one of his men.

Before he could tell the man to tend the freely bleeding wound, Amanda snatched the piece of her petticoat back. "Oh, no," she told him, "I've already seen how you and your men care for the wounded! I watched the way they brought him down from the cliff."

Webster burst out, "But he shot at you!"

David's man returned from where the bluebells grew at the back of the shallow canyon, where David had sent him to investigate the ledge upon which the stranger had fired. Amanda was spared voicing the scathing remark that came to her lips as every head turned toward him.

"No," the man announced to them all, contradicting Webster. "He shot this." He held up the thick, headless length of a large rattlesnake.

David was stunned. "Oh, my God." He took in the size of the snake and knew with terrifying certainty that if the rattler had struck his sister, she would have died.

Slowly, he turned to the man on the ground, his own face as pale as the wounded man's. "It would seem I owe you a debt of gratitude that goes beyond expression."

The prisoner-turned-savior glared his disgust at his white-faced captor. Then he ground his teeth together against a spasm of pain, groaned softly, and fainted, leaving them to their self-recriminations.

David turned to another of his men. "Take care of him while I make him a bed in the buckboard."

Reluctantly, Amanda surrendered the two pieces of her fine linen petticoat to the man and stepped aside. She stood watching, however, guarding against further rough treatment of the wounded man.

There was no need for her vigilance. To a man, the small group was chastened by the way they had treated someone who had obviously saved the life of one of their party.

As gently as if he handled a baby, Mason pulled the bloody shirt away to reveal the hole the bullet had made in the stranger's side. Blood seeped more slowly now, Amanda was relieved to see. She flinched slightly as Mason turned him to check for an exit wound and the unconscious man uttered a choked cry.

"It's clean. Bullet went right through. He's lucky," Mason said to no one in particular.

Amanda studied the man's face. The stubble of perhaps two days' growth of beard covered his lower face. His cheeks were lean and looked slightly gaunt, but she thought that was because his mouth was a little open rather than that he'd known hunger. She'd seen enough half-starved men, yes, and women, too, in the capital of the Confederacy, to recognize the look when she saw it. This man's body was lean and fit, not starved.

His teeth showed even and white through his parted lips, and he looked younger than she'd thought him—and much more vulnerable—as he lay there unconscious. The latter, she decided, wasn't hard to do. Awake, he had appeared self-possessed and dangerous in the extreme.

She remembered the defiance that had glinted in his clear blue eyes when he'd talked back to Webster, and felt envious admiration well up in her. She hoped that if ever she faced a hostile foe, she would prove as brave.

When David's men, their attitude toward the stranger having done an about-face, gently picked him up to put in the buckboard, she walked beside them. Amanda stood back and watched the expertise with which they lowered him to its flat bed.

The four men had learned to handle wounded in the crucible of the battlefield that was Virginia, she knew. This was the first time she had seen them do it. She was moved by the infinite care they took to settle him without causing him further pain.

He moaned once. It was a sound she was sure would never have escaped him if he'd been conscious. Then he was silent.

The men handling him looked concerned. "Easy now," Mason ordered.

How like men, she thought, *to wound, to maim, to kill, and then, when the heat of the moment passes, to care*. She shook her head. *Why is it that the caring always comes when it's too late to take back the wounding?*

She took a deep breath and spent it on a sigh. She would never understand them if she lived a hundred years. Hers was the nature of woman—to care, to nurture, to heal . . . never would she understand the nature of man.

Standing there, she accepted the idea that perhaps she was not meant to understand. Perhaps she was only to accept and temper, and most important of all, to balance their nature.

Rising on her tiptoes, she leaned over the low side of the buckboard to tuck the blanket the men had thrown over him up under his chin. "Keep him covered, please, Polly," she instructed her round-eyed maid. She knew how crucial keeping him warm could be.

Wondering how he would fare on the long drive to the ranch over such a rough trail, she sighed again and walked to where David waited to help her back to her seat. Climbing up, she settled her skirts and slipped her arm around a silent Laura.

No one spoke on this last half of their journey to the

ranch. The injustice of having gunned down an innocent man hung heavy over them. Shame and regret saddened the men's faces.

Their picnic had been left for the coyotes, their fire, dirt covered, to burn itself out. They were probably all hungry, but no one wanted to eat, so it didn't matter.

Amanda knew that David felt awful, and she felt awful for him. They had been close all their lives, and she could read his feelings easily.

She wished she could console him, but like the rest of the party, she could only listen to the occasional groan wrung from the wounded man by the jolting of the buckboard and wish the miles could somehow be miraculously shortened.

As the shadows lengthened, and the lights of the ranch-house came into view like tiny stars far away across a broad valley, fever took the wounded man.

Polly called softly, "I can't keep him covered, my la— Miss Amanda."

Stiff after sitting so long on the hard seat of the buckboard, Amanda stood cautiously, her hand on her brother's shoulder for safety, and moved with great care to go to the man tossing on the pallet behind them.

David steadied her, taking the driving reins in one hand while the other grasped her elbow. Laura helped by a solid clutch on her skirt near her hip after she had turned. She was grateful for their support, as her legs felt as if they belonged to someone else's body.

It was the matter of a moment, though, and she was settled beside him. She touched his forehead with an anxious hand. He was burning up.

She reached again for her petticoat and tore off another piece with which to bathe his forehead. The sound of a rider pressing close to the side of the wagon brought her head up.

Mason was there, a look of deep concern on his weathered face, holding his canteen out to her. Like most of the

LOVING HONOR

others, he'd been watching the man, and wishing there was something he could do to help.

Amanda smiled her thanks and took his canteen, rising to her knees and leaning over the stranger to do so. Settling back on her heels, she unscrewed the cap of the battered tin water bottle and saturated the linen cloth she'd ripped from her petticoat.

When she placed the cool, wet rag against his forehead, he flinched away from it as from a branding iron, and pushed weakly at her hand. "Nooo," he muttered. "Too hot. Too hot."

"No. It is not hot," Amanda told him matter-of-factly, as if some part of his mind might hear her. "It is cool water. It is you who are hot." She pressed a hand against his shoulder. "Now be still and let me help you."

She held the cloth firmly against his forehead in spite of his shaking his head. As she'd known he would, he stopped protesting when he registered the pain the movement caused him.

Fever as high as his would cause any head to ache.

She turned the cloth over when she gauged it to have been warmed to the point of uselessness by the heat radiating from his forehead. As she pressed the cooler side to his brow, she was deeply troubled by just how hot the side that had been against his brow had become.

Almost desperately, she looked across the wide valley to the slope on which the ranch house sprawled. Still the welcoming lights in the windows were mere pinpoints of brightness in the deep violet of twilight. They were still so far away.

David eased the brake on, and the horses began the long, gently sloped descent to the floor of the valley. Even the team drawing the buckboard seemed to realize the need to avoid jolting their passenger.

She looked around her at the faces of the men flanking

the wagon. Each expression ranged from serious to grim. They knew what fever meant in a wounded man.

The big black horse that Mason ponied beside him let out an earsplitting whinny, shoved forward, and tried to reach his head over the side of the wagon to touch his master.

His master tossed restlessly and muttered, "Thor. Good boy. Ahhh. Good boy." Then he fell silent.

The black horse was satisfied, though, and made no objection when Mason changed him to walk on the other side of his own mount.

Amanda was relieved. The horse had a wicked head for all that it was beautiful. She remembered the way the stallion had gone after Webster, and was thankful that his liquid brown eyes were filled only with anxiety for his wounded rider.

She removed the cloth again, and holding it over the side of the wagon, poured fresh water from the canteen on it. As she wrung it out, her gaze met with Mason's. His eyes smiled approval at her, warming his stern, soldier's face.

Amanda returned his smile. She felt as if she had just begun a new friendship.

She sat back again on legs that were fast going to sleep, and replaced the cool cloth on her patient's forehead. Pleased that he didn't flinch as badly as he had the first time, she was surprised to find the cloth was just as hot when she turned it as it had been the time before.

He was muttering now, disjointed fragments. Speaking to calm his horse seemed to have loosed a torrent of words. Most were incomprehensible, but she could understand "Look out!" and "Get down, men. Artillery on the ridge." And then, in a broken whisper, "Charge! Forward, boys. We'll . . ."

The words became incoherent babble and he struggled to rise, his eyes wide and staring at a scene that existed only in his mind. A single, shouted "Forward!" and he fell back and was still.

LOVING HONOR 31

Several of the men riding with them exchanged rueful grins. None of them were strangers to the order to charge.

Their attitude mystified Amanda. None of them seemed resentful that this man of whom they were taking such care just might have led charges against them and their fellows. After all, they'd no way of knowing to which army he had belonged.

He began to toss again, and Amanda signaled Polly to help her hold him down. Polly settled beside her and their combined strength soon had the fretful man subdued.

After what seemed an age, they reached the level floor of the valley. Amanda, through a haze of fatigue, heard David order, "Thompson, ride ahead and tell Rosa we're coming in with an injured man."

"Yessir!" Thompson wheeled his horse and plunged off in the direction of the ranch buildings.

As if acknowledging that they were almost home, Amanda finally permitted her shoulders to sag. It had been a frightfully long day, and she could no longer deny that she was exhausted.

Rosa, David's housekeeper and cook, would be ready for the wounded man. She could stop fretting about getting him into his bed. That knowledge comforted her.

Her gaze dropped to the man beside whom she sat and dwelt there. Who was he? Why had she been so strangely drawn to him from the moment the steamer docked?

Amanda wasn't prone to foolish, maidenly starts. She'd never been a dreamy girl, nor was she given to premonitions. She never had been. If she were, no doubt she would be weaving shining dreams about this heroic stranger.

So why, then, was she almost oppressed by the strong feeling that this man was going to prove unusually significant in her life?

Chapter 4

Rosa ran out of the house to meet them. Her smile radiated the warmth of her welcome. "Ah, *Señorita* Lady Amanda. *Bienvenida*." She ran down the two steps to the brick walk. "But you are so tardy. What has occurred to make you so late in arriving?"

She hurried around the buckboard to Amanda's side, neither expecting nor waiting for a reply. She clucked like a mother hen when Amanda tried to rise only to sink back again. "Wait, wait. You have been sitting too long on your legs."

She pressed Amanda back down, patting her maternally. Never missing a beat in the rhythm of patting Amanda, she turned to beam at her employer. "*Señor* David!"

David smiled and started to pass a sleepy Laura down to Rosa. Rosa gave Amanda a final pat, slipped an arm around the exhausted child and led her into the house.

David came carefully over the low back of the seat into the bed of the buckboard. His face was grave as he assessed the wounded man's condition.

Amanda saw that he moved stiffly. They were all travel sore. Even the men on horseback were dismounting as if the habitual spring in their movements had been used up by the long, slow ride. Having had to keep the horses to a walk for the sake of the wounded man had made the journey doubly wearying for all of them.

"Wait, Manda." David's voice was hoarse with fatigue.

Four of the men moved to the tail of the buckboard. Taking great care to support his body as they slid him free, they pulled the blankets on which the stranger lay off the flat bed of the buckboard.

Careful not to jolt him, they followed Rosa into the house. When they spoke it was in whispers.

Webster remained next to the buckboard. The only sign he gave that he noticed the obvious care the men were taking was a slight frown. Then all his attention focused on Amanda.

The wounded man's departure left room for David to assist his sister to her feet.

Seeing her unsteadiness, when she reached the end of the wagon, Webster swung her up in his arms.

"I can walk, Mr. Webster. Please put me down."

Webster laughed indulgently. "You'd fall, Amanda."

Amanda, annoyed by his attitude, asked again to be free.

Webster, with a superior, knowing smile, let her feet touch the ground while David jumped from the wagon bed.

Webster kept an arm around Amanda. The gesture was far too familiar, but Amanda found to her chagrin that it was necessary. Both her legs had gone to sleep in the length of time she'd had to sit on them.

Needles and pins shot through her legs with a viciousness that made her gasp. She couldn't even feel the ground under her feet.

She looked toward David. She was still angry with Webster for his earlier harsh treatment of the man she had already come to think of as her patient. She wanted to refuse his help. Even as she stood looking at her brother, her anger increased in direct proportion to the width of Webster's grin.

David looked so worn out, though, that she capitulated, and allowed Webster to carry her as far as the porch. Once there where she could hold on to something, she was determined to walk for herself.

"Thank you," she said firmly. "You may safely put me down now."

Webster lifted her higher against his chest. "Are you sure?" His deepened voice held a seductive note.

Amanda felt a sudden urge to pinch him. His mocking smile irritated her. She would walk if it took her all night!

"Quite sure, thank you." She made her voice deliberately cool and distant.

Webster looked faintly disconcerted.

Suddenly relenting, she bid him good night without the withering edge she'd had in her voice since the shooting this afternoon. She saw his relief at having regained her good graces, and was glad.

She still felt distinctly at odds with him over the rough way he'd dealt with the stranger, but life on a ranch was difficult enough without indulging in conflicts of personalities.

Cautiously moving up and down the porch on feet that seemed to delight in torturing her for sitting on them so long, she told herself that she must not measure men by women's standards. The two sexes were worlds apart. It was pointless to pretend any differently. She sighed as she admitted it.

An instant later, her sigh threatened to become a yelp as feeling rushed back into her legs. The blood returning to them set every prickling nerve screaming.

When she could walk without gritting her teeth and clinging to something, Amanda went inside. "Rosa?"

"*Sí, señorita?*"

"Where have you put him?"

"*Señor* David said to put him in the downstairs bedroom where I can check on him and still get my work done." She gestured in the direction of the bedroom that had been built off the family parlor. It was there for a purpose. Ranching was not without accidents that sometimes made stairs difficult.

Opening the door quietly, Amanda saw that the men had deposited their injured charge in the center of the huge four-poster there. Someone had placed pillows beside him as if he were an infant who might roll off the edge of the bed.

The thought of the man on the bed—this particular man—being treated like an infant brought a smile.

Then, even as she watched, he swung an arm out, groaned and tried to shift his position. Suddenly the pillows that the men had put there to keep him safe didn't seem so ludicrous.

She saw a ripple of pain tear through him, heard him gasp with it. With his other hand he was trying to push down the covers.

Amanda observed the flushed, dry-skinned look of him and decided that his fever had probably not gone down from the high point it had reached during the afternoon. Not even a little, it looked like.

As she stood watching, he began to roll his head back and forth on his pillow. His crisp dark hair contrasted sharply with the sun-bleached white of the linen pillowcase.

She moved to the bed and placed her hand on his forehead. He jerked away as if he would avoid her touch, but she stayed his pain-filled motion with a gentle pressure of her hand. Her guess had been right. If anything he was hotter than he had been in the buckboard.

Worry creased her smooth forehead. It was not a good sign. By now his temperature should have dropped just a little. The night was cooler, and most fevers were at their worst in late afternoon, she had learned.

Tired as she was, she realized she had no choice but to spend the night here at his bedside. She dragged the upholstered chair by the fireplace close to his bed. This way, she would be sure to know what he was doing, no matter how weary she was. With such a high fever, he could easily come to grief if unattended.

Turning to settle into the chair, she was surprised to find Rosa just behind her. "Oh, Rosa." In her anxiety over the man's fever, she greeted the woman like a lost relative. "I'm so glad you're here. I shall need some cool water and some of the linen hand towels, please."

"*Sí, señorita.*" Fussily adjusting the angle of the chair, she scolded, "This chair is too heavy for you, *señorita*. You must not try to do such things." With a smile to soften her scolding, she hurried away.

Amanda gazed at the man a long moment. She'd been right when she'd described him as ruggedly handsome when she'd first seen him there on the wharf. His features were too irregular to be called conventionally handsome. His chin was too strong, his nose, once perfect, she thought, had obviously been broken at some point in his life, and his eyebrows were just a touch heavier than the current idea of handsome. Amanda was surprised to find she much preferred his face to that ideal, however.

She touched the side of his neck where a pulse beat erratically. She felt woefully helpless. He needed competent medical attention, and there was none for half a day's hard ride. That was another penalty of life on a huge ranch. She sighed.

He kept pushing feebly at the covers, and she saw his chest was bare. Good, the men must have undressed him.

He'd be much more comfortable, and cooler, too, without the dark shirt and trousers he'd been wearing when he'd . . . She forced herself to think "shot the snake" instead of "been shot."

Rosa came into the room with a pitcher and basin set. Over one chubby forearm she carried a heap of the best linen hand towels.

"Thank you, Rosa." Relieved, Amanda was reaching for

a towel before Rosa had even set the bowl and pitcher down on the marble-topped washstand.

Rosa took the towel back from her. "*Señorita*, it is I who should stay here. You have traveled long, and are weary. Go to your bed and rest. I will keep watch over him."

"No!" Amanda startled herself, she spoke so sharply. Instantly she softened her voice. "I shall stay. It is my fault." To her chagrin, she felt tears fill her eyes. She looked away from Rosa to hide them. "I shall stay." Her next words seemed to be torn from her. "I must."

Sensing further protest would be useless, Rosa bit off her objections and looked speculatively at the slender girl for a long moment. She put a gentle hand on her shoulder and said in a soft voice full of wisdom, "I see. I understand." As if she conferred a special honor, she gave the linen towel back to Amanda.

Plunging the towel into water cool from the depths of the well, Amanda wrung it out, folded it, and laid it on the wounded man's brow.

He gasped and twisted as if to pull away, then moaned when the sudden movement caused him pain. Words poured from his cracked lips in an indistinct murmur.

He started up and seemed to search her face, holding her with the intensity of his stare. Then he frowned, bewildered by the pain that shot through his side. An instant later, his heavy lids covered his fever-bright eyes.

Amanda put a hand on his shoulder to press him back against the pillows. His skin was as dry as an autumn leaf and hot to her touch.

Over and over, her movements slowed by fatigue, Amanda changed the towel on his forehead, exhaustion pulling at her shoulders as she leaned over him.

Silently Rosa reentered the room. After watching a moment, she said, "You are very tired, *señorita*. You must rest. I will take care of the *señor*."

Wringing out yet another towel, Amanda ran it over his shoulders and chest.

"Oh, Rosa." She considered Rosa's kind offer. Why was she so reluctant to accept it? It was as if the man on the bed were her very own responsibility, and no one else's. Tiredly, she reasoned that he was. He'd been shot while saving her from the rattlesnake.

She realized that her thoughts were blurring. Her body was at that point beyond exhaustion where she almost floated in a senseless daze.

She gave up, and merely shook her head at Rosa. She would express her gratitude for Rosa's thoughtful offer tomorrow, when her mind was functioning again. Just now, she was determined to perform this service for the man who had undoubtedly saved her life.

She thought that he seemed to sense that she was trying to make him more comfortable. Hadn't he stopped muttering?

"Thank you, Rosa, but I must stay. He was shot saving my life, you know." She was thankful that she had to say no more. She was speaking to another woman, what she'd said was sufficient.

"*Sí, señorita. Yo comprendo.* Rosa understands." She left, closing the door softly.

Very early in the morning, Rosa returned to find Amanda asleep in the chair with her head pillowed on her arms on the bed. A pile of soggy towels filled the bowl she'd brought to the *señorita* last evening, and the man on the bed looked as if he were resting easier.

Gently Rosa touched Amanda's shoulder. When Amanda opened her eyes, Rosa ordered in a whisper, "To bed. You must now go to bed."

She wagged her finger, stemming Amanda's protest. "No, no. To bed. His fever will rise again in the afternoon.

You will see. That is when you will want to be here. So you must now rest."

Amanda bit back the refusal that rose to her lips. Finally, she nodded. Rosa was right, of course. She got up.

Leaning over the long, lean figure in the bed, she studied his face a moment. She saw with relief that the hectic color was gone, and he was breathing easier. His lips were softly closed this morning, his hands relaxed on top of the covers. He looked strangely vulnerable lying there motionless. Amanda felt an odd tenderness for him well up in her.

She touched his forehead. It was still too warm to suit her, but oh so very much cooler than when she had last felt it. She smiled in weary triumph. He was going to be all right, now, she knew.

Turning away from him yawning, she savored the comfort her relief brought her. She smiled up at Rosa, and let her lead her off to her bed.

Chapter 5

Laura rose early so that she could do as she pleased for just a little while before all the grown-ups started telling her what she should and should not do. Honestly! You would think that she was a complete baby, instead of almost eleven years old.

Why, didn't her father tell her once that the ancient Romans married at thirteen, conquered the world at nineteen, and died at twenty-one?

By that standard, her life was half over, for gosh sakes!

And still she got treated like a baby.

And talk about outnumbered! There were so many people telling her what was good for her that she felt like a Greek facing Claudius Dentatus at the battle of Thermopylae—overwhelmed.

She frowned at the comparison she had just drawn, then shrugged. That was the way it was for her. Her father was a scholar, and she was stuck with historical comparisons, and that was all there was to it.

Squinting up at her canopy, she stretched luxuriously, kicked off her covers, jumped out of the four-poster, and padded over to the washstand. Splashing her face with the tepid water in the washbowl there, she set about redoing her braids.

When she thought she was neat enough to pass muster with her father—he had picked up certain unfortunate ideas about the value of tidiness while he was in the army—she started downstairs.

She knew just where she was headed, and knew, too, that she'd better get there before Rosa came into the kitchen to start the cook fire in the big, black iron stove. Figuring she had only about a half hour before breakfast, she sneaked across the foyer to the family parlor.

The slightest noise carried clearly on the cool, early-morning air. Already she could hear sounds from the bunkhouse.

She glanced at a window. No light yet, but the minute there was, that darned old rooster would crow, and the whole ranch would explode into activity.

She hurried across the wide family parlor, and arrived at the downstairs bedroom door just as the first ray of the sun urged the ancient bird into action. He flew up onto a fence post and beat the stiffness out of his wings.

Slipping into the room, Laura put the boots she carried down on the floor next to the door. An instant later, she squeezed her eyes tight and winced at the loud, rusty-sounding crowing that split the peace of the dawn. Wishing it could shut out the raucous noise, she pulled the door softly closed behind her.

Tiptoeing across the room, she stood at the foot of the bed. She stared at the still form lying there for a long minute.

She liked what she saw. Here was a real man.

She had decided that yesterday when he'd been so sassy to Webster. It wasn't easy to act smart to somebody who had all the advantages. She knew that from watching the way the boys behaved at school.

She liked what she saw because he was pleasant to look at, too. She stood admiring his handsome, bearded face and the lean length of him.

To her, he seemed to embody the heroes about whom her father read to her. She could easily envision him in the short skirts Perseus and Ajax wore in her father's books. He had nice, long legs.

Being a child had certain advantages. One was that people ignored you for such long stretches that you were free to gather information by observation and make up your own mind about what you preferred long before your elders got around to telling you.

Laura knew what she liked. She preferred intelligence, agility, and elegance to what she considered stupidity, clumsiness, and bulk.

She'd made up her mind several years ago that she was going to fall in love with a tall, slender man like her father when the time came. Heavy bunches of muscle held no appeal for her.

When she'd told her Papa, he'd laughed and said that she was like her great-grandfather; she preferred Thoroughbreds to workhorses.

It wasn't true that every single man she'd seen who was heavy or muscular lacked intelligence, of course. She just didn't lean toward them in her personal preferences.,

She could lean toward this man. His defiance of Webster—to whom she couldn't seem to cotton for all the store her papa set by him—had ignited her imagination. If he could stand up to his captors like that when he was grievously wounded and half-unconscious, what wouldn't he be able to do when he was all well and himself again?

She hoped she'd be around to see. There was little enough out here on the ranch to occupy her active mind.

A sudden thought came to her. Maybe she could work out some way to keep this interesting person in her life. Why not?

As she was tussling with the idea, the man on the bed opened his eyes.

"Good morning," she told him.

He smiled, a tight little smile, but his eyes twinkled as if she amused him. "Good morning." His voice was a rasping croak.

Laura moved around the foot of the bed. "You sound as if you could do with some water."

"That's a fact."

She looked at the pitcher doubtfully. "I don't think this is fresh." Her gaze challenged him. "If I go get some more, they'll make me stay out of here."

He passed the test. He grinned, and she liked the difference it made in his face.

Suddenly they were fellow conspirators.

"Some of the water I've had lately hasn't been all that fresh. I guess I can risk it."

She grinned, too, and turned the waiting water glass upright, absurdly pleased that he wanted her company. Carefully pouring, she filled the glass almost to the brim.

Leaning toward him, she realized that if she tilted it to his lips, half of the water would run out all over him. "Hmmmm." She frowned at the glass. " 'Scuse me."

She poured part of the water back into the pitcher. "You're my first patient except for my dolls. You're gonna have to bear with me till I get the hang of this."

Reese lay there and watched this extraordinary child. She had her father's cool blond coloring, but her eyes held a silver-green light that was at variance with her father's blue. No doubt her mother's eyes were green.

He worked hard at not gulping the water she held to his lips. He was as dry as the Sahara. "Thank you."

He dropped his head back to the pillow. Damn, he was as weak as a kitten. Flame had burned in his side when he'd lifted his head.

"Would you like some more?"

He balanced the pain in his side against the need of his parched throat. Pain came in a poor second. "Yes, please."

The child poured him another half glass. This time, she supported his head with her other hand.

The second glass he could almost enjoy. He was not as frantic for it as he had been for the first. Nor, thanks to her help, was the pain as bad.

He looked at her curiously. This was an amazingly perceptive child. He wondered how she had gotten that way. "Thank you."

"You're welcome." She got right to the point. "What were you doing following us up there on the ridge?"

Direct. She still had a child's directness, for all her seeming maturity. He grinned in appreciation as he brought out the story he'd invented to answer any questions her father and his men might ask.

Lucky he had one ready, as he recognized he was, presently, far from being at his best. "I was riding out this way because a man in Port Arthur gave me an offer of a job." He smiled ruefully. "Seemed like a good idea to me at the time."

He was disturbed to see the girl blush.

She looked at him, her green eyes serious. "And you'd have been fine if you hadn't shot that snake and saved my Aunt Amanda's life."

When she heard her words, she realized they sounded a little as if she were willing to sacrifice her aunt for his safety. Well, that was certainly not true. She hurried to add, "And we were ever so grateful, once we found out what you were trying to do. Really we were!"

She blushed again, looked down, and dug her toe into the rug. "Only then it was too late, of course."

He considered the situation a moment. Looking at what had happened from her point of view, he could see he'd been a fool not to shout a warning before he'd fired. But there hadn't been time to take that chance. The young woman's hand had been inches from the ledge, and the snake had already begun to coil.

Regardless of the fix he found himself in as a result of his shot, he wanted to make everything right for the child.

LOVING HONOR

"Think of how it looked to your men. Some strange saddle bum lets off a shot at one of your party—and a woman, at that—what would you have done?"

Her eyes were grave as she considered it. "Yes. There really wasn't anything else to do, was there? I mean if you really had been shooting at Aunt Amanda, it wouldn't do to let you try twice."

He grinned. The child had a fine mind. "And at least you didn't leave me out there for the buzzards."

She saw the coaxing smile in his eyes.

She had more of an apology to make, though. It wasn't time for her to return his smile. She still had to distance herself and her family from Webster's cruelty to this man. So she didn't respond to the smile. She didn't deserve it yet.

Instead she informed him solemnly, "Neither my Papa nor my Aunt nor myself approved of the way our foreman treated you." Her eyes watched him, big and troubled. "There was no excuse for such brutality."

He was fascinated by the child's command of the English language. No, there wasn't much excuse for roughing up a wounded man, but he wasn't a stranger to the practice. He'd been too long at the war.

As for Webster, the time would come when he'd even that score. He'd already made himself the promise.

He saw her draw back from him a little, and realized his face had given his thoughts away. He must be in bad shape. Usually he was better than that.

Smiling around a deliberate grimace of pain, he touched his bandaged side. "Sorry. Plagues me a bit."

There. He'd given her an excuse for his grimness. He wondered if it would work.

She returned his regard without blinking. Then she made her decision. She decided to accept his explanation for the fleeting expression that had momentarily frightened her.

She was unaware he could read her so easily. Reese, for

his part, was amazed that she had decided to trust him, a perfect stranger.

Deep down inside him, admiration for the child stirred. He had to force himself to deny it. He put it down savagely. If, as he suspected, her father was the man responsible for Jacob Garner's death, developing any feelings for this strangely wise child would hinder his mission.

He'd permit nothing to do that. Jacob was dead because he had taken Reese's place commanding the payroll detail so that Reese could go home to Philadelphia for his mother's funeral.

That act of decency had cost Jacob his life. Nothing, absolutely nothing, was going to stop Reese from avenging the death of his best friend.

Amanda awakened slowly. She was somewhat stiff from the long trip in the unsprung buckboard, but rested. She stretched like a kitten, curling up in a tight ball then reaching far with fingers and pushing hard away with her toes, reveling in the tension that ran the last kinks out of her body.

She moved her head back and forth against her pillow and drew in a deep breath of the sunshine and meadow grass scent of her sheets. Heaven! It was sheer heaven.

She took another deep breath and this time she thought she smelled bacon cooking. Breakfast. She was ravenous.

Then memory returned like a thunderclap. Instead of luxuriating in her wonderful feather bed, she should be up and dressed and checking on her patient.

She leapt from the bed, grabbed her wrapper, and threw it on over her nightgown. She'd check on him briefly before dressing. He was bound to be sleeping deeply after everything he'd been through the day before.

Her slippered feet made no sound on the stairs. She ran lightly down them, crossed the foyer and the parlor, and quietly opened the door of the downstairs bedroom.

Slipping into the room, her back to its interior, she concentrated on closing the door without a sound.

"Good morning, Aunt Amanda."

Her niece's cheery greeting nearly startled her out of her skin. She whirled to face the room, and was flustered to see the man in the bed wide awake and watching her, his glance full of appreciation.

Cheeks flaming, she wished with all her heart that she had taken the time to dress. Refusing to give in to her acute discomfort, she smiled, squared her shoulders and came all the way into the room. Her fingers smoothed the broad ribbon that served as the sash of her wrapper. It was an effort not to pull the suddenly flimsy garment more protectively closed.

From the bed, Reese enjoyed the sight of her. Her long blond hair, tousled from sleep, hung in loose waves and curls down her back. Her lovely blue eyes, still soft from dreaming, were slightly confused, as if she had not quite completed the transition from sleep to waking. He thought she was a little disconcerted at finding him awake.

That was probably it. He knew with absolute certainty that she would not have come into a strange man's bedroom in such charming disarray if she'd known he would be awake to enjoy the sight of her.

Her lips were soft, still, not yet formed into the firmness that told the world that she was fully in control. Standing there in her lavishly lace-trimmed nightgown and wrapper, she was the fulfillment of every dream he'd ever had. Suddenly she was that woman of his dreams. Prompted by the picture she made, unbidden the part of the dream in which he, awakened by the morning sun, drew her into his arms rose in his mind's eye.

His gaze hardened. It was only in his dreams, where his rigid self-control refused to function, that Reese Rivers allowed a woman who required and deserved commitment from the man in her life. Never in his waking hours would he do so.

He had no intention of changing that. Not now, not ever. His soul, his honor, his commitment, were otherwise engaged. He hardened his heart and closed his mind against her.

Too bad, something in the back of his mind whispered. He ignored it.

Reese was not a man to make a commitment. Not anymore. Never again would he make the mistake of pledging his all—all that he was, all that he had, and all that he could be—to a woman.

Not any woman. And not any commitment. He didn't have to be set on fire twice to know he could be burned.

His expression hardened as he reminded himself. By the time the woman reached his bedside, his face was set and his eyes hostile.

Amanda saw the hostility in his face. She understood the man's attitude even as it filled her with regret. After all, the men of her party had shot him.

Heaven only knew what plans of his now had to be held in abeyance, what physical handicap loomed ahead of him when he was again on his feet. At the very least, he would be weakened by his wound, and it was all her fault.

Nevertheless she wished he could see his way clear to be forgiving. Her sympathy for him shone in her eyes.

Reese saw the understanding and concern on the woman's face, and almost hated her for it. Analise's face had seemed to be like that. Analise's face had readily displayed the sweetness and sympathy he, after an austere and painful childhood, had achingly longed for. His Analise had had the face of an angel, too.

What a fool he'd been, thinking that at nineteen he could capture and hold the love of a beautiful, worldly-wise woman like Analise. But he had thought so, conceited, lovelorn ass that he'd been, and he had been ecstatic when she'd agreed to be his bride.

Amanda Harcourt moved forward, intending to touch his forehead, but Reese was caught in the soul-draining vortex of his memories. He saw Analise smiling graciously as she accepted the check from his father. The more-than-generous check that guaranteed the dissolution of a marriage that was no more than a farce. The check guaranteed her desertion of her young husband and restored honor to his father's name—the Rivers name.

Analise had left the country. Joyously she had taken herself back to her greedy lover in her native France.

Reese's father had had the marriage annulled and declared that by removing the adventuress from the country he had given his son a chance to mend his life—and to become a credit to his family.

That day Reese had seen the face behind the mask of compassion and love that his beautiful wife had worn to snare the scion of one of the richest men in Philadelphia. That day Reese Rivers had become a man. A bitter man.

He moved his head abruptly away from Amanda Harcourt's gentle touch, still lost in the maelstrom of his past. What a fool he'd been.

Well, he'd picked up the pieces, stormed from his father's oppressive mansion, and made the United States Army his life.

His father had been enraged. He'd saved his only son from his adventuress wife with the intent of again taking control of his life and molding him to follow in his own footsteps. Reese's rebellion had come as a shock.

Reese smiled a twisted smile where he lay. He'd never regretted his choice. At least he could thank Analise for that. It had cost him his trust, his self-respect, and his ability to commit himself ever again to any woman, but the crushing ending of his brief marriage had given him something invaluable. It had given him his independence.

"Would you like some water?" Her soft voice interrupted his dark thoughts. She was leaning over him with a glass half filled with water in her hand, and he caught the light scent of roses from her still bed-warmed body.

He couldn't help himself. He didn't care. He snarled the word at her. "No!"

Amanda drew back, shocked at the venom in that single word, bewildered by the hostility in his eyes.

Laura was almost as shocked. The man had been perfectly nice to her.

She threw herself into the task of soothing the obvious hurt he'd given her aunt. "I gave him two glasses just before you came down, Aunt Amanda."

"Oh." Her voice was a little breathless. "I see."

She was momentarily shaken by the man's attitude. She had only tried to make him more comfortable. She fumbled the glass back down on to the bedside table, and drew her wrapper a little closer, as if it could act as armor around her slender figure—armor to protect her from the harshness of the man on the bed.

Deciding she would be better able to handle his surliness if she were dressed properly, she moved to the door. "I had not thought to find you awake. If you will excuse me, I shall return shortly."

Reese watched her, hot eyed. She moved with a grace that held his gaze captive. She was as beautiful, as charming as his wife had been. He resented it with a savagery that the rational part of his mind told him was unfair.

That part of his mind tried to tell him he was being unreasonable. In his pained and weakened state rationality didn't matter. He didn't care whether or not he was being reasonable. With all the enthusiasm of a man redressing a wrong, he'd transferred, for just that moment, all his long-held hatred for Analise to Amanda.

It blazed from his eyes like the flames from a blast furnace. It reached out to touch and scorch her where she

LOVING HONOR

stood at the door. He saw her parted lips and her gasp of shock before she frowned her bewilderment and left the room.

The satisfaction that he experienced shocked him.

Then he felt shame, hot and fierce. It was followed by a rushing, tearing release that left him limp.

He had no idea what had happened, but he felt lighter and cleaner than he'd felt since he'd left his father's home. For the first time in more years than he cared to remember, he was without the weight of his accusing memories. The vortex that had pulled at him for more than a decade disappeared with a whisper from his mind.

For the first time in his life, he felt a hint of inner peace.

His eyelids dropped heavily over eyes that were again becoming fever bright. The pain in his side intensified.

Deep in the thing he called his soul, however, Reese was beginning to think that being shot was not so bad a price to pay for whatever had just taken place in the former blackness of his inner self.

Laura almost crept as she came near, puzzled by the change that had taken place in her new friend. She placed a timid hand on his brow. He sure was a funny gent—all amused smiles and plain talk one minute and as surly as a bear with a sore paw the next.

She liked him, though, so she guessed she'd be back, but glory be, she sure hoped she never affected him like her Aunt Amanda had.

Chapter 6

Amanda swirled her hair into a simple chignon, took one last hasty look in the mirror, and wished she had been able to make a neater job of it. Her fingers were shaking with the anger generated by the hurt the wounded man had dealt her.

Now she only wanted to get back downstairs to her own breakfast—she was ravenous after skipping meals in the excitement of the preceding day—and she needed to order something that would serve as breakfast for the wounded stranger. She hoped to get something from Rosa that he *wouldn't* like.

How chagrined she was that her first thoughts on awakening had been of the sardonic man in the bed downstairs, especially in the light of his surly behavior. In her experience first thoughts so often set the order for the day, and Amanda wasn't so sure she wanted to spend the day worrying about him after the unpleasant manner in which he had treated her.

She liked to take her days one step at a time. Until her grandfather had asked her to go live in the family town house in Richmond, Virginia, to look after it in the family's interest, her first thoughts on waking were usually merely what to wear, and how to tell Polly to style her hair. That done, she then washed and dressed and finally allowed the affairs of the day to intrude and be put into her plans in order of importance.

She'd managed to adhere to that practice even in the besieged Confederate capital. That certainly hadn't happened today, though. Before she'd even opened her eyes, she'd been worrying about the fevered, tall, dark man with the bullet wound in his side.

She sighed, then scolded, "For pity's sake, Amanda Harcourt! You have sighed more in these two last days than in the whole of your life combined. Whatever is the matter with you?"

Polly surged into the room on the heels of a soft knock on the door and saved her from answering herself. "My lady!" She frowned at her mistress. "What in the world are you doing out of bed at this hour? Why, I haven't even ordered your tray yet."

Amanda caught herself on the brink of another sigh and swallowed it. "Polly." She felt the trappings and traditions of her position in life closing around her like an iron maiden. She said rather unenthusiastically, "Good morning."

Swallowing a second sigh, she wondered at what point she had so lost control of herself that sighs now came at the slightest provocation. Perhaps it was because of the helplessness she'd felt living among the gallant people of doomed Richmond. Perhaps it was her helplessness now over the wounded man. She sensed a lack of control, as if she were a pawn of destiny. She didn't like the feeling.

Whatever the reason, she'd certainly have to be on her guard against this lamentable tendency. Her immediate problem, however, was to avoid hurting her maid's feelings. "Polly, dear . . ."

Polly bridled instantly. She'd known her mistress since before her ladyship was out of the cradle, and was up to all her little tricks. She knew something was coming that she wasn't going to like when Lady Amanda used that faintly wheedling tone with her.

She closed her lips in firm disapproval and prepared to

do battle. She knew she wasn't going to agree with whatever was coming.

"Polly, aside from helping Rosa as well as you can..." One look at her abigail's face showed her it was hopeless to think she might detach Polly entirely from the responsibility of caring for her. She amended hastily, "And taking care of my wardrobe, of course..."

Polly sniffed loudly, and Amanda knew exactly what she thought of the meager wardrobe she had brought from Richmond. "And doing my hair for me now and again..." She saw Polly brighten a bit at that, and, with the open scorn possible only to a London-bred upper-class servant, lock her button-bright gaze on the untidiness of Amanda's hasty effort to fix her own hair.

Amanda forged ahead. "Then you could treat the rest of your time here as a sort of holiday."

Polly looked unimpressed.

Amanda tried, "Wouldn't that be nice?"

Polly regarded her stonily.

Amanda was desperate. She would scream if she were forced to wait for Polly to help her dress and undress and bathe and brush her hair.

She needed, truly, truly *needed,* just a little freedom from the constant petting and pampering she had endured the whole of her *entire* life.

She tried another tack. "Rosa needs your help, Polly."

Amanda saw a little light come back into Polly's eyes and was flooded with relief. Polly's resistance was fading.

She'd finally managed to hit the right note. Polly, bred to serve, would help Rosa now. She would probably help Rosa until Rosa would want to hit her with one of the big iron skillets in the kitchen. But she would help Rosa. In doing so, she would unwittingly permit Amanda to enjoy the freedom she had come to treasure on her visits to this sprawling ranch in Texas.

They left the large, sunny bedroom together, and went

down the stairs, Polly properly trailing two steps behind Amanda. When they reached the archway into the dining room, Rosa was just leaving it for the kitchen. Amanda called to her, "Rosa."

"*Sí, señorita?*" Rosa waited, removing her hand from the smooth surface of the paneled swinging door and turning back respectfully.

"Could you fix a soft-boiled egg and two pieces of toast for our guest, please?"

Amanda couldn't bring herself to say "wounded man." It was as if doing so somehow condemned him to a long convalescence. As a guest he would be obliged to recover faster, she had no doubt. She smiled at her whimsy.

Her smile died as she remembered his attitude. If it were true that a merry heart acted like a medicine, she would undoubtedly be forced to modify her hopes for his speedy recovery. That thought brought a faint frown.

Polly left Amanda to go to the kitchen for her own breakfast there after greeting the future Earl of Kennerley with a deferential nod. She might have known him all his life, too, but *he* was the heir to the title, and due her respect at all times—even if she did complain to his sister that he had better stop embroiling his English self in the quarrels of these colonials before he got himself killed with no heir to succeed him!

In the softly lamplit dining room, David rose from his place at the head of the table. "Good morning, Manda. Why the scowl?"

"Oh. Was I scowling? I do apologize. I was thinking of our guest." She smiled at her niece. "Good morning, Laura."

David allowed her to see him cringe. "Yes, well, there is that. Is he better? I must go in as soon as he is well enough to stand a bit of groveling."

"Somehow," she kissed him good morning and headed

down the table to her place at its foot, "I don't see you doing groveling particularly well."

His smile became sad. "I've learned a little more about it since you were here last."

Anger flooded her, and she strove to keep it from her face. She knew that he was referring to having gone, hat in hand, to the Union fort to beg for medicine for his beloved wife.

How they could have refused him, she could not, even now, understand. She would never understand war made on women and children.

But they had refused. And the reason they had given was that David had been known to serve in the Confederate cavalry.

It still shocked her to the core. The Union Army, at least the part of it that held sway in this part of Texas, had made war on her dear sister-in-law, on frail and dying Faith, and in her heart she knew that neither her brother nor she would ever forgive them.

It was a matter of wonder to her that her gentle brother David even attempted to do so. It was almost as if he had found some outlet for his frustration, some way to avenge Faith. But if he had, she couldn't think what it might be.

Webster's entrance set her thoughts flying. Big and overconfidently handsome, his face still damp from the pump in front of the bunkhouse, he breezed into the room. "Good morning, Miss Amanda. I trust you slept well."

He greeted his boss with a nod. " 'Morning, Dave." He received a nod in response.

"Very well, thank you." Amanda picked up her napkin from beside her plate, and deliberately became absorbed with its placement in her lap.

Webster sat down. "How's the saddle bum?"

Amanda bristled. There was nothing about the man in the downstairs bedroom to mark him a purposeless drifter, and she resented Webster's remark on his behalf. She closed her lips firmly, pretending she thought the question was addressed to David, and busied herself with smoothing every wrinkle out of the napkin in her lap.

David looked at her with gentle amusement. Adroitly he turned Webster's attention to himself. "I haven't looked in on him as yet, but Laura says that he is doing as well as can be expected."

Laura looked up from her place opposite Webster, and smiled at her father. It felt good to have him rely on her report of the stranger's condition. She was careful not to look in Webster's direction. After all, he hadn't even had the courtesy to greet her.

Webster spoke in the false, overly hearty tone so many adults used with children. "So, young lady. Do you fancy yourself in the role of a nurse?"

Laura told him drily, "Not particularly." She'd like to have added that if it weren't for his deliberate roughness with the wounded man she wouldn't have to spend as long in the role as she anticipated she now would.

She'd have liked to tell him, but she knew it would embarrass her Papa. So she didn't.

She'd like to stick her tongue out at him, too. She didn't do that either.

Instead she watched with distaste as he set about trying to turn her Aunt Amanda up sweet. She was pleased that he didn't seem to be having much luck at it.

Rosa came in with their plates, warmed in the big oven and holding just what each of them liked best for breakfast. As she placed the first plate from her tray in front of Amanda, she said, "If I have his food ready for you in ten minutes, will that give you enough time to finish eating?"

Usually Amanda lingered over her food so that she could talk to David, but today she would be glad not to, she realized with a little feeling of surprise. She told Rosa, "That will be fine."

Webster frowned. "Are you talking about the man I shot?"

"Why, yes."

A frown creased his forehead. "Why doesn't Rosa take care of him?"

"Rosa has enough to do, I'm sure." Amanda's voice was cool.

Webster subsided. He didn't want to get her mad at him again. Her frosty treatment of him yesterday had been quite enough.

He didn't much like the idea of Amanda personally tending to the insolent man he'd shot, though. There was something about the stranger that set his hackles up. He felt in his gut that the man was trouble.

He took a deep breath. If Amanda nursed him, the man was bound to heal faster and leave sooner than if he stopped her from doing so.

Not that he had the power to stop Amanda Harcourt from doing anything, but he wanted that power, and he was going to work like the devil to get it. Until he had it, he'd just put a bug in David Harcourt's ear whenever the need arose.

The need might be about to arise. In light of the attack they'd made on the Yankee payroll detachment, it just seemed best for him to keep any strangers out of the area. Especially cold-eyed ones that put a knot in his middle just by breathing. He toyed with his food while he gave the problem his complete attention.

Amanda finished her breakfast more quickly than she ever had before, and Webster frowned again. Half rising, she smiled at David and said, "Please excuse me. I'll go help Rosa with our guest's tray."

Webster leapt to his feet with an alacrity that threatened to upset his chair. In two strides, he was unnecessarily helping Amanda with hers.

LOVING HONOR

His reward was a murmured, "Thank you, Mr. Webster," and a formal smile.

David took more than his usual interest in his food to hide his amusement. Webster was obvious in his desire to please, and Amanda was just as obvious in her intention of keeping him from doing so. David found the matter lighter than so many of his thoughts and allowed it to entertain him. At the back of his mind, however, he knew he was relieved that his sister didn't find his comrade-in-arms attractive.

Amanda slipped quietly into the downstairs bedroom, a small breakfast tray in one hand. Someone had drawn the curtains and the room was dim.

The man on the bed turned slightly and moaned aloud. As the door clicked closed, he gasped and shot his gaze in her direction. "What the devil do you want?"

Even though she realized he was embarrassed that she'd heard him moan, she stiffened at his use of profanity. "I have brought your breakfast."

He didn't need the coolness in her voice to tell him he owed her an apology. "I beg your pardon," he grumbled. "You startled me." It was a lame excuse, but like a surly adolescent, he forced himself to make it. And like that same surly adolescent, he refused to elaborate on it to make it right.

Amanda stood with her back against the door a moment, just looking at him, letting him feel the full weight of her displeasure. His hair was an unruly mop that fell over his forehead. The truculent look on his face finally brought a smile to her own.

His obstinate expression, unblinkingly offered her, made her think of the cheeky urchins in the streets of London. Perversely, the thought endeared him to her.

She said with a gaiety his dreadful attitude engendered in her, "Here is your breakfast. An egg and two pieces of toast. When you have finished them, I'll wager you would appreciate having a toothbrush."

"God, yes!" His fervor took any offense from his answer.

Amanda crossed to the bed and set the tray down on the table beside it. "Would you like some light while you eat? Or do you prefer the curtains drawn?"

"I only like the curtains drawn when I . . ." He swallowed the end of his sentence. "Thank you," he growled, disconcerted. "I prefer the curtains open."

Amanda watched with interest the tide of color that rose up his bare chest above his bandage to color what she could see of his face around his beard. What in the world had he nearly said? She wondered what color he would turn if she asked him.

"Would you like me to feed you?"

"No, th—" By damn, she was *laughing* at him. He changed his mind. "Yes, please."

There. That ought to fix her. Having to find a way to get food down him without spilling it all over should keep her too busy to chuckle at his expense.

Not that she really laughed out loud, of course, but he'd caught the sparkle of laughter in those breathtaking blue eyes. That was enough to provoke him.

His teeth grated together. What the devil was making him so difficult? He couldn't blame it on his discomfort. It wasn't as if this was his first wound. And it certainly wasn't the most serious wound he'd ever had, or even the most painful. He was a professional soldier, after all.

Maybe it was because it had certainly been the most ignominious. It was the first time he'd ever been shot for doing a good deed. That was the God-honest truth!

At any event, he began to feel as if he were behaving badly to take out his disgruntlement on his beautiful nurse. Reluctantly he admitted that if he was stuck here in this bed for a while, he might as well make an attempt to be pleasant about it.

LOVING HONOR

Amanda crossed the room to a camelback trunk between two windows. Opening it, she pulled out two large pillows. "Here, I think if I can get these behind you, you could be in a little more comfortable position to eat." Sudden concern made her pause. "Unless that would cause you pain."

Why that stung him, he had no idea. Surely he didn't mind her thinking sitting up might cause him pain? It sure as hell was going to. Her very concern, however, caused him to be adamantly determined to sit up!

"Thank you," he said, ignoring his body's protest at his intended foolhardiness. "It would be nice to sit up."

He almost flinched at his own words. "*Nice?*" He sounded like somebody at a blasted tea party.

He plowed on, "Especially when you give me a toothbrush." Heaven knew he didn't want her to forget that.

"I'm sure you'd like to brush your teeth before you eat," she told him sympathetically, "but I want you to humor me and wait until after your meal." She smiled at him winsomely. It didn't make him want to smile back as she had intended. It made him want to curse.

When she'd smiled like that, he'd felt some of his bones beginning to melt.

"Please," she added.

The "please" was brisk and impersonal, as if she had not, just the instant before, been in sympathy with his plight.

Strange. Reese could have sworn he'd given no indication of the disastrous effect she was having on him.

Amanda had spoken her last word bracingly because she was nervous about the moment at hand. Putting the pillows behind him was going to occasion him pain. She hated the very thought of it.

"I shall have to help you sit up a bit so that I can get these behind you."

He answered her with a steady look.

She bent forward, and slid an arm under his shoulders.

His skin was firm and taut and hot. Her breath caught in her throat.

She felt his muscles tense as he tried to aid her effort. Amanda summoned all her strength to lift his considerable weight.

She saw sweat break out on his forehead as she slid the first pillow behind him. "Shall we rest a moment before we do the next one?"

She found she was breathing quickly. She was honest enough to admit to herself that it was only partly due to exertion. Part of this quickening of her heartbeat was from having been so rash as to come so close to him. She was now almost fearfully aware of the magnetism that emanated from him.

Amanda saw that his chest moved more quickly with each drawn breath. He was obviously in pain. Her making him move had caused it. Guilt swept over her.

Reese saw that she was flushed with the effort to lift his shoulders in order to slide the first of the two extra pillows behind him. He vowed he'd sit up unassisted if it killed him when she tried to add the second. He watched her warily to be ready.

She leaned over him again, and the same delicate, warm scent of roses wafted over him that had all but rendered him helpless earlier. He inhaled it deeply, wanting to fill his lungs to capacity with the taunting fragrance of her. Maybe that way he wouldn't have to cudgel his memory for the scent of her when she was gone.

She heard his quick intake of breath with a sinking heart. She was asking too much of him!

With a faint moan of distress, she pressed her body closer to his in an effort to help him more. Her arm gathered him tight against her as she tried to wedge the next pillow behind him. She willed all her strength into the task of easing his effort.

Reese exerted all his will to lift his own weight in an effort to spare her. It wasn't the pain that threatened to sap his ability to do so, it was her proximity. The scent of her, the pressure of her right breast against his shoulder, were driving him toward some precipice of the senses.

He let a groan escape him. She was killing him. His entire body flashed into flames, and every bone in it went liquid.

He turned his face into her shoulder to hide the hunger he knew was in his eyes. He heard her murmur sympathetically.

Fine. Let her think it was the pain of his trifling wound, let her think anything she wanted to. Just don't let her move away from him.

He gasped for another breath of her, and she pulled away.

"Oh, I have hurt you! I am *so* sorry."

He managed to look at her, hoping he could hide his amazement at the devastation she had wrought on his senses. She had no idea that she had set him aflame. Thank God. This desirable woman thought he was merely in pain!

He almost laughed aloud. This whole damn situation was becoming ludicrous.

Then he saw the tears in her eyes and was undone. He was overcome by the need to pull her, this woman he barely knew, into his arms and kiss each shining teardrop away. Instead, he turned his head away from her, certain he must be mad!

When he had regained his usual rigid control, he turned back to see her regarding him anxiously. Her distress forced words from him. "I'm fine. Only a twinge. You mustn't concern yourself."

The stilted words were both balm and lash to her spirit. She felt so *horribly* guilty about causing him pain. He was so incredibly brave.

She placed the tray in his lap as if she were erecting a barrier between them. Perhaps, she thought foolishly, she was.

She welcomed anything that could serve as a shelter behind which she could hide her shocking response to him.

She needed protection from further attack by her own senses. The last thing she had expected when she entered this room was that she would be brought to the point of conflagration by the mere contact of her arm with his body.

Somehow, she got through the task of feeding him. She broke it up into single actions, concentrating on one thing at a time. Fork to bearded lips. Don't notice how perfectly they were formed, how like the mouth of a Grecian statue his was.

Try not to watch the way his throat works as he swallows, she warned herself. Don't admire the strong column of his neck, the smooth way it joins his shoulder. Oh, why hadn't the men put him in a nightshirt?

Hold the toast for him to bite. Her senses ran riot as his lower lip, fever dry, brushed her fingers.

Don't let him know you see and understand his amusement. Don't admit, even to yourself, that this is all a silly gesture . . . doing that which he could do for himself.

If he would, that is. Her glance fell to where his strong, long-fingered hand lay relaxed against the white sheet.

He could, if he wanted to, feed himself his buttered piece of toast, at least. He really could. So why didn't she tell him to?

She did feel as if she'd helped by cutting up and feeding to him the piece of toast on which she'd broken his soft-boiled egg. She felt faintly annoyed, however, at the twinkle in his eyes when she offered him bites of toast that were only buttered.

The man knew full well that he was having an effect on her. She retreated into the safety of her habitual British reserve.

Reese lay there and wondered what in the world ailed her? For the first time in his life a woman was doing something for him, and just when he let himself relax and enjoy it, she was pokering up.

He let his eyes linger on her mouth. It was beautifully

shaped, the lower lip a little fuller than he'd thought it before this close inspection. It was deliciously rosy.

Her lips looked soft and moist. For one mad instant, he wondered how they would feel against his own dry, cracked ones.

He felt his stomach knot as he realized he wanted nothing more than he wanted to nibble at that lower lip instead of the perfectly toasted bread she proffered. He raised his gaze to her eyes, his own beginning to go smoky.

Amanda didn't meet his gaze. She didn't like being laughed at when she was making a sincere effort to atone for the awful way he'd been treated. If he was going to laugh at her efforts, then she would . . . she would . . .

What would she do? Just what *could* she do? Rosa, God bless her, already had too many duties. She couldn't dump his care on her. It wouldn't be fair.

Like lightning, inspiration came. She would send Laura to feed him. Laura seemed to like him.

So do you, her mind taunted. Pointedly, she ignored the small voice and concentrated instead on the fact that the two of them, this man and her niece, seemed to get along famously.

When he'd finished his last bite, she took the tray from his lap and rose, almost overcome by relief. "I'll bring you your toothbrush and powder," she said primly.

Reese watched her go. What the devil had he done? He cast his mind back over the last few minutes. He couldn't think of a thing he'd done that might have offended her.

He could have offended her. He could have so easily, he thought resentfully. He could have finished the sentence he'd bitten off.

When she asked him if he liked the curtains drawn, he could have just lain back against his three pillows, looked her straight in the eye, and finished his sentence.

He *could* have told her that the only time he liked the curtains closed was when he was making love.

Chapter 7

Laura brought him his breakfast.

By then he was accustomed to the discomfort he was constantly and deliberately causing himself by changing his position against the pillows that Amanda had left him. Discomfort was a price he was used to paying whenever he was called on to overcome a physical bother to get a job done.

And he had to get on with getting the job done. It was far too pleasant to lie there with the unusually bright Laura to entertain him.

He'd already wasted five days flat on his back, the last two when he could have been on his feet at least, forcing himself to walk around outside to get his strength back.

It was the sound of Laura's aunt's voice from the next room every now and then that tied him in place with silken bonds that held as surely as chains would have. He'd never be able to explain it. He'd given up trying.

Now that he'd figured out the reason for his strange lethargy, however, he was damned well going to overcome it.

"Kitten, do you have any canned goods on the place?"

Laura looked at him with interest. "Yes." She frowned, trying to puzzle out his reason for asking. "Rosa doesn't trust 'em, so every single can Papa ever bought is still sitting on the pantry shelves. Why?"

"I'd like to have a couple to use as weights."

"Weights?"

"You know." He grinned at her. "Cans are smooth, fit the hand well, and I can lie here and build a little strength back. Lying in bed makes a man fall apart."

Laura looked at him saucily. "You look like you're all in one piece to me."

"Cans?" He lowered his head and glared at her.

"Okay, cans." She looked at him a minute, delighted he'd let her get away with her teasing. "You mean right now?"

"Stop complaining. You don't have anything else to do."

"Bet I could find something." She flitted out of the room.

Reese smiled. He knew that she actually hated to go. She liked keeping him company. That gave him a damned good feeling. It had been years since he'd had the company of other than hard-bitten soldiers, raw recruits, and camp followers. And even they, who'd been better, warmer friends than he'd had in his own home, didn't compare with this pigtailed wonder.

He found himself watching the door, eager for her to return. He heard her light step just outside the door, and his smile broke out to greet her.

Amanda entered the room.

For just an instant their gazes locked, then she dropped hers and sought to hide the effect his smile had had on her. She was surprised. She'd thought him a gruff and secretive man, but for that first instant his face had been open and welcoming . . . and ten years younger, just as she'd thought him when he lay unconscious in his delirium.

When she looked up again, she was not surprised to see the guarded expression he usually wore. "Rosa sent me to ask if you would like your chicken for lunch in a sandwich, or with hot vegetables?"

He looked impatient, as if food were a subject beneath his notice. Then, aware he was being unappreciative, he relented. "Thank Rosa for me, if you will, and tell her I shall be pleased with whatever is easiest for her."

Amanda let her gaze linger on him. She was, however guardedly, impressed by this man. He was obviously well educated. His manners, when he chose to use them, were excellent. Everything about him proclaimed him a gentleman. She couldn't help wondering about him, every contact she had with him fired her curiosity.

There was a soft knock at the door. Amanda glanced toward the bed as if to ask whether to open it. At the patient's nod, she did, feeling a little rattled. That would teach her to stand around woolgathering.

David entered and smiled at her. "Hello, dear. Didn't know our guest already had company." He leaned down and pecked her on the cheek.

In the bed, Reese's stomach tensed. His emotions went to war in him, destroying what little peace he'd carefully constructed.

If this was the man who'd led the attack on the payroll detail, it was going to cause Laura and Amanda Harcourt more pain than all that he had suffered since first meeting them and more. And he would have to live with the knowledge that he had caused it.

Why the hell do they have to be such a blasted loving family? he thought, as Laura arrived and tilted her face up for her own kiss from David Harcourt. She had two of the newly invented tin cans clutched to her chest.

David's frown was puzzled as he watched her cross to the bed and hand them to Reese. "Here, Reese. I'm glad you think they fit into your hand nicely. I had trouble getting any kind of a grip on them, myself."

Amanda heard his name, and remembered that Laura had been the one to inquire it. Both David and she had felt remiss when Laura had told them.

David said, "Laura," in a voice that demanded manners from her.

"Okay. Here, Mr. Rivers," she grumbled as she handed over the cans.

Reese Rivers. Amanda liked it. The sound of it fit him somehow.

She didn't linger on that thought, though. Eyeing the cans, she asked, "What in the world?"

Amanda was no less puzzled than her brother. Both of them stared at the cans. David finally said, "I hope you intend to satisfy my curiosity."

For an answer, Reese took a can in either hand and bent and straightened his arms a few times.

Both David and Amanda laughed. Together they said, "Exercise."

Then David said, "Good idea," and at the same time Amanda said, "Do you think you should?"

Reese felt laughter surprised out of him, and was amazed to hear himself tell Laura, "There you have the basic difference between men and women, Kitten."

Laura tossed her braids over her shoulders. "Huh. I guess you know what you mean. Just sounds confusing to me."

David crossed the room to stand beside the bed. The expression on his face became serious as he looked down at his wounded guest. "I'm sure you are aware how we all feel about your accident."

Reese allowed him that. It would have been just as tough for him to say "for having shot you" if he had been in the man's place. He waited.

"I have no idea how badly we've inconvenienced you, but I hope you will tell me if there is anything I can do to make up for it."

Reese decided his course quickly. Returning David Harcourt's sober look, he said, "As long as I haven't missed out on the chance of a job herabouts, I'll be all right."

David looked a little uncomfortable. Webster had warned him last night that it would be foolhardy to offer this man a job here on the ranch, but what was he to do? He took his responsibilities seriously. It would be his fault if the man had lost his chance of employment because of being delayed by his wound—a wound inflicted by a man under his command.

Clearing his throat, he did the only thing he could do, the honorable thing. "I could use you here if you want to stay on after you're well."

Reese had to conceal the triumph that surged through him. Here was his chance to stay here on Coronet Ranch and spy out proof against the men he was almost certain had attacked the payroll train. He couldn't believe his good fortune.

"That's a mighty fine offer, Mr. Harcourt. I appreciate it."

Laura grinned. "Hey, that would be great. You can finish teaching me to play chess if you work for my papa."

Reese smiled at her. With pretended sincerity, he assured her, "I owe it to a man on a ranch up north of here to see if he still needs me, Kitten."

There was no man with a job for him up north, of course, just a Unionist who would back up his story if asked. In the interest of fair play he must search for other suspects—even though his gut feeling was that he would be wasting his time.

Unfortunately, more than his sense of fair play was at work. His affection for the child, Laura, demanded the search, and had him fervently hoping that he could find other suspects. Suspects who weren't led by David Harcourt. Who didn't have as their leader Laura's father. *And*, a voice he attempted to ignore added, *Amanda's brother*.

Laura's face fell at the thought of losing her new friend. She reached out and put her hands over one of his on the can he held. "I wish you didn't have to go." She made an excuse for the wistfulness in her voice. "You still have a lot to teach me about chess."

Her aunt came over and placed her hands on the girl's

shoulders in sympathy. "I know a little about chess. If it should turn out that Mr. Rivers can't work for your father, perhaps I can help you learn it."

Laura looked up at her. "I already play better'n you do, Aunt Amanda. Papa says so."

Amanda turned a startled face toward her brother. "Oh, does he really? Well! Thank you very much, David."

Harcourt colored slightly and grinned. "You know that chess was never one of your strong points, my dear."

Amanda decided to amuse her niece. Uttering a mock offended sound, she turned a pretended cold shoulder to her brother.

Reese felt the smile her actions brought freeze on his lips. Their banter was so full of affection, their love for one another so obvious.

They were such warm, comfortable people to be around.

How was he going to feel if he had to bring Harcourt to an army gallows?

The next day found Reese, pale and uncomfortable, saddling Thor.

Laura and Rosa watched. Laura gnawed at her lower lip, and Rosa twisted her hands in her apron.

"I wish, señor, that you wouldn't leave until *Señorita* Amanda and *Señor* David come back from their ride."

Reese didn't answer. In his present condition, he needed all his strength to tighten Thor's cinch. Leaving before he had to face Amanda was part of his plan. It didn't work out the way he wanted.

David and Amanda arrived at the barn just then. Blast it! He'd hoped to get away without having to say good-bye to them. To her.

David walked up from the barn leading his big chestnut gelding and ground tied him a safe distance from Reese's stallion. "So this is why you asked me to bandage you this morning." David wasn't accusing, he understood Reese's desire to spare himself a bunch of goodbyes. "If that bandage doesn't do its job, Reese, get back here immediately."

Reese almost bristled at the tone of easy command in his host's voice. Even though the man was expressing concern, it rankled Reese, partly because he was irritable from pain, partly because of his suspicions.

In the light of Jacob's death, his resentment far transcended the fact that their ranks were equal, and that David Harcourt had no business giving *anyone* orders in the army to which Reese had devoted his life.

On top of it all, riding him like some fiend, was the fact that he was beholden to the man's sister and daughter. Hell, to the man, too. None of that made his job any easier. In fact, it made his job tougher than hell, and him surly as a bear.

Realizing his anger came from his utter hatred of the situation in which he found himself didn't help. He was still unable to overcome it.

Knowing he had to make some kind of response, Reese pulled his hat brim lower. There. Harcourt could easily take that for a salute, and since it was a gesture he habitually made to get ready to ride, it didn't cost Reese too much.

Amanda joined the little group, smiling. When she saw his packed saddlebags, she was startled. Her patient had been healing fast, she knew, but she hadn't realized he was well enough to leave.

She was surprised . . . and a little disappointed. No, she admitted honestly to herself, she was *very* disappointed. In truth, she felt a poignant sense of loss.

He had evidently asked David to bandage him, and that worried her. Obviously, he was pushing himself. Surely he shouldn't leave until he was healed beyond the point of needing a bandage? "Are you quite sure you are well enough to leave, Mr. Rivers?"

He answered her with a nod.

Instinctively, she knew that he was afraid that if he

spoke, she'd hear the pain in his voice. Something inside her clenched hard and hurt her.

David said, "My sister learned a lot nursing soldiers in Richmond, Rivers. If she's concerned, maybe you should wait a while."

Reese felt fierce anger. So she'd nursed Confederates and sent them back out for him to fight. Men who rode like centaurs and seldom missed their shot. Men who killed his friends. His face hardened.

Amanda wondered at his expression. Had he taken exception to her nursing Confederate soldiers? Had *he* been a Union soldier, perhaps?

Suddenly she was fearful for her brother. Would this man to whom she was so strongly attracted pose a danger to David?

Unconscious of the gesture, she touched her hand to her fluttering heart. No. She couldn't believe it. There was simply no way she could be drawn to anyone who might be a danger to her family.

Surely it was because Rivers feared the loss of the job he'd been promised north of them somewhere that he looked so grim. Nevertheless, she shot an anxious glance at David.

Looking at him, she relaxed. David was such a noble creature. This far from the battle lines, there was no reason anyone would want to do him harm. She was just experiencing ungrounded womanly qualms.

Heaven knew her emotions seemed determined to keep her in a constant state of turmoil. They had from the first moment she'd seen Reese Rivers standing below her on the wharf in Port Arthur. She would just have to get her feelings firmly back under control. Failing that, she'd just have to ignore them. She was English, after all.

So was David, she mused as she returned her thoughts to the immediate present. She knew her brother had a true English Lord's concept of noblesse oblige. It caused him to take everyone else's good to heart. Surely David would say something now to save Reese Rivers the long ride to the ranch of the man to the north.

She waited for him to demand that Rivers stay and become completely well before he attempted to leave them. To her surprise, David stood silent.

Helplessly she watched the wounded stranger swing aboard his horse. She saw the outline of the bandage that encircled his body just above his waist as his shirt pulled taut over its bulk. She heard, too, the catch in his breath that told her he'd suppressed a grunt of pain.

Still David said nothing. She wanted to shake him. She framed words to goad him into doing something to keep Reese from further pain.

Before she could speak, however, she realized Rivers was saying, ". . . and I surely do appreciate all you've done, ma'am."

The moment to force David to take action had passed. She could only answer the man on the tall black stallion. She murmured, "Of course. It was the least we could do." She felt like a ninny. Nothing was happening as it should.

Laura looked from her flustered aunt to her father. What was the matter? Nobody was behaving correctly.

She looked up at Reese, frowning fiercely. She hadn't missed the way he'd stiffened when her Papa had said come back if the bandage didn't work.

Turning it all over in her mind, she decided everybody was sure acting peculiar. She was busily filing it all away for further consideration when Reese touched the brim of his hat to them and signaled his stallion to move off.

There was nothing she could do. She was just a kid. So she stood waving as he rode out of the yard and away.

"Darn," she said in a mournful voice. Her throat started aching with tears she wanted to cry. She felt as forlorn as an abandoned kitten. Why did Reese have to go?

Frustration welled up in her. When she was grown, darned if she'd act so foolish.

She had a pretty good idea her aunt was as sorry to see him go as she was. And she was a grown-up. She could've stopped him.

Afraid she'd say something that would get her in trouble—or even worse, she amended as she noticed the look on her aunt's face—make her Aunt Amanda feel worse, she sighed mightily, and ran down to the barn to visit her pony.

The adults walked up to the house. David, aware of his sister's depression, slipped an arm around her waist.

Amanda smiled up at him and touched her cheek to his shoulder. But it didn't make her feel any better. Still she ached with worry for the man who had saved her life and, she feared, stolen a little piece of her heart.

Reese didn't make it more than a few miles from the ranch house. He knew that he was going to fall off Thor if he didn't get off. He looked around for a place to camp.

He freely admitted he wasn't strong enough to make this attempt, but he had to try. He had to go search for someone else—anyone else—who might have committed the murder of his best friend.

He'd had to leave Coronet, ready or not. Another day spent under David Harcourt's roof might have compromised his honor. He was becoming too attached to the child. He forbade his mind even to consider how he felt about the woman.

Without honor, a man was nothing.

After years of rejection by his mother, who had never wanted him, and years of failing to measure up to the perfection his father had demanded, he'd learned to take refuge in his own hard-won code of honor. After the years he'd spent living up to it, he knew he couldn't live without it.

His honor was his mainstay, just as was his inflexible father's to him. Reese had only that, and the aristocratic blood that flowed through his veins, in common with his sire.

If Reese had ever had any chance to become less inflexible than his father, it had been swept away by the disaster that had been his brief marriage.

Even now, after ten years in the army, his soul still cringed when he thought of her. Analise. What a fool he'd been.

"Hell!" he snarled.

Thor flinched under him at the force of the expletive. He turned an anxious ear backward.

His mount's sudden movement sent a shock of pain through Reese. "Hell," he groaned softly, a hand pressed to his side.

He shook his head to clear away unwelcome thoughts. Usually he refused to entertain them. "What the blazes is the matter with you, Rivers?"

Obviously, he wasn't his usual self. Surely, it was only his present physical weakness that allowed these thoughts that tormented him.

He'd always considered introspection the fool's road to madness. Damned if he was going to start down its path now.

He turned Thor's head toward a cliff that rose on his left. He knew there'd be a cave under it that he could take shelter in until he felt up to continuing his search.

Right now, his only thought was to get out of the saddle and exist until the gnawing pain in his side stopped eating away at his mind.

Chapter 8

Laura stifled yet another yawn, and looked up from the inlaid chess board struggling for just the right words to tell her aunt she was being bored to death without hurting her feelings.

Amanda caught the look on her face and smiled ruefully. "Would you rather go for a ride?"

"Are you sure you'd like to?" Laura's face lit with relief in spite of trying to look wistful.

Amanda laughed. "I should much rather take you out and try to reach you to ride than to continue boring you to death with my indifferent chess."

Laura leapt to her feet, her eyes incredulous. "I can already ride!"

"Indeed you can." Her aunt chuckled. "As well as any wild Indian, and, I am forced to add, in exactly the same style." Extending her hand, she rose. "It remains my task to teach you to ride as befits an earl's daughter." She rolled her eyes heavenward in mock distress. "I only pray that I shall prove equal to the task."

"Ooooh." Laura couldn't think of a single reply that might be acceptable to her elegant aunt and still express her feelings. She didn't think any of the comments crowding her mind would be well received.

She took her aunt's hand, and together they walked to the stairs.

Amanda gave her a quick hug. "Run along and change. I shall go on out to the barn and get Mason to saddle our horses."

"Don't get him to put that silly contraption on my Warbonnet. I don't want him to end up lopsided."

Amanda just laughed and said firmly, "Sidesaddles do not make a horse lopsided."

She pushed open the screen door and headed for the barn. It would be wonderful to ride for a while. She needed to get out of the house and get busy. Busy enough, she thought ruefully, to stop thinking every moment of Reese Rivers.

She'd already driven herself half-crazy wondering if he were well, if he had enough good food, and if his wound were completely healed. And, of course, she wondered whether he'd gotten the job he'd gone after.

Secretly, in her heart of hearts, she hoped not. She hoped that she'd look up one day, and there he'd be, telling David that he'd be working for them after all.

Then he'd be here, where she could be certain he was all right. She told herself that the interest she took in the man was commensurate with the service he had done her.

It was only natural that her interest in his welfare should be on a grand scale. She was alive thanks to him.

These were the things she told herself when, over and over, her heart nagged her about him. Never would she admit that there was more to her concern than gratitude, the sort one felt for a friend.

She smiled as she crossed the hard-packed stable yard. Friend was a funny word to use about Reese Rivers. He'd never been very friendly to anyone in the house except Laura. In fact, she herself could remember getting only scowls and guarded looks from the man.

Nevertheless, she could call him by no other name. Whether or not he liked it, he had unquestionably proved a friend to her when he'd saved her life.

She heard hoofbeats and looked up to see Pete Webster heading toward the house. She hurried to put the barn between them before he saw her.

As she did, Mason ambled out of the shadowed center aisle, walking stiffly. He was still unaccustomed to the high-heeled boots needed for dogging cattle. "Good afternoon, ma'am. How can I help you?"

"Would you put my sidesaddle on a horse for Laura and saddle Evening Star for me, please."

"Why, sure, Miss Harcourt." He walked back into the cool interior of the barn. "She don't want Warbonnet, I take it?"

Amanda laughed. "Absolutely not!"

Mason chuckled. "Still sure he'll end up lopsided, is she?"

Amanda followed him as he walked back into the barn. "Absolutely!" She said it to amuse him, and Mason laughed, too.

Amanda was pleased at his banter. Mason had been so much less cheerful this trip than he had any of the previous times she'd seen him. While she knew the war was changing a great many men, she was disquieted by this change in Mason.

A shadow fell across the dirt floor at her feet. Pete Webster appeared in the door of the barn, a tall silhouette against the bright Texas day outside. "Amanda. How are you? Are you going for a ride?"

Mason corrected him, "*Miss* Amanda's goin' to give Miss Laura a lesson on her sidesaddle." He regarded Webster steadily.

Webster ignored Mason and turned his full attention to Amanda.

With a little sense of shock, Amanda realized there was an undercurrent of animosity between the two men. It was startlingly easy to see.

Wanting to bridge the awkwardness, she told Webster,

"Yes, Laura is willing to try to learn to ride in the style she must when she returns home."

Webster laughed as if she'd made good joke. "Willing but not enthused, right?"

Another shadow joined his on the barn floor. Laura spoke from behind him, her voice cool. "That is correct, Mr. Webster." She trudged into the barn, awkward in her flat-heeled English boots, the long skirt of her handsome habit dragging. "I am willing to comply with my father and aunt's wishes, but I myself am, indeed, less than enthusiastic about riding sidesaddle."

There. That should have sounded ladylike enough to turn her aunt up sweet for at least a week. If it put Webster down, as well, she'd be more than grateful.

Webster guffawed. "Hoity-toity."

Laura decided she was not going to feel guilty anymore for not liking him.

He said to Amanda, "By the way. Coming in from town, I passed that saddle bum riding this way. You might want to ride toward the west so you don't bump into him." He crammed his hat back on his head. "I have to go find Harcourt. Excuse me, ladies."

"Gladly," Laura muttered.

Amanda pretended not to hear. She was glad, too. Glad to have Webster leave, and glad beyond her wildest expectations to hear that Reese Rivers was on his way back to the ranch.

To keep her feet on the ground, she turned to start a conversation with Mason. He was brushing Evening Star with his jaw clenched, and the mare didn't like it. She switched her tail vigorously to tell him so. Mason didn't seem to notice.

Amanda thought that was strange, Mason was usually very much aware of the reactions of the horses he handled. Amanda thought him the best horse handler she'd found in America.

LOVING HONOR   81

In an attempt to lighten his mood, Amanda chatted with him while he finished saddling the horses.

She marveled again at the ease between classes here in America. She would miss it sorely when she had to go home again.

She would never chat with a stable hand at her Grandfather's. If she did, and the poor man survived the shock, he would probably give his notice immediately.

Laura, clad obediently in one of the habits Amanda had brought her from England, began poking her blouse more firmly into the waistband of her skirt. She'd dressed in haste and needed a bit of neatening. She saw her aunt look at her.

"I hurried." She felt she had to offer some explanation. The riding habits her aunt had given her were beautiful. She wouldn't want her to think she didn't appreciate them.

She didn't, though. If anything, she resented the darn things. It didn't matter how beautiful a riding habit was if it made it impossible to ride her pony astride. Like her aunt, Laura had her own ideas about personal freedom.

When she saw that her aunt's mount had a stock saddle on she erupted. "That's not fair!"

Amanda, secretly agreeing with the child, swung into the saddle without comment. She sat there quietly waiting for her mutinous niece.

Laura glared at where, with interlaced fingers forming a cup for her foot, Mason waited to toss her up on her horse's back.

"C'mon, little honey. Ya know we only have one of them things. Your aunt *has* to ride astride so you can have it." He shook his head and coaxed her. "Ya gotta learn. Might's well git it over with."

She stepped into his hand then, and a minute later was riding out of the yard with her aunt. In perfect accord they turned their mounts east, toward the road from town. Clearly, they had both heard Webster.

Amanda rode in silence. Out of the corner of her eye, she watched her niece try to make herself comfortable on the sidesaddle. She'd instructed her well, and knew that it was just a matter of adjusting to the drastic change in riding style.

She waited until Laura stopped squirming, then turned and smiled at her. "See. You are making very good progress. Soon you will be as proficient at sidesaddle as you are astride."

Laura scowled.

Amanda ignored it and went on. "I have ridden that way for years—all my life except for the little bit of time I got to spend here. And here, I've had to become used to a new style—riding astride. You can switch, too. You'll see."

Laura wasn't convinced. Furthermore, she didn't care if she ever learned. It seemed pretty silly to ride sitting nicely straight on the horse and then try to manage him with both legs on one side.

They hadn't gone a mile, and she already had a stitch in her side. She'd try though. Her Papa wanted her to learn. Besides, she didn't want to hurt her aunt's feelings.

After returning Amanda's smile with a tight little one of her own, she allowed her gaze to wander. Suddenly she straightened and squinted into the distance.

"Look!'" Laura pointed toward a distant hill.

Amanda's gaze followed the direction in which she pointed and saw the solitary rider she'd been looking for. Her heart almost jumped out of her chest.

The big black horse was instantly recognizable. His rider, slumped in his saddle instead of tall and straight, less so.

Amanda demanded anxiously of her niece, "Is it Mr. Rivers? Or has someone borrowed his horse?"

Her last question had a trace of fear in it, and Laura knew Amanda was afraid something might have happened to Reese. Laura guessed that she feared the stallion had been stolen, so changed was the formerly upright posture of their friend.

Laura knew better. She knew Thor wouldn't tolerate anyone but Reese on his back.

She knew firsthand, because she'd tried to sneak a ride, and Thor, shaking his head, the bit firmly in his teeth, had politely trotted over to the pile of soiled straw from Mason's cleaning of the barn and bucked her off into it!

She didn't think she ought to tell her aunt that, though. Instead she yelled, "C'm'on!" She spurred with her left heel and slapped the silly little whip her aunt had forced her to carry against the horse's right side, where she had no leg with which to spur.

"Silly damn way to ride," she muttered as the cow pony Mason had pressed into service for her finally sorted out her mixed signals and charged off in the direction of the distant hill. "Damned silly!"

Amanda followed, lying low over her horse's neck as she urged the animal to cover the ground to the lone rider. Neck and neck they flew over the treacherous ground. The child had no thought of danger, the woman no care for it.

It was the big black stallion that first noticed them. He stopped and threw up his head, watching them come. The movement alerted his rider, who roused himself and sat up straight. After a moment he cantered to meet them.

When they came close enough, the girls could see that he was grim. The three of them pulled up as they met, Laura's horse plunging as he stopped.

"Dratted saddle. How am I supposed to rein in with my knee up here in the way like this?" She looked at her aunt, hot-eyed with frustration.

Amanda, however, had no attention to spare her niece. Every bit of hers was on the gaunt figure before them. "You're so thin!" Her worried gaze ran over him. "What have you been doing to yourself?"

He didn't even hear her. His eyes blazed and he shouted

at her. "What the devil do you mean racing over that ground? What if your horse had stepped in a hole? You could have been killed!"

His anger was like a dash of cold water to Amanda. It extinguished her concern. She knew there were no prairie dogs here. What right did this colonial have to tell her she had endangered her mount?

Nothing she'd encountered here in the state of Texas, no, nor Virginia either, compared with the territory she rode when she hunted back home with the Quorn. That was the trappiest fox-hunting country in all England. He'd probably break *his* neck if he tried it, and she'd ridden to hounds there for years.

To be chastised for an easy gallop over an almost flat plain was not something that gave her charitable feelings toward her chastiser. She looked him over boldly, not caring in her anger whether or not she seemed unladylike.

His color was good, so her anxiety disappeared. His wound must have healed nicely in spite of all her worry.

She noticed there were shadows under his eyes. She would have been upset to see them if he hadn't been so offensive.

As it was, she decided that he seemed to have the usual complement of arms and legs under all his dust, and in her present mood, contented herself with that. With his attitude, he deserved no more.

Laura grinned at him. "We know where all the holes are, Reese. But I sure do think it was nice of you to worry."

She defeated him with that. He sure as hell had no intention of telling Amanda Harcourt how upset he'd been to see the two of them tearing over ground that might have sent their horses somersaulting.

There was no way she was ever going to know how he'd felt at that moment. There was no way she was going to learn where he'd been or what he'd been doing, either.

LOVING HONOR

Something in him wanted to tell her, though. Wanted to tell her at the top of his lungs.

He'd been riding over the whole of this part of Texas, pushing himself beyond his impaired strength and diminished endurance. He'd been pushing himself to find someone besides her beloved brother who might have been responsible for the raid on the army payroll detail. He couldn't tell her, of course.

Unfortunately, much as he'd longed to, he'd found no one who even remotely resembled the group described by the lone survivor of the raid. There was no one—no one but David and his men.

Unable to tell her that, he lied as he had before. Hating every word, he lied to her.

Lying might not set well, but he was skilled at it. And he was willing to use that skill in a good cause. "I went to the man who had offered me the job, but I was too late."

He looked away from them, tortured by the way they accepted his lie without the slightest hesitation. When he spoke again, his voice was tight. "So I went all over trying to find another."

Laura blurted, "Then why haven't you come to us? You were supposed to come back to us. I heard my Papa tell you so!"

Amanda answered for him. "He didn't want to embarrass your Papa, dear." Her voice was soft with regret, vibrant with sympathy. "He didn't want us to know that we had cost him the job he'd counted on—the job he wanted."

Reese thought he would choke on his lies after she said that. Never had he come so close to loathing himself.

"That's so, isn't it, Mr. Rivers?"

Amanda's question was so quiet that he barely heard it over the movement of the horses. He looked at her directly, and refused to lie again. Let her think what she would.

She took his silence for assent. "Come. Let's all go back

to Coronet. Rosa will have lunch ready by the time we get there."

"Coronet's an odd name for a ranch." It was his effort at conversation.

"Yes," Laura picked up on his effort. "Great-grandfather is a man of strange vanities." Her grin took the sting out of her words. "He named the ranch Coronet after the one he wears on occasions of state back in England. He's an earl, you know. And someday Papa will be."

Reese looked at Amanda, an eyebrow raised.

"Oh, yes." Her smile was bittersweet. "I'm afraid that's quite right. David is Grandfather's heir. With our father dead, he's next in line for the title." Then she smiled as if she wanted to soften a blow. "David will be the next Earl of Kennerley."

"I'll be . . ." Out of deference to the ladies, he didn't say what he'd be. That David Harcourt was to be the next Earl of Kennerly would certainly complicate matters. He didn't exactly relish the diplomatic nightmare he'd create if he had to haul a British peer of the realm off to be hanged for the massacre of the Union payroll detail.

And, he thought, *things are too blasted complicated already*. He looked at the child of whom he'd grown so fond, and his heart actually ached. If he had to arrest her Papa . . .

His jaw clenched. He forced himself to remember, Jacob had children, too.

He refused to let himself think of Amanda Harcourt. He couldn't admit that he shied away from hurting her. Even so, he remembered how she'd defended him even before she'd seen the dead snake. The picture of her defying the men around him for his sake rose in his mind.

That and other memories of Amanda Harcourt had frequently haunted him. He put this one down even more savagely than usual. He had no time for foolish dreaming. He was here on a mission for the army.

And he had no intention of risking his heart. Not ever, ever again.

He almost laughed aloud. As if there would be the slightest chance of putting his heart at risk. Not once he had destroyed her brother to avenge the death of his best friend!

With a knot in his middle that hurt him more than the bullet in his side had, he rode on toward Coronet.

At least one thing was going his way. Unless he missed his guess, his two charming companions were going to see to it that he had a job just where he wanted to be.

Chapter 9

"Rivers! Good to see you well." David said the only thing he could say with real sincerity. Having this man around might be dangerous.

Warned by Webster that Reese Rivers was on the ranch, he'd made his decision. In spite of his second-in-command's vigorous objections, he was going to offer the man they'd shot a job. He refused to let this war strip him of every vestige of honor.

"I hope you'll work for me now." As he made the offer, Webster's cautions lay heavily on his mind.

Reese saw his slight reluctance, but ignored it. "Thanks, Mr. Harcourt. Much obliged."

Reese was grimly elated to have the right to be on Coronet, instead of having to skulk on and off like some blasted Confederate raider. He'd have a lot better chance of finding evidence of the payroll theft.

If, of course, anyone had been careless enough to leave any.

He'd learned early in life not to underestimate the abilities of his enemies. Measuring Harcourt's intelligence accurately, he knew he'd be out of luck if everything had been left up to that particular man.

There were others involved, though, and none of them came near Harcourt for brains. He was hoping one of them might have been careless—or greedy.

"Put your gear in the bunkhouse," Harcourt was telling him. "Mason will take you over and help you pick a relief horse from the remuda." His grin was almost boyish. If Reese read him right, he was relieved to have done the right thing. "That stallion doesn't look very much like a ranch horse." His appreciative smile as his gaze went to Thor took any offense out of his words. "Maybe you had better pick two cow ponies."

As David's smile widened, his eyes still on the black stallion, Reese knew that Thor had earned high marks with the Englishman. He damped his quick pleasure firmly. He wasn't about to make a friend of a man he was hunting.

Mason appeared as if conjured up by the mention of his name, and walked with Reese across the yard to the stables.

"Ain' all of us gets to put our horses in the barn. Best with a thin-skinned Thoroughbred, though."

Reese noticed the man watched him closely the whole time he was settling Thor. Mason was sizing him up and making up his mind about something. He wasn't eager to accept a stranger. Reese gave him credit for that, and placed the wiry little man on the list with Harcourt. It was a list of men he wouldn't expect to find had made mistakes.

Ten minutes later, they headed toward the bunkhouse. The long, low building sat under a canopy of the yellow-green leaves of a stand of cottonwoods.

Reese was glad to see the shade. Nothing was hotter than a building that sat all day in the Texas sun. He knew. He'd served at posts and outposts at which the barracks and quarters had done just that.

Sleep came hard in a sun-baked box. Even with the nighttime drop in temperature, they cooled slowly, leaving a man to toss and turn in his own sweat.

Rounding the bunkhouse, Reese saw benches and rough-fashioned chairs in a shaded circle in front of it. Horse trough and pump, and a hitching rail at a comfortable distance under another big cottonwood finished the picture.

Reluctant though he was to be there, he was nevertheless impressed by this effort to make the ranch hands comfortable. Not every rancher cared how his men lived.

Inside, there was enough space to give a man a sense of having a place of his own. Windows, with shutters to cover them when the weather got really bad, let in plenty of light, and the bunks were all on the floor, with no upper tier to make a man feel hemmed in. A potbellied stove sat at each end of the long room, promising comfort in the winter months.

"Pretty nice, huh?" Mason must have read his mind.

"Yes."

"Down here's a spare bed." Mason led him to a bed under a window. "Air's good in the summer. In the winter, I add a blanket, close the shutters, and put my feet toward the window." He was looking hard at Reese. "That's my bunk next to it."

Reese read the man right. He'd made up his mind about him and was offering him friendship.

Reese steeled himself against it. He was in no position to accept friendship. It wouldn't suit his purpose to alienate the man, however, so he forced a smile and said, "Looks mighty good to me."

Plopping his saddlebags down on the tautly stretched blanket, he wondered how many other signs of military life he'd find as he went along. This bunk would have passed a West Point inspection.

Glancing around, he couldn't find a single item out of place, nor any dirt on the floor. All shipshape and Bristol fashion was the phrase that popped into his mind. All ready for inspection was another, and that one probably fitted.

Mason stood watching him. When Reese, glancing around to figure out which was his to use by the arrangements, put his saddlebags into the small trunk at the side of his bunk and straightened to look to him for the next move, Mason nodded as if he'd come to a decision. "If you wanna choose a couple of horses, come on. That Thoroughbred you ride won't be any good working cows, I can tell you."

Reese swallowed the indictment against Thor meekly because Mason was absolutely right. Thor had been chosen to put distance between him and tight places at top speed, not to hold on to the other end of a rope from some bawling steer.

He trailed after Mason out to the big corral beside the barn. There, what was left of the remuda loafed in the sun or stood quietly dozing in the shade. Several looked up alertly as the men approached.

Mason climbed up to sit on the top rail. Reese joined him, keeping his eyes on the horses.

Several more of them looked over when the men climbed the fence. One spun away from them, playing spooked.

Reese kept his selection to the few that had looked up when he and Mason had first come toward them. He made a mental note to avoid the one who'd pinned back his ears at them. Half the time a horse laid his ears back he was bluffing, but why bother to find out?

He studied the other three. One had a shoulder so straight that riding him would be like sitting on a pile driver—hazardous to Reese's spine. So he told Mason, "How about the bay with the blaze and the chestnut with the star?"

Mason looked at him a long moment. "Good choices. They both ride purty well, and the bay's a good worker. The chestnut'll give ya trouble if ya let him, but they're the best of this lot." He grinned at Reese. "Remuda's been picked over by the other hands, but those two are still good. They just need a bit more ridin' than the boys wanna do when they're working cows. You got an eye for horses."

Reese wasn't about to tell the wiry little man beside him that he'd learned just about all there was to know about horses. He'd done it for self-preservation.

In an effort to escape the cold, formal mansion into which he'd been born and the father determined to mold him to follow in his footsteps, he'd spent a hell of a lot of time with horses. The stables had been his sanctuary.

As a child, he'd run down to the stables to tell his pony his troubles. No one else had cared.

There he'd been taken in tow by an acerbic groom. Reese had never known whether Patrick Witherspoon had been trying to help him, or whether he was just bored and letting the boy Reese fill his own empty hours.

He was grateful, nonetheless. Witherspoon and his down-to-earth attitudes had probably been what had saved Reese from being just like his father.

Most of all, he'd been pathetically grateful for the crumbs of approval he'd won by absorbing and repeating back all Witherspoon taught him. It was the only approval he ever remembered having won in all the time he'd lived on his father's estate.

None of that was anybody's business. Not here on Coronet. No, nor anywhere else. So he just grinned lopsidedly at Mason, and wondered why the devil so much of his past was surfacing all of a sudden.

Even after he'd chosen his two horses from the ranch's herd, they were subject to no more than easy riding. Neither horses nor man were doing much ranch work.

"Sorry, Rivers. You get to bed the stalls in the barn again today." David looked sympathetic as he gave him his orders.

The other men chuckled. The whole ranch knew that Amanda Harcourt saw to it that her brother kept Reese Rivers on a short string. He was always given the lightest of chores. And every one of them knew he would be until Miss Amanda felt he was well and back up to the weight at which she'd first seen him. They all laughed about it in the bunkhouse. Even those who'd suffered similar indignities after an illness or injury when Amanda Harcourt had been in residence. Usually they were the ones who pushed it the hardest.

Somehow, none of them wanted to push it too far, however.

Reese didn't find it funny. He made the best of it, though, and used his all but free time to search the ranch for some clue that might pin the payroll theft on the men of Coronet. When he was asked to police the yard or—damn it all—to *tidy* the flower beds, he made good use of his assignments.

He used the chores to look for any signs of loose stones in the foundation of the house behind which something might have been hidden, or for a spot of soft earth that could indicate buried evidence.

So far he'd had no luck. All his searching had been in vain, but he hadn't been able to get far afield as yet.

Thanks to the good intentions of the beautiful Amanda he was tied to the ranch house and its blasted flower beds. Sometimes he wanted to wring her neck.

He had a nagging hunch that he needed to get out to the line shacks and poke around. Reese had learned, the hard way, never to ignore his hunches.

He'd get to the line shacks as soon as the lady of the manor let him off his tether. In the meantime, he took a lot of teasing from the rest of the men, and gritted his teeth, waiting for it to be over.

Carrying great pitchforks of straw to rebed the stalls that Mason was cleaning was easy work. He'd given up trying to buck Amanda's iron hand, and was enjoying the fresh clean smell of the straw and Mason's laconic company.

He guessed that once Amanda Harcourt was satisfied, he'd be let off his leash to pull his share of the load around Coronet. Then he'd make it his first priority to have a look at the line shacks.

"Hey! You don't have to bury me!"

"Sorry."

Mason said something Reese wasn't meant to hear as he dug straw from the neck of his shirt, then, "I'll sure be glad when you get on with work out on the range, Rivers. You're gettin' to be a pest."

Reese laughed at him. In spite of himself, he liked Mason.

Then the fact that he might have to hang the man hit him like a blow to the pit of his stomach. For a moment he was nauseated with the thought.

Walking over to put his pitchfork away, he vowed he'd never take on a task like this again. It didn't make him feel any better that he'd been the one to insist on this assignment. No better at all.

From now on, he'd stick to ordering troops around. There was no satisfaction in getting to know the men you hunted when you found yourself trapped into liking some of them.

Reese could feel his soul squirm.

Relief came. Webster appeared in the doorway of the barn, his face sour. "Rivers!" He peered into the dimness, his eyes dazzled by the sunlight from which he came. "Oh, there you are." He sounded less than pleased to have located Reese. "Miss Harcourt and the kid want to go in to English Bend."

Reese moved toward the door. Here was one man he was in no danger of liking. He stood looking at him neutrally. He wasn't ready to let Webster know just how much he despised him, not yet.

"Are you telling me you want me to drive Miss Harcourt and her *niece*?" He put heavy emphasis on the word niece.

Webster ignored Reese's correction. "That's 'yes, sir,' Rivers."

"Really?"

Webster slammed his fists to his hips. "Yes, really, Rivers."

"Very well." Reese reached down the double harness for the buckboard team.

Webster reddened. "I said—"

"I heard what you said, Webster." Reese looked at him levelly. "But you're not my boss, Harcourt is." Reese heard the hiss of his own voice with cool interest. "And this isn't the army. You're damned lucky I didn't just tell you 'okay.' "

Mason popped out of the stall he'd just finished. "He's got a point there." His voice became loaded with meaning, *"This isn't the army."*

Webster glared at the older man. "It is if I want it to be. I'm foreman here."

Reese kept quiet and watched them.

Mason said, "Maybe you better check with the cap . . . with Mr. Harcourt."

Webster's handsome face was taking on a purple hue. "Maybe you better butt out, Mason."

Mason fluffed up like a cockerel. "Maybe I done that once too often already."

Webster's face blanched. His eyes burned at the smaller man. "So that's what's stuck in your craw." His voice was deadly.

Reese cursed silently as a buckle on the harness jangled in the tense atmosphere. Helluva time to remind Webster he was there. He was sure he'd been on the brink of learning something.

With a mighty effort, the foreman got hold of himself. Spinning away from Mason's accusing eyes, he snapped at Reese. "Get that buckboard ready, Rivers. Pronto!" With that, Webster stomped out of the barn.

Reese looked after him pensively, then transferred his gaze to the steaming Mason. "What was that all about?" He made his voice casual. He didn't expect an answer, but it was worth a try.

"Just a thing we disagreed about back a ways." Mason

spoke as if to himself. "He killed some men I just couldn't see needed killing. . . ."

Mason's attention was still on the departing Webster. If it hadn't been, Reese knew, he'd have said a lot less.

Catching himself, Mason gave a snort, whacked his Stetson against his thigh, and marched out of the barn, muttering about old fools with flapping tongues.

Reese stood with the heavy weight of the harness dragging at his arms. He was positive now that he was on the right track. What he'd just heard was probably as close to an indictment of Webster as he was ever likely to hear.

Standing in the silence of the cavernous barn, he harshly promised his friend, "Soon, Jacob."

As was his habit, he tucked the matter into its special compartment in his mind. He was then able to go about the task he'd been assigned as if he had nothing more on his mind. Tossing the harness onto the seat of the buckboard, he grabbed up two halters and went to fetch the matched bays that made up its team.

Victory was his. Now he was certain of it.

Why, then, did it taste like ashes on his tongue?

Reese drove the buckboard to the house where Amanda was waiting quietly on the front porch, her brother beside her. As Reese halted the bays, Laura came running over from the well where she'd been listening to it echo the phrases she sang down it.

"Reese! Hello! Why haven't you come to play chess with me?"

Amanda moved out from under the porch, opening her parasol. "Mr. Rivers," she emphasized, "has his work to do, Laura. And he needs his rest. Where is your parasol?"

"*Parasol!*" Laura looked at her aunt as if she'd just asked her to bring her chamber pot.

"Parasol." Amanda's tone brooked no disagreement.

"English ladies carry parasols to protect their complexions from the sun."

Laura tried a mild snort.

With excruciating politeness her aunt inquired, "I beg your pardon?"

Laura squirmed and her rebellious flare subsided. Meekly walking back into the house, she thundered up the stairs and returned in a rush. Opening her parasol with a snap that nearly turned it inside out, she climbed up beside Reese to await her aunt.

David, with a smile exactly balanced between approval and amusement, helped his sister to her place beside Laura. "Thank you, Rivers. I know you'll take good care of them."

"Good-bye, Papa."

"Tell Rosa we'll be sure to be back for dinner." Amanda added mischievously, "And tell Polly that I'll watch out for Indians."

David just smiled and waved. Reese drove them out of the yard and off toward the road to English Bend.

Fortunately, the team followed the dusty track without much help from Reese. Reese was experiencing difficulty keeping his mind on driving.

His senses were under assault by Amanda Harcourt's proximity. Having Laura between them in no way lessened his awareness of the woman.

It was going to be a long afternoon.

Chapter 10

As he assisted her down from the buckboard, Amanda made it a point to smile at Reese Rivers as if he were no more to her than any other of the men from the ranch. "Thank you, Mr. Rivers." She made her voice cool and impersonal, and kept her gaze focused on the storefront, instead of where she longed to look—at his face.

Reese had been annoyed by the aloofness she'd exhibited all the way from the ranch. It had really gotten under his skin. That puzzled him. He couldn't understand his own attitude. The last thing he wanted was an entanglement with the beautiful Amanda. Wasn't it?

Now he was even more annoyed with the undisciplined streak that was showing up in his own nature all of a sudden. It was as if some part of him wanted her to notice him as a man.

For her, or anyone, to take special notice of him was the last blasted thing he needed. The whole idea was to be able to go about his investigation without being noticed.

So he held her by the waist at arm's length as he swung her down. He was careful to keep even her skirt from brushing against him. He was as wary of any contact as she seemed.

As soon as he'd placed her on her feet and removed his hands from her waist, Amanda turned her back on him. Scowling, he climbed easily up into the seat of the buck-

LOVING HONOR

board and moved the team to the shade of some trees across the dusty street.

"Come, dear." Amanda sailed into the spacious general store with Laura in tow for all the world as if she couldn't wait to see what had arrived on the latest freight wagons from Port Arthur.

Laura tagged after her, wondering what Reese was so irked about and why Aunt Amanda sounded like she didn't have quite enough breath to summon her niece to heel. Life was sure getting interesting.

There had been freight from the port. Some things were even from England, run in by Confederate blockade runners to raise funds for their war effort.

Goods were indeed scarce with the war in the east, but that didn't explain Amanda's haste. Her haste was born of a need to hide from Reese Rivers the color his touch had brought to her cheeks. Fortunately, he couldn't hear the way her heart had beat faster as he'd put her down.

It was cool inside the store. She'd soon recover her good sense in its quiet atmosphere. She stood breathing deeply to calm her silly fluttering.

She glanced out the big front window. Endicott's Mercantile Establishment, she read, turning the words painted on the glass around mentally. She refused to admit that she was really looking to see where he had gone.

Why Reese Rivers had this effect on her she could not imagine. Worst of all was the fact that he had done nothing to cause it.

In fact, she thought as she moved toward the sunbonnets she wanted to look at for Laura, the man had done nothing but scowl and snarl at her through the whole of their early acquaintance, and treat her with an almost resentful coldness through the latter part of it. That sort of thing shouldn't cause her heart to race.

He'd done absolutely nothing to elicit the feelings he aroused in her.

Except nearly lose his life saving hers.

Amanda stopped dead, and Laura had to go up on tiptoes to keep from running right into her.

Even as Laura studied her aunt's luminous expression, Amanda shook her head and said softly and without much conviction, "Preposterous."

Laura decided to head for the penny-candy urns. Grown-ups. They certainly made a chore out of life.

Amanda broke out of her reverie and looked around the store. A good dose of intelligent shopping would get this fantasy about Reese Rivers out of her head. She fished out her list.

Her gaze went over the items on the list, but her thoughts stayed on Reese Rivers. He was a perfect stranger. And he wasn't even English!

She shook her head. Sternly she forced herself to concentrate on the list in her hand.

The store was arranged with fanatical neatness. That was hardly surprising, as the owner, Ralph Endicott, who was a demon for organization, saw to it that his two employees were never idle.

As a result, though the store was a delight to see, some of his customers were annoyed by the constant scurrying of the help. The woman clerk and the young boy who assisted her always looked as if they were about to drop.

Once Amanda had even tried to tell Mr. Endicott that she wished he would spare his employees a bit—that they could, in her opinion, use an occasional rest, and that they would undoubtedly be even more efficient if they had one.

Her confidential chat with him had had disastrous results. Endicott had felt it indicated Amanda's personal interest in him.

The last thing Amanda wanted was to be courted by Ralph Endicott. Even though he was a handsome man, and a successful one who owned the hotel and the saloon as well as this store, as well as the livery stable and the feed store—in fact most of the businesses in English Bend—Amanda was not impressed.

Her thoughts were mercifully interrupted. A mouse-colored woman in a mouse-colored dress came to her side. "May I help you make a selection, Miss Harcourt?"

"No, thank you, Mrs. Beame. I shall just look around for a while." She saw the woman's crestfallen expression. "Unless, of course, you have something that you would particularly like to show me."

Elvira Beame smiled and her face became really pretty. "Oh, yes, there is a lovely bolt of India cotton that came in. I can't imagine how it got here, but it is so cool and lovely." She sounded wistful. "It will make up beautifully."

"But where would I get it made?" Amanda had no idea where gowns were fashioned in this part of the world, she realized with a start.

Mrs. Beame whispered shyly, "I sew, Miss Harcourt."

Amanda wondered when the fragile woman would find the time, with the hours Endicott demanded of his help. But she wasn't so dense that she didn't realize the woman had told her of her skill for a reason. "Would you sew for me, then? You will have to tell me your prices, for I have no idea what is charged here in America."

Mrs. Beame smiled radiantly and quoted her a string of figures for various articles of women's apparel as if she were sharing her favorite dream. And perhaps she was, Amanda thought.

Her maid, Polly, might have a fit if Amanda had clothes made by a colonial, but Amanda said, "Show me the India cotton, please. With you to fashion it for me, I'm certain I shall have to have it."

Mrs. Beame was smiling as she led the way to the bolts of fabric. Taking pleasure from the woman's enthusiasm, Amanda was actually beginning to enjoy her shopping trip, the strain usually present in the mercantile being absent with its owner.

She glanced across at her niece and saw she was engrossed in selecting candy. Smiling back at the clerk, she gave herself over to the inspection of the new fabrics.

Seeing the loving way Mrs. Beame smoothed and draped the fabrics was a revelation. The little mouse exterior hid the creative spirit of a true designer. Amanda was enchanted.

Across the shop near the front door, Laura studied the selection of hard candies in the glass apothecary jars. Ben, the boy who assisted Mr. Endicott and Mrs. Beame but mostly just did the sweeping up, angled over to her.

Ben was about her age, she thought, but he was taller than she. Ben didn't talk enough for her to tell whether or not he was a little older. She secretly hoped he was.

"Hallo, Miss Laura." He was pretending to sweep near where she stood, and his eyes darted toward the curtain over the door to the storeroom. Laura knew, then, where obnoxious old Mr. Endicott was. She hoped he'd stay in the storeroom doing whatever he was doing until she'd a chat with Ben. She knew her aunt would enjoy her shopping better if she could finish it up before he came out and oozed oil all over her.

She noted with satisfaction that both her aunt and Mrs. Beame were keeping their voices even lower than usual. They must not want Mr. Oily Endicott to hear them, either.

"Hallo, Ben. How you been doing since school's over?" She was careful to ask quietly.

"Getting a lot more sleep." He grinned at her, his own voice conspiratorial.

Laura knew that he'd had to work nights here at Endicott's Mercantile Establishment to make up for the time he spent in the little one-room schoolhouse they attended. Ben had gone all winter on less than six hours of sleep a night. Laura thought that was a shame, and that the shame was Ralph Endicott's.

Ben was lucky he got to go to school at all. Endicott

LOVING HONOR 103

hated to let him attend, but the women of English Bend had put pressure on him, claiming it would be of benefit to Endicott later, and the whole community, too, if the boy were educated.

Endicott's compliance had been brought about very simply. When Endicott had balked at letting the child go to school, Mrs. Whistlebury, leader of the townswomen, had told him it would benefit Endicott *now* to let Ben go to school in the form of continued patronage of his store by the women of English Bend.

Endicott had postured and argued, but his heart hadn't been in it. Since Mr. Whistlebury ran the local freight and passenger transport company, and his wife dictated the behavior of every decent woman in town, Endicott had capitulated. Now he never failed to point out that he was seeing to his young clerk's education.

Tom Whistlebury sometimes wanted to know why the boy had to work at the store until one and two in the morning, but the boy was the sole support of an ailing mother, so the town took what it could get for him and shut up.

Laura offered, "Want some candy?"

Ben's eyes gleamed for an instant before his face closed.

"To take home to your mother?" Laura added so hastily that it seemed to be all one sentence. "I bet she might like some. I know I do. And," she fabricated hastily, forestalling his refusal, "if I don't spend all the money my Papa gave me for today, next time he'll give me less."

That made it all right with Ben. "I guess I gotta say yes, then. It wouldn't do for me not to look after Mr. Endicott's getting all you brung . . . brought to town to spend."

"That's just good business, Ben." They put their heads together and, whispering, gave the candy all their attention.

Ralph Endicott burst through the curtain over the door to the storeroom. "Ben, why aren't you sweeping?"

Laura fixed him with an imperious look that she'd practiced ever since she'd seen her aunt use it to advantage on a presumptuous clerk. "I've asked Benjamin to help me decide on my purchases, Mr. Endicott."

Watching him take a breath to reprimand them, she took delight in adding, "Like Mrs. Beame is helping my aunt." She almost giggled to see him deflate, his unpleasantness gone in an instant at the thought of Amanda being nearby.

Without another thought for the children, he turned to look around for Amanda Harcourt.

"Amanda! How nice to see you."

Amanda turned and regarded him coolly. She couldn't remember giving him permission to use her first name. She didn't *like* Ralph Endicott.

"How do you do, Mr. Endicott."

"Are you here for long, Lady Amanda?" He picked up her hand and stood smiling at her over it. "Terrible news about David's Faith. Such a dear little thing. She will be greatly missed."

Amanda wondered if he knew the first name of her grandfather, and if so, when he'd pull it out. She worked her fingers free of his clasp. "I have come to stay with my niece until we return to England together."

His face fell at the news that she was planning to return to England, but he rallied with a wide smile. "Ah, yes, little Laura."

He missed the terrible face Laura made behind him, but Amanda didn't. She frowned quickly at her niece and Laura grinned back, totally unrepentant. When Amanda returned her attention to the storekeeper, he was saying, "How fortunate she has so lovely an aunt to come and look after her in her mother's absence."

Amanda saw the grin fade from Laura's face and wanted to leave Endicott standing there while she went to comfort her niece for the hurt he'd so carelessly inflicted. Ben, bless him, slipped an arm around Laura's shoulders and told her something that brought an effort at a smile. Amanda stayed where she was.

LOVING HONOR 105

Finally she could stand Endicott's fulsome comments no longer and said impatiently, "Would you check to see if there are any letters for us, while Mrs. Beame shows me the rest of the fabric she thinks I might want to buy?"

The double shot galvanized Endicott into action. Soothed by this assurance that she was going to stay long enough to purchase something, he allowed the pride he took in being postmaster of the region to blossom.

Shoulders unconsciously squared, he went to the section of the store that had a small separate counter with a series of pigeonholes on the wall behind it. Flipping up one end of the short countertop to gain entrance, he muttered "Harcourt, Harcourt," as if he didn't know exactly to the inch where he'd put the letter that had arrived from England just the other day.

Handling the heavy vellum with reverence, he gazed down at the coat of arms on the envelope and drew in a deep breath. Such glamour, elegance, and power. He thought he could feel it radiating from the parchment like heat.

It was his imagination, of course, and he knew it, but knowing did nothing to diminish the burning determination that filled him. Someday he would make such things a permanent part of his life. He glanced at Amanda possessively. She would serve as his entry into that world that he knew only in his dreams.

Just then, the bell above the door jumped, tingling on its spring, and Reese Rivers entered the store. Opening eyes he'd closed for his last three sunlit strides to the door so they'd adjust immediately to the dim interior, he stared straight at the shopkeeper.

Dislike rose in him. The blasted man was all but slavering over Amanda Harcourt. Reading the shopkeeper's look for exactly what it was, he could feel the hackles rise on his neck like those of a cur about to defend his bone.

Tall and meticulously dressed in the latest fashion, the

man returned Reese's look. Silhouetted as he was against the light from the large area of glass at the front of the building, Reese knew his face couldn't be read. It was just as well. He wouldn't want to scare this dandy.

As the man approached, Reese stifled the impulse to wring the insufferable pup's citified neck. By the time the store owner neared him, however, he had his reaction to the man's presumption under control. He wasn't really going to hit him for looking at Amanda Harcourt with such a proprietary air.

Reese's expression was neutral. "I need some shells."

He was faintly amused to hear his words come out in a growl. Maybe he didn't have his reaction to this popinjay as well under control as he thought.

The popinjay bowed slightly and announced, "I am Ralph Endicott, the owner. As soon as I have given this letter from the Earl of Kennerly to its recipient, Lady Amanda Harcourt, I shall be free to assist you."

Reese didn't bother to respond, he merely leaned a hip on the counter in front of the shelves holding the ammunition and waited. His gaze, seeking Amanda's, was derisive.

She saw his look, and colored. The man was exasperating.

She might agree with his—surely contempt was too strong a word—his . . . *whatever* he was thinking of Endicott, but she resented Rivers sharing it with her so confidently.

Flustered, when Endicott presented her grandfather's letter with a flourish and a little bow, she almost snatched it. Carelessly she jammed it into the pocket of her skirt.

She wished with all her heart that she might, with the same amount of force, jam Ralph Endicott into one of the neat postal pigeonholes of his overly neat mercantile establishment.

"Thank you," she snapped at him, and turned away.

"But—"

"Mrs. Beame is all the assistance that I require, Mr. Endicott." One of her eyebrows rose. "If you wish to oblige me, please attend to my niece and my driver so that we may be on our way."

Amanda wasn't sure which of the two men staring at her had done the most to raise her level of irritation to fever pitch, but she knew which one was going to bear the brunt of it, because only one of them was going to drive her home.

Chapter 11

His teeth were gritted so tightly his jaws ached by the time he dumped Miss Amanda Acid-Tongued Harcourt at the front door of the big ranch house. "And she's damned lucky she made it that far!"

Several times he'd been tempted to ask her if she'd prefer walking to being driven by him. Once he'd even considered handing her the reins and walking the rest of the way home himself.

She'd chided him for every rock any rim of any wheel passed over. When there were rock-hard sets of ruts carved into the road by heavy freight wagons, she'd accused him of deliberately choosing to drive in the worst. By the time they were only a third of the way home, Reese was ready to throttle his beautiful Amanda.

Thank God the off horse had waited to stumble until they were turning into the ranch yard! He would have choked the life out of the nasty shrew if she'd had more than a minute or so to elaborate on his trying to lame one of her brother's horses!

Slamming the gate after he'd put the team into the corral, he shot the bolt home and lugged the heavy double harness back into the barn. Dumping it, he went for a bucket of water and the harness soap.

He was lathering his hands and running them over the long, smooth driving reins when, unbidden, the memories came.

Analise, gently telling him he was the best driver she had ever ridden with. Analise assuring him that no one could handle horses in traffic with the skill and precision he did. Analise with her soft voice telling him that everything he did was superlative or perfect or the best of its kind that she had ever encountered. Analise leaning over to whisper that he was a magician when it came to discerning which ruts to select to give her the smoothest ride. Analise . . .

Then cynical laughter hit him. There was no Analise in Amanda Harcourt, that was for damned sure. She had criticized, nagged, and carped all the way home from English Bend.

He'd sure as hell not detected the least bit of flattery in the tall English termagant who had ridden home from town with him just now. She hadn't cared if she reduced him to rubble with her criticism of his driving skills. In fact, for a while there, he'd been perfectly sure that that was her intention.

Remembering, he swore under his breath. There was a good lesson to be learned here. Women were poison. One way or another they'll thrust in the knife and turn it if you're fool enough to get close.

Reaffirming the promise he'd made himself long ago that he'd stick to dance-hall girls and the hot-eyed wives of other men, he finished the harness. His promise had made good sense when Analise had finished mauling him, and it made better sense now. He picked up the clean harness and hung it on the pegs where it belonged.

There was still a twisted smile on his face when he left the barn and headed for the bunkhouse. Damn. There was nothing to be found in Amanda Harcourt of the flattering little French charmer who'd cozened him into a disastrous marriage, but she was just as bad in her own way. He told himself he could repeat that for emphasis, and he did.

The only good thing he could say about Amanda Harcourt was that she obviously hadn't a single *deceitfully* charming bone in her body. Today, in fact, he'd have sworn she hadn't a charming bone *of any kind* in her body.

The men drifting in from the range and heading for the bunkhouse stepped aside to let him pass. When a man like Rivers had a look like that on his face, it paid to give him a little room.

Amanda decided to retire early. She didn't need the concerned glances of her brother and his daughter to tell her she was behaving badly. She knew she was. The trouble was that try as she might, she couldn't seem to stop.

Early bedtime was the only solution she could come up with. She probably wouldn't be able to sleep, but at least she'd be able to put her beloved family out of their misery—by taking it to bed with her.

As she passed the window on the landing between the first and second floors, she saw Reese Rivers sauntering out of the barn. Remembering the ride home from English Bend that her behavior had made so miserable, she felt a little tug of conscience.

It didn't make her want to apologize to the man disappearing toward the bunkhouse, however. It made her wish she had something to throw at him.

The next day things were back to normal. Amanda came down to the breakfast table with dark smudges under her eyes and a contrite expression on her face. "I was abominable. Please forgive me."

"Nonsense," David said bracingly.

"You sure were," Laura assured her. "Boy, I thought for a minute one time that Reese was either going to throw you out of the buckboard or jump out himself." She laughed and warmed to her topic. "You should have seen her, Papa. Aunt Amanda was a real grouch."

She noticed the look on her father's face at that point. "Uh-oh. I guess that's not the right thing to say, huh?"

"What's not the right thing to say?" Webster breezed in for his breakfast. "Good morning, everybody."

Laura hated being grateful to Webster for anything. It made her itch all over.

She noticed that the whole time Webster was drooling over her aunt, her father was watching his favorite sister with a speculative expression on his face. She wondered if his speculation had anything to do with the way her Aunt Amanda's behavior had been so radically changed by a day spent in the company of Reese Rivers.

Come to think of it, she'd thought it a little strange herself. Not knowing her aunt all that well, she'd just put it away on a mental shelf. Now, suddenly, in light of the look in her Papa's eyes, Aunt Amanda's peculiar carryings-on yesterday in the buckboard took on new interest for her.

Thinking about it helped her get through another breakfast with the obnoxious Webster. Gosh, why was it everybody thought *he* was so wonderful?

There was a restlessness in Amanda that she couldn't explain. She knew that she had to fight it off, however. Work was always the best way to get rid of restlessness, she'd discovered.

Deciding to see if she could be of any help to Rosa, she headed for the kitchen. Her hand on the door, she heard Polly say, "Yes, I know just how that is. We had the same thing happen once when her ladyship was just a tyke."

"Ah, then you do know how it is," Rosa said eagerly.

The conversation, though animated by their shared experience of the topic at hand, was easy and low voiced. Amanda was delighted. Polly had finally given up the animosity she'd felt at "being put in the position of mere kitchen help" and was enjoying her new acquaintance.

Amanda smiled and moved away from the door. Not for all the world would she intrude and risk interrupting the rapport developing between them.

She'd find a book to read, instead. Her tread was firm as she took herself to the library.

Reading was her favorite pastime. It had been her escape and refuge since she was a child. Many were the long, happy hours she had spent on a tropical island, marooned with Robinson Crusoe, or flashing down the lists toward another armored knight with Ivanhoe.

Surely in reading she could rid herself of this strange . . . what? She thought the French had given the world the best word for it. It described her feeling exactly. *Malaise.*

She scanned the shelves. *Ivanhoe* was there. It had always been one of her favorites. She pulled it from the shelf, let it fall open and perused a page. "Sorry, Mr. Scott, but no," she murmured, disappointed. She shoved the leather-bound friend back into place. "I'm simply not up to the tale of two unrequited loves today."

Shakespeare's sonnets tugged at her, but she shook her head. His tragedies got a "No. Something cheerier, I think." The comedies got ignored as well, however.

Pride and Prejudice! There was a book she never tired of. She found the Regency period fascinating. England passing from the bold and open Georgian era into the much stricter society of the Regency always made for interesting reading.

So many things had changed in England during the Regency. It was during that period that Beau Brummel's friendship with the Regent had resulted in English society accepting the idea of bathing. "Thank Heaven," she murmured.

As she pulled Miss Jane Austen's best work from the shelf, Amanda wondered if she were homesick. "No," she mused. "That's not the answer. I do wonder what in the world is the matter with me, though."

Pride and Prejudice fell open to the scene in which Elizabeth refused Darcy's clumsy proposal. She snapped the book shut. She loved it, but it wasn't her answer today.

"Not Austen either?" She shook her head as she replaced the book on the shelf. "You are indeed hard to please, today, my girl."

Obviously she was being as impossible today as she had been the day before.

Restless, unable to stand her own company, she went looking for Laura and David. They were absorbed in a game of chess.

She saw that they were both content. She was on her own.

She tiptoed away from the study, and stood for a while at the front door. Drawing a deep breath of the sun-scented air, she felt her spirits lift.

That was it! She needed fresh air. This dreadful discontent must stem from the fact that she hadn't gotten any exercise for the past few days. Sitting in the buckboard trying to be as unpleasant as she could had not been any kind of *physical* exercise.

While it had certainly been *an* exercise in both bad manners and frustration, her behavior on the ride home from English Bend hadn't gotten her blood flowing. Not in a healthful way, anyhow.

She determinedly ignored the reprimand her conscience was trying to give her, and the nagging thought that skirted the edges of her mind—the thought that she knew the answer to it all, but wouldn't let herself admit it. Instead, she concentrated on her earlier idea. That was it, she decided. Exercise was the solution to her present mood. She just needed some time to blow the cobwebs out of her mind.

Suddenly, taking Evening Star out for a ride seemed the very thing. She wanted to go alone, however, so that she could roam wherever she pleased. She wanted to ride at whatever pace she pleased, too, without the constant precautions the men of the ranch were always attempting to put on her.

Slipping quietly from the house, she made her way to the barn. Luck was with her, and Mason was nowhere to be seen. She told her mare, "We can have the day to ourselves, Star. Won't that be nice?"

The mare nickered as if she understood, and Amanda laughed. She felt better already. Except for the nagging thought.

Minutes later, they were headed out to the hills. The clear blue sky beckoned them onward.

At one point, Amanda caught sight of a lone rider in the distance. She pulled her mount into a stand of cottonwoods. "We don't want company, do we girl?"

They rode in the opposite direction, and finally came to a low formation of rocks that looked familiar. It proved to be the place Amanda had hoped she remembered how to find. Entering it through a narrow canyon, they followed a faint path that led slightly down from the level of the ground outside.

Star picked her way carefully to a little pool in the rocks that Amanda remembered from a long-ago visit. "Oh, look, there it is. I remembered."

Dismounting, she loosened Star's cinch. "Better?" She smoothed her hand down the mare's long, satiny neck, then hugged her impetuously.

Amanda felt as deliciously naughty as a child escaped from the schoolroom. She pulled off her boots and socks and slithered down into the cool water of the pool. "Oh." She wriggled her toes in the cool, clear water. "How wonderful."

While Star dozed shot-hipped in the shade, Amanda walked the length of the small stream that fed the pool to where it spilled from the crevice in the rock that was its source. Delighted by the cool clarity and smooth bottom of the little run, she began to play the game of prospecting that she and David had shared as children.

All the cares that had weighed on her for the last few years in Confederate Richmond slipped away as she made selecting pebbles from the bottom of the stream the most important project of the moment. There might be no golden nugget to excite her now, any more than there had been one when she and David had played here, but she didn't need one.

There had never needed to be one then, as the hunt had been the thing, and there was no need for treasure of that sort now. Treasure enough was the peace of this golden moment.

And suddenly, with her mind clear of all other thoughts, the one she had been avoiding slipped in. She was in love with Reese Rivers. She straightened from her search of the stream bottom in astonishment.

It was true! She who had refused the cream of English nobility was head over heels in love with a man who was called a saddle bum! She stood considering it, a bemused smile on her face. Then, with another quiet smile and a shrug of acceptance, she went back to her prospecting.

Before she knew it, the hours had slipped away in a happy daze, and with it the bright sunniness of the day. A whicker from Star brought her back to the present. She looked up to find that the sky had darkened ominously, and a rising wind was stirring through the canyon.

She scrambled hastily out of the stream, dropping the pebbles she'd picked up back into it. As she yanked her socks and boots back on, she told her mare, "Oh, dear, Star. We'd better hurry home. I don't like the look of that sky, and if the wind is this strong down here, it's probably a lot worse out in the open."

She sprang up and dusted the bottom of her divided skirt. "If a storm's on its way, we'd better get home before it catches us."

Her worst fears were confirmed when they reached the mouth of the canyon. The wind was blowing forcefully, sending grit flying. The sky was uniformly dark, and split occasionally by distant flashes of lightning.

She should have remembered that Texas weather could be unpredictable at this time of year and kept better watch. She reined Star back into the protection offered by the steep walls of the little canyon while she tried to decide the best course of action.

Staying in the canyon wouldn't do, she realized. The path they'd followed into it was one carved by centuries of rain running off the range. In a thunderstorm like the one that was fast approaching, it would quickly become unsafe to remain where she was.

She knew being out on a horse on the open range in a thunderstorm was not only foolish, it was downright dangerous. A rider became an inviting target for lightning over a flat plain.

"Thank heaven we didn't bring Laura, Star." With a little shiver she heard the tension in her own voice as she told the mare. "We're in trouble."

Amanda watched the mare flick her ears nervously back and forth. Star didn't like the storm any better than she did. She held the mare firmly as she sidled and stamped, obviously eager to run for home and the safety of her stall in the big barn.

To let her do so was to expose them to the very real danger of being struck by lightning. They couldn't stay where they were, though. The wind was screaming, now, and Star was on the verge of panic. "Where can we go?"

She heard the edge of panic in her own voice. This wouldn't do. It was all right to be nervous, indeed, there was very little chance of not being nervous in her present situation. The trick was not to let it render her incapable of finding a solution to her dilemma.

Suddenly she remembered. "The line shack! There's a line shack a mile or two from here, Star. I can keep you out of the open under this bluff for most of the way there."

Relieved now that she had made her decision, Amanda rode out into the storm.

Chapter 12

Good! There was a storm brewing up fast over on the horizon. Reese straightened up from the calf he'd just tied, wiped the sweat from his eyes with a shirtsleeve, and assessed the lowering clouds with satisfaction. A good storm was all the cover he needed.

"Okay, men," Webster bellowed. Already, he could hardly be heard over the wail of the rising wind. "We better head in until after this storm passes."

The hands, squinting against the blowing dust, coiled ropes and gathered up the rest of their gear with quick efficiency. They were more than ready to head in to shelter until this squall had passed.

Reese set the calf free, smacked it on the rump, and watched it scramble, bawling, for its mother. Then he packed it in, too.

He took his own sweet time about it. Narrowing his eyes against the blowing grit, he turned his face into the wind, relishing the illusion of coolness brought by the first strong breezes as they touched his sweat-drenched skin.

The storm was a personal gift. It would keep the men pinned down in the bunkhouse, and free Reese to go take a look at the first of the line shacks he wanted to investigate—the one out near the bluffs.

He'd tried to get to it the other day, but he'd run into a couple of the men rounding up strays from that area, and he'd decided not to chance it. No need to give them the idea that he was interested in the line shacks.

That was the last thing Reese wanted. Instead, he'd helped them bring in the steers.

Today, with that lightning building up the way it was in the dark clouds he was watching, he'd be willing to bet that there wouldn't be anybody over that way. Nobody wanted to take a chance on getting fried. He wasn't too keen on the idea himself, but he had a job to do.

He trailed the other men back to the ranch buildings. When they'd all gotten their horses back in the corral, they lit out for the bunkhouse, eager to escape the blowing dust.

Reese didn't join them as they hurried, spurs jingling, to shelter. Instead, he sluiced off at the pump beside the horse trough. When his hair felt halfway clean again, he rinsed the salty sweat out of his shirt. Putting it back on wet to cool him down more, he sauntered off to the barn.

As he saddled Thor, he listened to the distant rumble of thunder and weighed the idea of pulling the big black's iron shoes to keep him a little safer from lightning. Unfortunately, given the shale and rocks over in the direction Reese wanted to go, that would probably result in a lameness for the big stallion.

In the end, he decided to try to race the storm to the shack and sit it out there. Then he could come back in perfect safety after the weather cleared.

If he were going to make the plan work, he'd have to get a move on.

Saddling up took only a few minutes, in spite of the restless excitement Thor was picking up from the echoes of the distant storm. Reese swung up onto the horse and rode him out of the barn into the darkening day. Setting him on the trail to the bluff they could no longer see in the gathering darkness, Reese gave the big horse his head.

Sitting his mount's smooth, ground-eating stride effortlessly, he gave himself over to enjoyment of the wild day.

He drew a deep breath of the clean air coming from the black clouds on the near horizon and smiled.

The storm touched something primitive in him. A storm was something safe to pit himself against. A challenge without a penalty. Meeting it was like combat . . . combat with no regrets.

There were no wives of the storm to widow, no children to orphan. He could throw his frail human strength against its elemental force without a qualm of conscience.

He had only to win the race he had set for himself to the bluff to win against the storm. And the storm had only to stop him.

Simple. That simplicity set him free.

Thor caught his rider's mood and bucked once, jarring Reese to his back teeth. Then he settled down to prove that a Thoroughbred could cover ground like no other horse alive.

Reese laughed exultantly as they flew through the wind-torn, fading daylight toward the bluffs.

Hugging the base of the low bluff, Amanda and Evening Star were not laughing. The little mare had all she could do to make progress against the howling winds driving straight at her from the rain-heavy thunderheads hanging over the cliffs behind the line shack. Every time a piece of brush from the cliff edge above sailed down over their heads they both flinched.

Then they arrived at the end of the bluff. Now they had to face the full force of the wind as they crossed the floor of the next canyon in order to reach the shack.

The only shelter for miles, it huddled beneath a rock overhang on the far side of the canyon. To Amanda, it seemed miles away.

Reluctantly, they left the windbreak provided by the bluff. Star staggered when the full strength of the wind hit her.

Amanda hung on to the saddle horn for all she was worth. Her hat was torn from her head with such force that the narrow cord that held it cut into her throat.

Sand and dust flew at them, blinding them. Amanda squinted her eyes and threw up an arm to protect her face from the stinging sand. Even so, she could barely make out their destination.

In the featureless lash of windblown dust before the coming rain, there was only the stark outline of the old tree beside the shack to guide her. She fastened her gaze on it and watched it through the tangle of her eyelashes, afraid to lose sight of it.

They were almost across the canyon. Star struggled for every step.

With a searing whoosh, lightning singed through the air and down. The tree disappeared in an explosion of blue light.

Star reared and fell heavily as she twisted away, screaming. Her head slammed into a rock as she landed.

Amanda was blinded by the blazing strike. The force of the impact sent her senses flying. She lay pinned, helpless, under her unconscious horse.

Reese saw the lightning strike, and knew it had hit in the vicinity of the line shack. Knowing the rain was coming now, he told his skittish mount, "Whoa, Thor. Steady, boy." Then he pulled out and donned his slicker. Thor sidled nervously at the crackling sound of the thing being flapped around behind and over his head, but he held his ground, quivering, obedient to his rider's voice.

With a sound like the rending of the very heavens, torrential rain came pouring down. Reese crammed his hat down even more firmly, and rode to meet the downpour. "Good boy, Thor. Good boy," he rewarded the stallion.

When the rain hit them, Thor, oblivious to any protection

LOVING HONOR

he might have afforded his rider, bogged his head low and kept moving resolutely into the storm.

Reese accepted his now completely exposed position stoically. At least Thor was willing to move into the teeth of the storm. He'd ridden a few horses that would have just turned their tails to the driving rain until its fury had abated no matter what the rider wanted.

The big black, streaming water like Niagara Falls, slowed to a trot and followed the bluff toward the line shack. Sheets of water hurtled off the top of the bluff now, bringing rocks and bits of brush with it. They stayed out far enough to miss being hit by the debris.

They came to the end of the bluff. Thor whinnied sharply and skidded to a halt.

"What the hell? What is it, boy?"

Reese peered ahead through the driving rain. It was too heavy to see what had caused Thor's abrupt stop.

They'd come too far together for him not to trust the big stallion, however. He dismounted and moved forward cautiously.

Good God! A dead horse and rider! Making his way toward the sodden hump with Thor just behind him, he prayed. There wasn't much he could do for a poor devil hit by lightning except pray for his soul.

When he neared the downed horse, his heart stopped beating. He recognized the dainty mare. It was Amanda's!

Frantically he plunged forward the last few feet. His stomach turned to jelly.

"Ahhh, God," he heard himself groan as he fell to his knees beside her. "Amanda! Dear God! Amanda!"

The words were torn from him by a searing agony. He reached for her and saw that his hands shook. He wiped them down the sides of his thighs, as if the gesture would take away their unsteadiness.

When he put out a hand toward her again it was no better. With shaking hands he reached for her. She couldn't be dead. She couldn't . . . but he had to know.

He froze in the next flash of lightning, his hands inches from her shoulders. Crouching immobile, he looked down at her. He realized that he was afraid to touch her, afraid to confirm the fear that was tearing him apart.

Her pale hair fanned out against the golden soil of the canyon floor, wheat pale in comparison when the light from the storm touched her. Any moment now the rain would turn the earth under her to a sea of mud to trap and tarnish the glow of those strands.

He could never permit that!

His mind refused to do his bidding, refused to sharpen and solve. It spun with the enormity of the loss he felt at seeing her there, lying so still.

"Damn you, Rivers!" he roared, and shook his head, baffled. Never before had his abilities betrayed him. What the bloody hell was his problem?

His curse released him, and he shifted her head and shoulders to cradle her in his lap. His mind working now that he had her safe, he made a tent over them with his slicker, protecting her from the torrent that fell from the sky.

Thank God! She was alive, warm and breathing, her breath feathering lightly against his neck. And *he* came alive again.

He reached out a rock-steady hand to feel the pulse that beat steadily under the mare's jawbone. Good. Amanda thought a lot of the mare. He was glad she was all right.

He had to get Amanda into the line shack. He ran his hand over the sweet curve of her hip and down her leg to as far as he could thrust his hand under the horse's side.

They were in luck. A ridge of rock in the canyon floor was holding most of the mare's weight off Amanda's leg.

He clawed a small ditch to channel some of the deluge down beside her leg to where it was pinned under the horse.

Quickly he dug the girl's leg loose as the rainwater softened the dirt around it. With a strong pull, he drew her free.

Gathering her into his arms, he cradled her against him. His whole body shook with relief, as if he'd moved a mountain to free her. Thank God he'd gotten her loose without causing her pain.

He smoothed her hair back from her forehead in a gesture touched with desperation. As the rain pelted a tattoo on the surface of his slicker just over their heads, he fought an absurd desire to cover her face with kisses.

She stirred and opened her eyes. They were soft with confusion. An instant later, by the blue light of another near strike, he saw that they had focused.

When a sizzling fork of lightning rendered his slicker almost transparent and tore the dark away, she recognized him. Tentatively she reached out to touch his chin.

Then the lightning was a personal thing. This lightning blazed through him at her touch.

"Is it . . . truly you, Mr. Rivers?"

Greater relief exploded in him like fireworks. "Yes." The single word sounded surly. He added, his voice harsh with tension, "Are you all right?"

"I . . . I . . . think so. My leg is caught, but otherwise I'm fine." Panic filled her eyes. "Star! Is Star all right?"

Gently Reese ran his hand down the leg he'd freed from under the mare. It troubled him that she thought it was still pinned under the mare. He could feel no break.

She started at his touch and flinched her leg away from his hand. "Oh!" She said it wonderingly, still not herself. "You have got me free." She sounded a little breathless.

He thought it safer to go to another subject. His touching her seemed to have too strong an effect on both of them.

He was still fighting his way back from the awful pit he'd descended into when he'd believed her dead. He needed time to recover fully.

Carefully he stretched his slicker into a better position

around them both. He tucked it under his knee to secure it against the wind, making a safer little tent under which to talk with her.

"Are you certain you're all right? You weren't hit by the lightning?"

Asinine question. She wouldn't be alive if she'd been struck by lightning.

He'd had to say something, though. With her seated where he'd lifted her into his lap to keep her above the rivers of rainwater now running over the canyon floor, it was hard for him to think coherently.

He forgave himself the asininity.

"No," she said with a little shiver that moved her soft weight against him. "It was a near thing, though. The lightning struck the tree by the line shack just as we started over from the shelter of the bluff."

In the almost complete darkness under their makeshift shelter, she peered at him, determined to know whether or not his next answer was the truth. "Star reared when the lightning hit the tree. She fell." She couldn't keep the anxiety out of her voice. "Will she really be all right?"

Reese, still coping with the effect her little quiver of emotion had had on him, saw the tears glittering in her eyes by the light of the next flash. He knew how he'd feel if that were Thor stretched out on the rain-soaked ground, and concentrated on that, instead.

It wasn't in his nature to reassure if he wasn't certain his reassurance would be the truth. Since there was nothing he desired more than to tell her her mare would be fine, he was glad he thought it was so.

Just as he started to promise that he'd see to the mare once he had *her* safe, the wind ripped his foul-weather gear up and almost away. Driving rain slashed at them, putting an end to any thought of reassurances.

Scooping her up in his arms, he drove to his feet, snatched up his slicker, and ran toward the line shack.

"Thor!" he yelled back over his shoulder, "Get that mare up!"

Reese crashed into the door of the shack and jabbed the latch with his elbow. He sent it slamming back against the flimsy wall of the cabin with his back and shoulder and reeled inside. Standing back in the shelter of the doorway, he watched to see how his stallion fared at his assigned task.

When Amanda tried to see, too, he pressed her face into his shoulder with enough force to see that she kept it there. He had no guarantee the mare would get up, now or ever.

Thor took to his task with an enthusiasm that would have appalled the girl grieving for her fallen mare. Pinching with his big yellow teeth and biting at her, he brought the mare, shocked and complaining, to her senses.

"She's come around," Reese told Amanda. Then he fought for breath as she relaxed in his arms, and the sweet weight of her rested closer against him.

Outside, Thor backed off and let the mare curl up and lie still a moment with her head up, swaying dizzily. Then the thunder rolled ominously, and his patience ended.

Mercilessly nipping, he drove the squealing mare to her feet and herded her after his master. Thor found shelter for them between the shack and the cliff wall. There, protected by the rock overhang from the downpour, they dropped their heads and turned their tails toward the storm.

Inside the shack, Reese fought to hang on to the control that was trying to slip away from him. No woman had ever had such a debilitating effect on him.

He sure as hell didn't like it.

Braced easily against Amanda's slight weight, he scanned the tiny cabin. He'd no intention of setting her down anywhere until he'd seen for himself that the shack was clear of any snakes or wild visitors.

Spying a lamp standing on the table in the center of the room when lightning flared through the open door behind them, he crossed to it with her still in his arms. Holding her tightly in the circle of one arm, he felt around the tabletop for matches or a flint.

Amanda sensed an unfamiliar tension in him. Her uneasiness about it made her breathless.

Light flared and danced on the tip of a lucifer. Rivers turned as if surveying the room, the match held high.

Seemingly satisfied with what he had or had not seen by its light, he permitted Amanda to slip down his side to a standing position. She felt his muscles quiver with the strain of having held her with only one arm. She stepped away from him quickly.

Reese lifted the chimney of the lamp and ignited its wick. He took his time about it, as if he performed some sacred ritual against the dark.

He was too aware of her proximity. At least, he was pleased to see that his hands no longer shook.

He went to the door and stood there breathing in great drafts of the lightning-tinged air. What was this effect Amanda Harcourt was having on him?

Concern for Amanda Harcourt, he corrected himself sternly. It was his concern for her that had him so shaken.

He was shaken because when he'd first found her he'd thought her dead. That was what had thrown him off so. Nothing less could have rattled him like this.

God knew no woman could. Not after Analise. He was proof against them all, thanks to her.

Himself again, he turned to tell her. "I'll be right back. I'm going to see to the horses."

Without waiting for her answering nod, he plunged out into the rain. As he expected, Thor had brought the groggy mare to the little corral behind the cabin. She still looked a little dazed, but she'd soon get over that. She looked fine otherwise.

As he approached the two horses, he talked to them in a voice loud enough to be heard over the thunder. He had no intention of being kicked into the next world because he was too dumb to let storm-spooked animals know he was coming up behind them.

Stripping off their bridles, he uncinched their saddles and left the corral lugging the tack over one shoulder, latching the gate as he left them. When he'd regained the relative safety of the cabin, he plopped the heavy saddles down on their horns to dry off, and tossed the bridles on top of them.

Amanda made an impatient sound, and picked up the bridles. She looked around for pegs, or even nails to hang them from. When she saw Reese watching her she said, "There's no need to have them twisted as they dry."

He merely grunted. If she wanted to hang bridles, let her. He'd felt the coolness of her rain-soaked body when he'd had her in his arms, and his own first order of business was to get a fire going to warm her up.

There was plenty of firewood stacked beside the crude fireplace. He tossed off his slicker and began laying a fire.

Amanda came right behind him. The bridles were now safely on wall pegs meant to hold cowboys' heavy coats during winter stays in the cabin. She picked up his slicker, gave it a shake that sent rain scattering through the small space, and hung it on a third peg.

He could feel her implied criticism of his behavior in dumping things. He didn't give a damn. Nights got cold up here, and this one was coming early. Seeing to it that she didn't take a chill was the most important thing right now, whether or not she had sense enough to know it.

Reese could feel her standing behind him. It made the hairs on the back of his neck want to rise. Why the devil was he so aware of her? Of everything about her. He could even hear her soft breathing.

That's quite a trick, Rivers. How the deuce do you think you can do that? This storm is making one helluva lot of noise!

He could, though. There was no way he could deny it.

His nerves itched with awareness of her.

It was going to be a long night.

Chapter 13

The cabin creaked as the screaming winds of the storm tore at it. Chinks in its walls made it almost impossible to heat, as the wind whipped the warmth away through them.

Amanda sat huddled in a blanket in front of the rude fireplace where Reese had put her. Her derriere was numb from sitting on the crudely fashioned wooden chair, and she was heartily sick of being bossed by the taciturn Reese Rivers.

More than anything, she wished he would pronounce her dry enough so that she could move about. She tossed her hair back and informed him, "I'm dry now. Surely you can't object to my getting up and walking around."

He crossed to her from where he'd been watching the storm through the one tiny window. Without so much as by-your-leave, he thrust his hand into her cocoon and felt the back of her neck where her still-damp hair touched her sodden collar.

Amanda fought an urge to gasp as his long fingers touched her nape. The man seemed made of the lightning that still flashed outside. Tingles shot through her to her toes. So did a new and wondrous knowledge.

So this was what happened when the one you loved touched you. She kept her smile secret.

"You don't seem dry to me," he stated flatly.

"Well," she answered him with some asperity as soon as

she got her breath back, "I am quite dry enough. I'm weary with sitting here, and I don't intend to do so a minute longer."

She rose purposefully and turned to face him. Suddenly she was aware of just how big he was. He loomed over her, his lean, athletic body seemed to fill the cabin.

She fought the impulse to recoil a step.

He was a dark figure, fire touched. Something about his stillness made her heart beat faster. The same something suddenly made her aware of just how alone they were.

Willing her hands to be steady, she deliberately folded the blanket, concentrating on the task as if it were the most important thing she'd ever done. Perhaps, her mind told her, it was.

Electricity that rivaled that of the storm had filled the cabin. Amanda felt as if her hair would dry in the currents that sizzled between her and the tall, silent man before her. That was, if it hadn't already from the heat the touch of his fingers had caused at the nape of her neck.

Something caught in her throat, and her breath began to come in short little efforts. She clamped her will down on the tendency, and took a deep breath to stop it.

She saw his gaze go to her breasts as they lifted to accommodate that breath. Instantly they became alive with a tingling she'd never experienced before.

She held her breath, locking it in the base of her throat, and turned back to the fire. She refused to gasp. The effect his glance had had on her made it difficult not to.

She could *feel* him behind her. She knew, to the inch, exactly how far away he was.

She had no need to see him with her eyes to judge the distance. She could feel him there with her skin, with her hair.

So this was love! Never in her entire life had she been so aware of another being's presence. Her body wanted to tremble. Only her pride held her steady.

How was she to get through it if she had to spend a night in this cabin with this man? Her body's response to him shocked her. She seemed incapable of behaving naturally.

She tried to swallow, but couldn't. Why didn't he say something? Anything. This was impossible!

Reese stood stock-still. He was frozen to immobility by the shock of his reaction to Amanda Harcourt's simply drawing a breath.

His own breathing became a matter for thought. He felt that if he didn't command his lungs to expand and draw in the air he was starved for, they'd let him die of suffocation.

What the hell was the matter with him? He wasn't a callow youth to get overtaken by lust just because he was alone with a beautiful woman.

Sharply he called his raging senses to order. He'd better get a grip on himself.

If he didn't watch out, his odd behavior would frighten her. It was sure as hell coming damn close to frightening him!

This attack of desire he was suffering could make her uncomfortable. He certainly didn't want that to happen. One word from her to her brother would send him packing before he'd accomplished his mission.

That thought steadied him.

He reached out and took the blanket she was folding from her. He ignored the spark that leapt between them when their fingers touched.

"Electricity. From the friction," he said gruffly, though there had been none in spite of the blanket's being wool.

The spark that had flashed between them had been born only of attraction. Attraction, pure and simple.

He saw by her eyes that she knew that. He also saw that, like him, she preferred the easier—less dangerous—explanation.

Neither of them could find anything else to say. Finally she broke the spell by looking away.

He watched her smooth the back of her split riding skirt against the back of her legs and sit on the edge of the lower bunk. She looked toward the fire, away from him.

He tried not to think about that smooth, firm line of her hip and the way it had comforted his hand when he'd traced it out there in the rain and the mud on the canyon floor earlier. He refused to think of the silken feel of her bare leg as he reached to bring it out from under her fallen horse.

Instead, he concentrated, hard, on harmless observation. She was short enough so that she could sit comfortably erect without her head touching the slats of the upper bunk.

Sitting there so erectly, she looked so proper, so very British. He almost smiled.

Standing she had barely reached his shoulder. She'd fit comfortably under his arm. For a moment, he could actually feel the soft length of her there, warming all down his side. And his left arm felt empty, for he would have held her there, nearest his heart.

Before he could save himself, memory overwhelmed him. She had fit *in* his arms. Perfectly, with exquisite precision, as if she been made to be in his arms always.

Outside in the canyon when he'd lifted her into his lap to keep the mud from touching her, she'd fit very nicely in his arms. His manhood remembered her weight in his lap. Madly, achingly, he tried to recall her fragrance. She was . . .

Cursing under his breath, he felt his body respond to his thoughts of her. He went back to the window to watch the progress of the storm.

Amanda watched Reese.

She tried to think of something to say, but the man's intensity seemed to forbid idle talk. She wondered if she should attempt to thank him properly for saving her, again, by pulling her out from under Star.

She surely owed him thanks. She might have lain there for heaven knew how long before Star revived and scrambled off her leg. And even then she might have had her trapped leg mangled, or been severely injured by the iron-shod hooves of a scrambling, disoriented horse.

Just how did one thank a man like Reese Rivers, she wondered?

She cleared her throat to speak, but at the same instant he said, "It looks as if it's clearing. I'm sure you'll want to get back. I'll saddle the horses."

"Thank you." She hated saying the words. It was wisest to leave, of course, but she realized that she didn't want to go. Not just yet. Irrationally, she knew there was something that must be settled between them. She didn't want to leave this place.

With an aching confusion, she knew that there was something that kept her here. What? What was it she wanted? Was it time alone with him, to get to know him? To ask him who and what he was?

She was confused and a little shocked by the impropriety of her feelings. They were all so new, so strange and puzzling, and their strength frightened her. What *did* she feel for this man, this stranger? Why was she . . .

She sighed in frustration. They couldn't linger. There was nothing else to say now anyway. Whatever it was she wanted, it was part and parcel of the restlessness she had been experiencing lately. And it was impossible to share that with him. It was too late to say anything, even if she'd known what it was she longed to say. The moment had passed.

The least she could do was to help tack up the horses, though. She jumped up, and moved briskly to bring the bridles down from the pegs where she had hung them.

Distracted, she forgot to watch where she was going. Her foot struck one of the heavy saddles, all but invisible in the dimness of the cabin, just as Reese reached for them. She lurched forward with a little cry, and threw out her hands to break the force of her fall.

Reese leapt to catch her. As he did, one of his hands chanced to brush her breast. Suddenly she was clasped in his arms. He held her, fiercely crushed against his chest. Not safe against his chest. Oh, no, she didn't feel safe at all.

The palms of the hands she'd thrust forward to catch her were trapped against his chest. She felt the lean hard muscles there . . . and the sudden acceleration of his heartbeat.

Her lips inches from his, she looked up into his eyes and saw there whatever demon he'd been fighting all evening. Her breath left her lungs, and she was conscious only of her blood singing in her veins . . . and of *him*.

She wasn't restless anymore. She was helpless, mesmerized by the fierce possessiveness in his gaze . . . and the realization that he was losing his fight.

Overcome by the lassitude that filled her, she felt as if she were as old as time. She felt as if she were every woman who had ever been held in the arms of the man she loved.

She felt as if she had come home. Not safely home, but daringly, dangerously home. She felt . . . triumphant.

She parted her lips to ease her breathing.

It was all the invitation he needed. With a groan Reese covered her mouth with his own, plundering from her lips the response he'd dreamed of in the nights that he'd lain listening for her voice, her footsteps, the mention of her name.

He crushed her to him with a strength that should have made her cry out, yet didn't. He was exultant that she did not.

He'd waited so long to touch her, to feel his hands on her silken skin.

So many times she'd touched him—her hand against his forehead to see if his fever was down, her fingers lightly skimming him as she adjusted or changed his bandage. In his memory, he could feel again her hands brushing his chest above his bandage as she tried to lower his raging body temperature by bathing his burning skin.

She'd touched him, driving him half mad, and he'd blamed it on his delirium. But now he knew that he'd been wild to respond in kind. He'd been nearly out of his mind to reach out to feel her skin in answer to her touch upon his own.

Here in the line shack, her nearness had been tearing at him all evening. As the storm had echoed through blood already pounding in his veins with the effort to keep his hands off her, he'd suffered the tortures of the damned.

Now an accident had thrown her into his arms, and he could see that she was in no hurry to leave them. His hand touching her breast had been his undoing. At the brief, accidental contact, the last vestige of his control gave way.

He'd been tantalized all through the storm by her presence in the cabin. Now her willingness to rest in his arms drove him past caution.

When she entwined her arms around his neck and pulled him closer, he gave in to the wild urge to touch her breast again. When she moaned as he cupped it, his senses reeled.

He could feel the insatiable hunger he had denied having for her sweep over him like a storm tide. It dashed away all restraint.

Running his hands down her back he brought her hips closer, comforting the hardness of his body. "Amanda," he murmured against her lips. And again, "Amanda."

Then he kissed her eyelids and her throat and the swell of her breasts, before he returned to claim her mouth. He was gentle, at last, calmed by the knowledge that she was his.

Since the long moment she had stood indecisively in the doorway of his sickroom in her silken wrapper, he'd fought the knowledge that he wanted her more than he'd ever wanted any woman. He'd used all the talismans at his disposal to keep himself from admitting that his every desire was for her. But now she was his. A gift from the storm gods.

He looked down into her half-closed eyes, and saw the clear blue of them was smoked with passion. He let his gaze travel to her lips, soft and bruised by his kisses. He fought the urge to kiss her again, and said instead, "Say my name." His voice was a husky whisper.

She heard it mingle with the distant rumbling of thunder from the retreating storm, and smiled. "Reese," she said obediently. It sounded like a benediction.

He growled low in his throat to hear the languorous note in her voice. She was his! He knew it with a savage certainty.

He had only to lift her to the bunk and stretch out beside her and spend the long night lovingly teaching her what love between a man and a woman could be.

Smiling, he bent to lift her to carry her to the narrow bunk. Desire for her roared through him. He started toward his goal, his pulse hammering in his ears.

She kept her gaze locked on his lips, letting him know that she, too, admitted this was preordained. No missish airs marred her regal acceptance of this, their gift from fate.

Never, in his wildest, most fevered dreams had he known that he could feel as he felt now about Amanda. Never had he thought that he—

One step short of the bunk, he heard Thor whinny.

The sound was like a cold dash of water. He'd brought Thor to help him accomplish his mission. He'd brought the big stallion to help track down the killers of his best and truest friend.

What the hell was he doing?

He'd been about to claim the girl in his arms! He'd been about to take her and brand her as his own just as if he had a right to bind her to him forever with a night of lovemaking. As if he had the right to pledge to her with his body.

Fool! What would she feel if she then discovered that

he'd come into her life for the express purpose of hanging her brother?

Dear God! Wasn't it enough that every minute she'd known him had been a lie?

Self-contempt scalded him. *Would you take the sister, then turn her love for you to unspeakable hatred when you hang her brother?*

He stood rock still, cherishing the precious weight of her in his arms. Despair washed the desire from his body like an icy river.

After a moment that seemed to last a lifetime, he lowered Amanda gently onto the bunk, and took her arms from around his neck. Dizzy with the effort it cost him, he stepped back.

He thought the pain that tore through him must be like that suffered by the damned.

Quietly he said, "I'll go saddle the horses."

Chapter 14

Amanda hadn't been able to look at him even once on the ride home. She knew she was going to die of shame. One glance in his direction would have severed her very soul from her body.

The pain and bewilderment she'd felt when he'd left her curled in a miserable, shamed little ball on the bunk in the line shack was gone now, and in its place was utter humiliation.

She didn't know how she was going to live with it.

"I think it would be best if I let you ride in first." Reese spoke in a voice she could hardly recognize. "It might be better, too, if you let them think you weathered the storm in the line shack *alone*."

She heard the emphasis he put on the last word. She nodded, silent, still refusing to look at him.

Yesterday she would have been startled at his suggestion. A little insulted, she would have told him in no uncertain terms that her brother would have known that nothing improper had passed between them.

Today . . . Today was a different matter. For today she knew herself to be . . . She couldn't even frame the words in her mind.

Tears threatened her composure. She willed them away with every force at her command. If she cried in front of Reese Rivers she knew she would die on the spot.

Not trusting herself to speak, she nodded to show that she understood his gallant attempt to save her reputation. Still without a word or a backward glance she rode on toward the ranch house.

Only when she heard his stallion turn and gallop away, no doubt to approach the ranch from another direction, did she give in to the luxury of tears.

"Amanda! Thank God!" David rode to meet her. Behind him the ranch hands smiled their relief, and turned back to leave the brother and sister alone.

She was glad, then, that she'd been unable to give full vent to her upset and humiliation a few minutes ago. She was grateful now for the terrible bred-in reserve that had limited her to a token tear or two.

Hot shame flared in her. Reserve. She wondered where it had been when she had so willingly played the wanton in Reese Rivers' arms!

She'd thought the agony of having been denied the relief of tears would kill her at the time. Now she was glad. The few tears she'd been able to shed could be mistaken for tears of joy at safely returning.

"David! You were mounting a search party for me?"

"Of course, my dear." His smile was full of relief. "We were worried about you, out in that storm. Thank God you're all right."

"I managed to make it to the old line shack out near the bluffs."

"Thank God. Laura kept telling me you'd be all right. That you, and I quote, 'had a head on your shoulders.'"

Amanda startled herself by laughing. Evidently she hadn't completely died of humiliation when Reese Rivers left her to go saddle their horses.

Strange. She'd been sure she had.

"Laura is waiting for you at the house. She says she's not

the least bit worried, but you'll be flattered to know she doesn't even realize that there was no supper tonight."

Amanda turned in her saddle and gave him what she was sure was a travesty of a smile. "Splendid, I am ravenous."

David laughed with relieved delight. "There. Now I am truly reassured. You've always been fine as long as you had an appetite."

He leaned over and squeezed her hand. He drew back, holding it, concerned. "Amanda. Your hand is so cold." He peered at her, trying to see her expression under the shadow of the brim of her hat.

She forced a smile. "It's just nerves, dearest." So she was right. A part of her had died up there under the cliff. Died of humiliation and . . . and what?

She forced herself to admit it . . . of longing. No, she told herself savagely, tell the truth. Of desire.

To David she said, "I'll race you to the house. That'll get my blood flowing again."

As they thundered down the trail to the big ranch house, she wondered if her blood would ever again rush, singing, through her veins as it had when she'd been in the arms of the man who had spurned her.

That night when she was safe in her bed, the tears came. Floods of quiet, self-hating tears. Never again would she permit herself to show her emotions as she had when Reese Rivers had held her in his arms.

Even as she thought his name, her body flamed into life and wanted him, achingly.

She turned on her stomach and punched her pillow with all her might. She punched it as if it were *him,* and when she had worn out her anger and dropped her head on her battered pillow, she was still afire at the simple memory of his kisses. Of his body, hard and lean and urgent against her own.

"Ooooh." She lunged from her bed to stand at the window. She lifted her hair to let the night breeze cool her fevered nape. The gesture only reminded her of his touch there in the cabin. It had been that touch that had set all this . . . this *hunger* loose in her.

She let her hair fall, shutting her mind to the thought of his touch. "This is impossible!"

She paced the floor for a few moments, then returned to the window and its cool breeze. "If only I could leave. If only I could take Laura and go to grandfather's town house in Richmond."

She couldn't, of course. If the news was true, Richmond was all but destroyed. There probably wasn't even a house left to return to.

Standing in front of the window, she grasped the neck of her nightgown to pull it away from her and allow a breath of air next to her . . . "Yes, Amanda," she told herself in a jeering whisper, "admit it . . . your *passion-heated skin!*" She flailed herself with her contempt.

Fierce humiliation rose again to engulf her. She had *wanted* him. *Wanted!*

Never had she thought that she would feel such hunger and yearning for a man, any man. The women in her family were cool and self-contained. They knew their duty, and they did it without complaint. That was the family tradition.

It had been Faith who had been the first woman of her acquaintance to blush and smile and sigh and seem to look forward to the night. When it drew near she had been full of blushes and shining eagerness to go up the broad marble stairs with David.

The others had smiled indulgently or frowned disapprovingly depending on the bent of their particular personality. Both groups, however, had tolerantly attributed Faith's enjoyment of the marriage bed to the French blood of her émigré grandmother.

Amanda had no French blood. So what was her excuse?

Suddenly she saw him out there in the shadow of a tree at the edge of the yard. She knew with a shocking certainty that it was him. Not some other man, walking off sleeplessness. It was Reese Rivers.

Anger, cold and hard as flint rose in her. How dare he come to stare at her window? How dare he come to add to her humiliation at his rejection? How did he dare?

She wished she was the sort of woman to throw things.

Instead she whirled away from the window in a fury. Let him wait there until his feet fell off! He wasn't going to have the satisfaction of seeing her standing there yearning for him. He could jolly well roast in hell before she would ever again let him, or any man, know that she went weak with wanting at the mere sight of him!

She threw herself across her bed and began counting sheep with a determination passed down to her from the Magna Charta barons. Finally, hating Reese Rivers with every fiber of her body, she slept.

Outside in the storm-washed darkness, Reese stood looking up to her window. The remembrance of her in his arms was a torment that meant sleep was not to be his any more than Amanda Harcourt was.

He let his senses relive the memory of her clinging to him, her pulling his head down for her kisses—her pressing her body closer. He felt as if she were imprinted on his very flesh, in his very soul.

"Amanda." Passion broke the whispered name.

Heat seared through him, an agony of desire. He wrenched his thoughts away to safer ground.

He remembered how quiet she had been on the ride home. How noble and restrained she had been, when he knew he had all but killed her woman's pride by his seeming rejection.

If only she knew the true state of his mind. If only she understood how he sought to protect her. How could he have loved her with his body once he found he loved her with his soul? Not the way things stood. There was no way. The future was closed to them.

Any hurt she was suffering now was as nothing compared to what she would have suffered when she realized she had bound herself, soul and body, to the man who was going to destroy the brother she loved. To see to it that her brother was hanged. How would she be able to live with herself bearing that knowledge?

He'd no doubt that if he'd lain with her on that bunk in the line shack and drawn from her the wild passion that lived under her cool exterior, she would never have forgiven herself later.

There was no doubt in his mind that he could have drawn that passion from her, could have played her silken body like the fine instrument of passion it was.

But stronger than the aching need to quiet the raging hunger of his body for Amanda's was the fierce need to protect her from himself and from the searing self-recrimination that would fill her when she learned who he truly was, when she discovered that he had come into her life, not as a lover, but as an avenger.

No matter what the cost to himself, he must spare her that.

He stood watching her window until the first rays of dawn stole, rosy and golden, above the eastern horizon.

Chapter 15

Amanda found it easier than she'd expected it to be to return to her old self. Though she knew that a profound change had taken place deep inside where she had always imagined her soul lived, she was able to be the Amanda that David and Laura knew, notwithstanding.

After some initial panic induced by the fear of an accidental meeting with Reese Rivers, she relaxed. She realized that there was actually little chance of that. His work took him out on the range with the other hands, and it was a simple matter, most of the time, to find out where they were working and simply go in another direction.

At times when he was likely to be around the barn or corrals, she stayed inside. Finally, something dawned on her.

Whenever she appeared, he disappeared.

Evidently he was as eager to avoid her as she was to avoid him. In spite of the fact that it worked to her advantage, that knowledge brought tears to her eyes.

"What are you going to town for, Aunt Amanda?"

Amanda left off her miserable thoughts and turned to smile at her niece. "I thought I'd try to get fabric for some more outfits to ride in." She looked down at herself ruefully. "This one seems to have suffered a little in the storm, and I certainly don't want to have to wear an English habit."

Today they rode astride. Even so, Laura fought a temptation to scowl. Boy, did she ever agree about the English habit! Aunt Amanda had brought her three lovely ones from England. They were beautiful and elegant. They were what her aunt called stylish as well. And as far as Laura was concerned, stylish was just another way of saying uncomfortable!

There wasn't much she hated worse than being asked to don one of the dratted things for a lesson on her aunt's sidesaddle. Except, maybe, riding sidesaddle.

Instead of sharing that with the giver of the habits, however, she just looked at her aunt's mud-stained split riding skirt. "Yep, I'd say you could use a new one."

Amanda looked ahead. "We're almost there."

Laura looked up eagerly. "Race you!" And she was off, leaving a startled Amanda to tear after her.

They agreed to draw up while still a little distance out of town so that they could walk their mounts until their breathing quieted. Horses left standing at hitching rails while their blood was still pounding developed leg problems. Neither Amanda nor Laura would permit that.

When they entered the general store, Amanda saw, to her relief, that the owner was waiting on a customer.

"Ah, Lady Amanda. I'll be with you in just a moment, your ladyship."

"That's quite all right, Mr. Endicott. Mrs. Beame will help me. I'm here to buy fabric."

Smiling, Mrs. Beame rushed toward her. Amanda was pleased that the little clerk's haste was induced by her pleasure at the thought of helping Amanda select fabric rather than Endicott's usual subtle bullying.

"How may I serve you?" Mrs. Beame's smile transformed her to dainty prettiness again.

"I have ruined my riding skirt." Amanda gestured at it. "I was caught out in the storm the other day."

"Oh, dear. I'm so glad you're all right. It was dreadful, and it lasted so long."

Amanda agreed. *An eternity.* And for a moment *he* filled her mind and sent her thoughts flying.

She shook her head impatiently. "Yes, it was. I was lucky I was near an old line shack, otherwise I might have drowned." She forced herself to laugh lightly.

Was it always going to be like this? Was she going to be taken unaware like this by memories of the strength of his embrace and the passion of his kisses? And would she always be rendered a mere shell of herself? Was she to be drained of all normal emotion by this desire that coursed through her at remembering?

She was horrified to think that she might become, without warning, some sort of mindless creature going through the motions of daily life while her heart took flight to cling to traitorous memory. Her teeth grated with the effort of will it took to deny it.

Never would she allow Reese Rivers to do this to her. Never.

Mrs. Beame was holding a bolt of fabric out for her inspection when she came back to herself. "It's blue, you see, but it's the same tone as the fawn you're wearing. And . . ." She ran lightly to the other end of the large table of fabric. "With this," she said as she held up a lighter shade of the same blue with a pretty white figure in it, "for a shirt to wear with it. . . ." She looked at Amanda eagerly. "With your blue eyes . . ."

Amanda smiled, she was glad to see the tiny widow so animated, and was pleased, too, with her color selections. "Yes. That's a lovely combination. What others do you recommend?"

At that moment the bell at the door tinkled to signal the departure of the matron Ralph Endicott had been helping.

With a little gasp of dismay, Mrs. Beame slowed in her enthusiastic rush to choose a print to go with the medium gray gabardine she clutched to her chest. "I . . . I'm sure Mr. Endicott will want to help you now."

Amanda thought ruefully that he certainly would. Now she would be put to the trouble of getting rid of the pesky man so that she could continue her selections without getting the little clerk in trouble.

"Now," he announced his arrival, washing his hands in dry air, "How may I be of service, your ladyship?"

She turned to Endicott, suppressing a sigh and forcing a smile. "You must have far more important things to do than to help me select fabric, Mr. Endicott. Please don't trouble yourself."

"Oh, but I assure you, gracious lady, it is all pleasure to serve you. A pleasure I have no intention of denying myself, I assure you."

Laura had come over to see what her aunt was doing. *Boy,* she thought, *Mr. Endicott must have made a special trip to that castle in Ireland to kiss that Baloney Stone.* She shot a disgusted look over to Ben.

Ben responded by sticking out his tongue and holding a hand to his midsection as if he had a stomach ache. Ben and she always understood one another. Laura nodded her satisfaction with his response and turned back to watch her aunt try to slip away from the oily Endicott's clutches.

"What do you suggest, then, Mr. Endicott?"

"This dark brown gabardine for the skirt, and this tan plaid for your shirt." He pawed over the bolts and dragged out a black one. "This black for the skirt, and a white shirt for contrast."

Amanda had trouble not scowling at him. Brown was a color she never wore. Black made her look as if she were ready for a coffin, and one affectionate nudge from her mare would send her back into the house for any shirt but a white one.

When he turned away to look for another piece of gabardine, she cast a despairing glance at Mrs. Beame, and settled down to making her own choices.

She picked a medium green gabardine obviously designed with a lady's traveling suit in mind, and a light cream cotton with a stripe that nearly matched the green for the shirt.

"Oh, no, my dear. That is far too light for the purpose to which you wish to put it." Endicott took the bolts from her.

She resisted the impulse to hold on to them. "Oh, but Mr. Endicott, they are light enough not to show the dust that I fear would soon mar the perfection of that lovely black skirt you suggested." She turned her most radiant smile on him. "Why don't you just let me have these I have chosen made up before we decide on anything else?"

Turning her back to Mrs. Beame, she held her crossed fingers behind her where the clerk could see them and asked Endicott, "Would you happen to know where I could have these made up? It's silly to buy them all unless there is someone who can sew well here in English Bend."

"Surely your ladyship's maid . . . ?"

"Polly?" She widened her eyes at him. "Polly *cares* for my clothes, Mr. Endicott. She'd have no idea how to *fashion* them."

Endicott was at a loss. "Well . . . I don't know. Of course, I can make inquiries. I have my own clothes tailored and sent from . . ." He blushed and didn't finish his sentence, and Amanda was certain that he had his beautifully tailored suits made in Philadelphia or Boston. He'd hardly like to bandy that information around in a state that had sided with the South.

Since she was after his approval of Mrs. Beame as her seamstress, Amanda let him off the hook he'd almost impaled himself on. "I understand, Mr. Endicott. But I really don't think we need to be that particular about this. These are merely riding clothes, after all."

She cocked her head to one side as if thinking hard and

turned slowly to Mrs. Beame. "I wonder if you could help Mr. Endicott with a suggestion, Mrs. Beame. I'm sure you know the ladies of English Bend better than a gentleman might. Is there someone upon whom you might prevail as a favor to Mr. Endicott?"

The little clerk's eyes sparked with so much mischief that she was forced to look at her own toes as she answered.

Endicott didn't notice. His help were all but invisible to him at the best of times.

"There is one way I could help, I suppose. I might try to find the time to sew them up for you."

"Mrs. Beame," Endicott began repressively.

"Oh, how nice," Amanda said over him. "When shall we do it?"

"Oh, very well." Endicott's tone was one of resignation.

Just as if, Amanda thought, annoyed, it were up to him to dictate what his employee might do or not do on her only free day. The man certainly had more than his fair share of unmitigated gall.

"You will have to come to my house. I have no way to go anywhere, I'm afraid. And it will have to be on Sunday. You don't mind doing things on Sunday, I hope? It's my only day off."

Amanda knew better than to try to win a free half day for Mrs. Beame. She knew the clerk counted herself lucky that she'd been allowed to sew for Amanda.

So Amanda smiled and said, "My grandfather always says, 'the better the day the better the deed' when he wants to do something on the Sabbath. I shan't mind at all."

"Then could you come at two o'clock? That will give me time to get home from church and finish the dinner dishes."

"Lovely. I'll just stay in town for luncheon at the hotel after church services."

"Splendid." Endicott plunged back into the conversation. "You will let me be your host for luncheon, of course, your ladyship." Ralph Endicott bowed as if he were at St. James's.

Amanda suppressed a sigh. She was trapped. Since he owned the hotel, she would probably have been caught by him anyway.

She told herself that it would be no worse than being led in to supper by a bore at a London ball. Heaven knew she'd survived that more than once. Who was Ralph Endicott for inducing boredom anyhow, when one compared him with the dreadfully dull Duke of Ashroth?

Forcing a smile, she said, "If you don't mind including my niece in your invitation, that will do nicely." She ignored the scowl Laura shot at her, and the delightful way Endicott's face fell.

"I hope," she said, turning to Mrs. Beame, "that you won't mind sewing for Laura, as well. I think the lovely brown-and-tan combination Mr. Endicott chose would do so well on her. She has a bit of red in her hair. She will look lovely in that soft tan." She nearly laughed out loud as Laura pulled a face at the word "lovely."

"And," she added as Laura crossed her eyes at her, "the green that I chose I'd like made up for her as well." She beckoned Laura forward. "Is there anything else you would like, dear?"

Laura muttered something unintelligible. Amanda knew better than to ask her to repeat it. "Just look over the table, and choose anything you think you might like, dear."

Laura ducked her chin down and pretended to look at the fabric. It was the least she could do, but her heart wasn't in it.

Mrs. Beame produced a tape measure and stood quietly beside Amanda. Both women looked pointedly at the store's owner.

"Oh. Oh, yes, indeed. You will want me gone, of course. Please excuse me, your ladyship." He bowed, spun around, and marched off, leaving the two women to decide how much fabric would be required for Amanda's new acquisitions.

The two of them finished their calculations and the material was cut, folded neatly, and set aside to go home with Mrs. Beame. They had just reached the counter at the front of the store where the account book was kept, when the bell beside the front door jangled and jumped on its spring.

Neither of them paid the slightest attention, as Endicott was marching forward to take care of the newcomer. "How may I help you, sir?"

Instantly, before the customer answered, Amanda became aware of him. Totally, painfully aware of him.

It was just as it had been in the line shack. She could feel his presence. Every part of her vibrated with the certainty that the man who had just entered the mercantile was Reese Rivers!

She could feel the blood drain from her face, then rise to stain her cheeks crimson. How thankful she was that her face was shadowed by the wide brim of her riding hat.

Every muscle in her body tensed. If she hadn't been wearing the riding gloves Laura had given her on her last birthday, she thought inconsequentially, her nails would probably have dug into her palms.

She fought for composure. She was nearly undone when she heard him say, "You're busy. I'll come back later."

"No, no, no." Ralph Endicott got across the wide room in a rush. "I am perfectly at liberty. How may I help you?"

The man to whom he spoke handed him two letters to post and a list, but his eyes were fastened on Amanda Harcourt as if he could never get enough of the sight of her. When he said, "Mr. Harcourt asked me to take care of this," his voice was charged with an emotion Endicott could not identify.

Somehow, Endicott was not sure he wanted to know what that emotion was. The cowboy was a handsome brute..

If, he added mentally, you admired men who had such a dangerous air about them. He didn't.

He didn't like the hungry way the man looked at Amanda Harcourt, either. After all, *he* was determined to woo and win her himself. She was to be his passport into the elite world of the British aristocracy.

Looking Amanda's way, he saw the cool, stern look on her face and was relieved. Obviously she knew how to keep this upstart in his place. Endicott busied himself with the list the man had given him, dismissing him as a potential rival.

Amanda stood fighting for composure. She'd heard the note of strain in Reese Rivers's voice. It made her feel a little better. At least the man had the grace to feel *something* after what had happened between them in the line shack.

She wished she had the courage to look at his face to try to read just what it was that he might be feeling at this moment, but she hadn't. Resolutely, she kept her eyes glued on the figures Mrs. Beame was writing in the large, gray accounts ledger.

Endicott snapped, "Letters are mailed in the post office section," and led the way to that part of his store. When Amanda heard Reese Rivers move quietly away after him, she had to quell a sigh of relief. Then suddenly she was angry about the position in which she found herself.

Lifting her head, she took a steadying breath. She would prefer to be eternally damned rather than hide from that man for the rest of her stay at the ranch.

She vowed she would refuse, from this minute onward, to react as if anything had passed between them in that cabin. Even if her heart were breaking with the shame and hurt and humiliation that filled her, she vowed she would never again let it color her actions.

She was a British aristocrat, after all, no matter how she resented Ralph Endicott's constant harping on it, and British aristocrats knew how to hold their heads high and face life with a stiff upper lip. She had generations behind her who had done so under far more trying circumstances down through history.

When she had thanked and said good bye to Mrs. Beame, she unconsciously lifted her chin. Working hard at turning her head casually, she said, "Thank you, Mr. Endicott. Good day, Mr. Rivers."

She was absurdly pleased to hear her own voice. It sounded beautifully cool and impersonal.

In light of that triumph, she didn't even mind that there were tears in her eyes as she exited the mercantile. She knew she could blink them away before Laura's sun-dazzled eyes could discern them.

Chapter 16

Reese Rivers stood as if turned to stone. The sound of her voice, cold as ice on a January morning, had slashed at him like a whip. His body was reacting to the assault on his senses as if it had been a physical attack. It was all he could do to stand steady.

Oh, God, Amanda. Amanda. His beautiful Amanda. She must be so hurt. She must be humiliated.

He closed his eyes as the agony of what he'd done to her washed over him. He knew he'd never forgive himself for inflicting such pain on her if he lived to be a hundred.

Without hesitation, he'd give his right arm if there were anything he could do to make her understand. If only he were at liberty to tell her the truth! If only he could tell her that it had taken all the strength of will and every ounce of self-control he had in him to turn away from her in the line shack.

It had taken more than that. Much more than that.

He was the man who was going to orphan her niece by hanging her brother. There'd be nothing she could do, then, but hate him with every fiber of her being. He couldn't let her hate herself as well.

He saw Endicott looking at him oddly and instantly pulled himself together. "How much?"

Endicott frowned at the cowhand's impertinence. "I'm

sure Mr. Harcourt will want the charges for postage placed on his own Coronet Ranch account."

That was the first time Reese had heard of paying for the transport of letters through the U.S. Mail in that fashion, but he kept his mouth closed. The dandified storekeeper had obviously measured him and found him wanting. That suited him fine. He didn't feel any need to press the man into changing his mind.

"Thank you." He turned away from Endicott, dismissing him from his thoughts. As he passed the little lady clerk, he startled her by saying, "Good day, ma'am."

"Oh! Good day, sir." Elvira Beame watched him as he walked to the door, her eyes bright with interest. Without realizing it, she pressed a hand to her heart.

The door closed quietly behind Reese Rivers and Endicott walked over to Mrs. Beame. "Odd sort of fellow."

Mrs. Beame was surprised to be addressed about anything other than the work her employer expected from her. "Oh," she managed, "do you really think so?"

"Tell me," he said pensively, refraining from frowning at her with an effort, "how do you see him?"

"See him?"

He turned to frown at her now, impatiently. "Yes. Yes. As a woman. What do you see when you look at that man that just left?"

Mrs. Beame knew she was on thin ice. She took refuge in her grandmother's favorite adage, "Tell the truth and shame the devil." "Well," she tried to soften the blow as she admitted hesitantly, "from a woman's point of view, Mr. Rivers is very handsome ... in a rugged sort of way. And ..."

"And what? And what?"

"And there *is* a certain fascination about him." She shrugged apologetically.

"What sort of fascination?"

"Well ... it's as if he were in some way ... dangerous."

"And you women find that fascinating?" Endicott was aghast.

"I'm afraid so. At least most of us do."

"Why, in heaven's name?"

She frowned thoughtfully. "I suppose it's because we feel as if a man like that can keep us safe from anything." She tried to look calm and judicial about her statement, but even as she voiced it she felt her heartbeat quicken.

"Oh." Endicott lost interest. Amanda Harcourt could never be attracted to a rough like the departed cowhand. "Well. Thank you, Mrs. Beame. Please get back to work."

When she'd hurried off to straighten the fabric table, Endicott found himself considering the strange behavior of the "dangerous" Mr. Reese Rivers.

The man had obviously been much affected by the mere presence in the store of Lady Amanda Harcourt. He remembered the raw, aching hunger in Rivers's face when the man had thought himself safely out of her sight.

The fool had looked as if he couldn't live another minute without a kind word from her. As if Amanda would give such as he the time of day!

Remembering that look on the tall cowhand's face truly upset him, however. Mrs. Beame's face, particularly the light in her eyes when she'd described to him how she thought women would see the man, had upset him, too.

He didn't like what he remembered. He hated things that upset him.

He gave the matter serious thought. It was perfectly obvious that Lady Amanda didn't know the man existed. *That* was certainly a relief to him. He took great comfort in the knowledge. Still, it might be a good idea to get rid of Mr. Rivers. There was no sense in taking chances.

He considered his options. Unfortunately, he had no influence over Viscount Harcourt. He didn't even dare call the arrogant man by his title to his face.

There was always Webster, though. Yes. Webster was

acting as foreman of Coronet. And Webster frequented his saloon on Saturday nights faithfully, and a few nights during the week, as well as Sunday if he wasn't hungover.

He smiled. That would give him ample opportunity to influence Webster. He began to feel like himself again.

He'd begin to sow seeds of doubt and discord in the mind of the foreman as soon as the man showed up at the Golden Bough again. That would end by ridding him of the tall, dark, "ruggedly handsome, dangerous man."

Yes, Webster would take care of Mr. Rivers, he told himself with satisfaction. Washing his hands in the air, Endicott got back to the business of Endicott's Mercantile.

He'd think up something that would finish Rivers with Webster later, when he had more time to devote to the project. After all, he wanted to be sure to do a proper job of it.

The sermon had been shorter than usual, and the entire congregation was grateful. They were in a cheerier frame of mind than usual as a result.

David leaned down and whispered to Amanda, " 'Brevity is,' it would seem, indeed, 'the soul of wit.' "

Amanda laughed, and pointed surreptitiously to where several of the young men who'd sat in the back pews were already heading off toward the river with long fishing poles over their shoulders, their strides jaunty.

"I think Reverend Potter made several people happy, at any rate," she told her brother sotto voce. Then she smiled down at Laura. "Did you enjoy the sermon, dear?"

"I liked the part about the fourth man appearing in the fiery furnace. That was great."

David looked pleasantly surprised that his daughter had paid any attention to the sermon at all. He bent his head down again to whisper, "Great Scott, Amanda. The child *listened*. Gad. I think I was sixteen before I actually heard what the sermon was about."

"And," his sister laughed at him, "that was only because you'd gone dotty over the vicar's middle daughter, I'll wager."

He grinned ruefully. He didn't deny her accusation. Instead he asked his daughter. "Why did you like the fourth man's appearance? Did it mean something to you?"

Laura looked at her father earnestly. Surely he was testing her. Certainly he already knew the answer to that question.

She obliged him anyway. "When Shadrach, Meshach, and Abednego were put in the furnace," she recited in her best schoolroom voice, "it was because they'd stood up for God. It was only right that God sent his son, the Lord Jesus, into the furnace to protect them from harm. What that means to me is that if I ever have a serious trial, He'll be there with me, as well."

She looked confidently at her father for the praise she expected.

"Well done, dearest," he told her in a rather breathless voice. "How it gladdens my heart to see that you understand so well."

Amanda looked at him steadily.

"Laura," David said, "why don't you run ahead and save a table for us at the hotel dining room."

"Yes, Papa." Laura was off like an arrow shot from a bow.

"Understands so well?" Amanda asked him with her eyebrow almost up to her hairline.

"Whew! I think I'd better begin to pay better attention to Reverend Potter."

"To make up for all the years you didn't?"

"For my sins." He held open the door to the hotel and bowed her gracefully inside.

Laura waved from a table near the front window of the dining room.

Unfortunately, so did Ralph Endicott. He stood, dapper

and smiling, beside the chair at the head of the table with a hand on the one to his right that he obviously had every intention of seating Amanda in.

"Oh, dear," Amanda breathed to her brother.

"For your sins," he said with evil amusement.

She dug her elbow into his side in retaliation, and his grunt made her smile genuine.

Endicott drew out the chair for her and smiled. "How lovely you look this morning. I attempted to sit near you in church, but all the space was taken in the pews surrounding you. Did you enjoy the sermon?"

David suggested with a perfectly straight face, "Laura seemed to get the most from it. Perhaps you would enjoy discussing it with her."

Endicott shot a glance his way, saw only a bland expression, and decided just to ignore his suggestion. "Frankly, I've never seen what harm it would have done for the three of them to do as the king commanded. They could easily have simply complied and then gone back to doing as they pleased when all the furor was over."

David was struck dumb by the very idea.

Amanda added Endicott's lack of understanding of the basic concept of honor to the long list of things she didn't like about him, and studied the design on her plate.

Laura, without the long experience of wearing a mask in social situations that her aunt and father possessed, blurted, "But that was the whole point! The whole idea was to remain true to God." She looked at him with the full weight of her disapproval showing on her face. "To do as you said would have compromised their honor at the very *least*. And this went far beyond honor."

"Oh, really?" Everyone in town knew that Endicott found children boring in the extreme. "From the seriousness of your tone, you'd think there was nothing of greater importance than honor."

Before his daughter could answer, David said in a quiet voice, "Only God."

Endicott looked at him, but before he could say whatever he was about to, Amanda broke in. "What do you suggest we order, Mr. Endicott?"

She squeezed her niece's knee under the table, then patted it reassuringly, and Laura subsided without muttering the words she longed to say.

Endicott preened himself like a peacock. "I hope you don't mind, but I've taken the liberty of ordering our dinner especially for us."

David raised an eyebrow. Laura stirred restively.

Amanda rushed into the breach again. "How nice. I'm sure it will be delicious."

Talk became desultory as they waited, most of it fulsome compliments to Amanda that had Laura and David exchanging glances that threatened to send the child off into gales of laughter. Amanda was certain Laura would have bruises on her knee by the time they got back to the ranch.

"Mrs. Beame tells me you were out in the storm the other evening."

It was merely a way of making conversation, she knew, but Amanda started guiltily. Her mind filled instantly with the memory of that which had transpired between Reese Rivers and her.

Color drained from her face at the pain of the memory, then rose again to give her a becoming rosiness. She was in better control now as the passing days built a buffer for her savaged emotions, but still could not control her blushes.

"Have I distressed you with my mention of the storm? I do apologize."

"Oh, no." She was glad to hear that she sounded cool and collected. "I was merely remembering how exhilarating it was to be out in it." She offered him a small smile. "At least," she added, "as soon as I remembered there was shelter nearby."

"What a brave girl you are to find such a beastly storm 'exhilarating.' " Endicott smiled at her in pretended approval. "I would have thought you'd have been wishing yourself safely at home where you belonged."

Laura watched her aunt with suddenly increased interest. She knew, if Mr. Awful Oily Endicott didn't, that he'd just done two things to land himself in the soup.

Aunt Amanda didn't like being called a girl, for one, and if there was one thing that really made her see red, it was being told that she belonged at home.

One of the things Aunt Amanda hated about most men was the way they thought that women were helpless bits of fluff to be pampered like expensive pets, and ignored any thoughts they might have. It was something she couldn't seem to tolerate even in people she liked otherwise. And Laura knew very well that Aunt Amanda couldn't stand Ralph Endicott.

Come to think of it, she felt very much the same way. That was why she liked Reese Rivers so much. He was a man who treated her as if she had something interesting to say, and seemed to enjoy talking things over with her.

She watched her aunt. Amanda was paying particular attention to what she was going to put on her fork next. Laura hoped she was framing a good set-down to put Mr. Oily Endicott in his place. She was really disappointed when finally her aunt spoke.

"I enjoy storms. And I like being able to ride about alone, Mr. Endicott. That is the thing I like best about this country, in fact. At home I am always chaperoned, and have many appointments to keep and duty calls to make. I'm almost never allowed to do as I please. Unless, of course, I am on one of Grandfather's country estates. And even then I have a groom tagging along in the distance behind me half the time."

Amanda's eyes were grave, as if she really wanted him to understand. Laura thought that she was just taking comfort in expressing herself aloud.

"I love the freedom of the colonies . . . I beg your pardon, this country. I shall be sorry to have to leave it and go home again."

Laura scowled. In all those words, her aunt hadn't slapped at the smiling Endicott once.

Endicott leaned forward as if he'd finally been given a long-sought opportunity and declared passionately, "But, your ladyship, there is no need for you to return to England. You could, if you desired to do so, stay here for the rest of your days. There is one here who would be the happiest man in the world if—" He stopped as if he were aware, suddenly, that he was overstepping his bounds. "That is to say, you might decide to marry an American. Then you would grace our fair land for the rest of your days."

David was thunderstruck.

Amanda had long known that Endicott, confident in his good looks and the wealth he had amassed from his various and successful enterprises, had been entertaining the notion that he should attempt to attach her. Several remarks he had made on her last visit had warned her he wanted nothing more than to be able to brag that he'd married into a titled English family.

So many feelings warred in her that she was unsure how she would answer him. David saved her from it.

"Yes," he said drily. "There have been quite a few men who have offered for my sister's hand as a means of granting her this silly wish to spend more time in this country. Our Grandfather, however, has an attack of the gout every time the subject comes up." He looked piercingly at Endicott. "Very painful, the gout."

Endicott looked at the Viscount as if he thought him a bit mad. "Yes," he said at last. "I have heard that it is. Very painful, I mean."

Somehow, the suggestion that Amanda marry an American didn't come up for the remainder of their meal.

Laura gleefully filled the rest of the time they were in the restaurant by regaling a crestfallen Endicott with wild tales of her Grandfather's terrible behavior during his mythical bouts with the gout.

❀ ❀ ❀ ❀ ❀ ❀ ❀ ❀

Chapter 17

Amanda could easily have walked to Mrs. Beame's house. In fact, David, well aware of his sister's typically English love of walking, stared at her in amazement when she asked him to drive her the short distance to the little clerk's home.

He reassured himself that Amanda was not ill as he realized she'd asked because it was impossible for more than the three of them—and that only because both Amanda and Laura could squeeze together on half the seat of the gig—to ride. Obviously there was no room for Ralph Endicott. Just as obviously, to David and Laura, at least, that was why Amanda insisted on being driven two blocks down the dusty street and around a single corner.

"Good day to you, Mr. Endicott." David spoke with all the dignity he could muster. "My sister and I thank you for a most excellent meal. You have been all that one could wish for in a host." He turned his head toward his daughter with a stern look. "Say thank you Laura."

"Thank you, Mr. Endicott." Laura had to struggle not to giggle. She had never heard her father express himself so stiffly.

"You are very welcome, all of you. It was my very great pleasure. I assure you, I enjoyed your company immensely, more than I can say. Immensely." He waved his hat in a wide sweep to emphasize his words, and David had to hold his horse firmly. "I hope we shall be able to do it another time. Every Sunday if you would like. I should like it . . . immensely."

He clapped his hat on his head, and Laura stopped holding so hard to the edge of her seat. Maybe they weren't going to be run away with after all. She was a little disappointed.

David eased his pull on the reins. He was grateful the idiot had stopped waving his hat before the horse's mouth had gone numb from the pressure on the bit.

"Please. Be my guest every Sunday. I should love it. Truly."

Amanda was torn between being sorry for the man and utter irritation that she would now, probably, have to give up her church attendance to avoid other torturous hours at the dinner table with Ralph Endicott. She smiled as nicely as she was able and said, "Thank you, Mr. Endicott. That is very nice of you."

At that moment David let his horse start forward. "Sorry, old man. Thank you, again." He let Pickwick behave outrageously, permitting him to break into a canter on Main Street, and only pulling him down to a sedate trot when he'd raised enough dust to nearly suffocate Endicott.

"David!" Amanda's protest was halfhearted, at best.

"I won't apologize, sister mine. Besides, it is all your fault." He guided Pickwick expertly into the little side street between the livery stable and the feed store.

"My fault!" She tried hard for indignation, but fairness hobbled her from the first word. "Oh, dear. How I wish we could blame it on someone or something else."

"Well, actually," her brother shot her a teasing glance, "I suppose if you really wanted to be freed of all blame for the suffering we just endured with that very good dinner, we could lay it at the door of Grandfather and his title."

Amanda laughed. *"Merci du compliment, mon cher frère!"*

LOVING HONOR

"Ah," David looked down at his daughter with a very serious expression. "You see, my dear, what a pet a reigning beauty can work up when she hears that one of her admirers has an eye to other than her delectable self. Just see how she flies into the boughs to call me 'dear brother' in a tongue not my own." He threw a glance at his sister. "One, I might add, in which she was always able to best me, much to our tutor's gratification." His refined accent gave way to that of the Liverpool docks. "Thanked me for me compliment in nasty sarcasm, she did."

"David Harcourt, I think I'd like to push you out of this gig."

Laura laughed. "You don't have to push him out, Aunt Amanda. He'll get down peacefully. We're here."

David got down peacefully and reached up to help Amanda. With his most charming smile he asked, "Am I forgiven?"

She pecked him on the cheek by way of answer, and they walked up to Mrs. Beame's door smiling. "You were," she murmured, "sorely tried, after all."

The little house was of unpainted clapboard, but the porch was swept clean, and the yard was as neat as a pin. Flowers grew in tidy beds along its front, and pretty little ruffled curtains showed at the windows.

Mrs. Beame threw open the door before David had even lifted his hand to knock. "Oh, I am so glad you have come. I hope you had a nice dinner. I saw you in church."

Amanda smiled with real pleasure. Mrs. Beame had just said more than Amanda had ever heard from her in the general store, except for sparse comments that were all business. Without conscious thought, she labeled Ralph Endicott oppressive.

She looked around the little parlor. "What a delightful room!" Everywhere she looked, there were little touches of comfort or beauty. Patchwork pillows were on every surface anyone might sit upon, ready to furnish further comfort by propping up an elbow or easing a back. On the walls hung several pictures made of scraps of fabric cleverly pieced, as well.

Amanda's attention was caught by a dressmaker's dummy that had obviously seen better days standing in one corner. It wore a dress of simple fabric, ornamented only by tucks running diagonally across the bodice from one shoulder to the waist. The neckline was a simple vee, cut to follow the line of the tucks.

Amanda asked, "May I?" gesturing toward the dummy.

Mrs. Beame colored with pleasure. She clasped her hands together tightly. "Oh, please." Her expression was both eager and apprehensive, her gaze locked on Amanda.

Her visitor walked to the dummy and peered around it to see how the little seamstress had treated the back of the gown. More tucks ran down from the back waist matching those in the front of the gown, giving interest there without destroying the beautiful simplicity of the creation. "How talented you are, Mrs. Beame!" Amanda looked at her earnestly. "This dress is lovely. And I can tell you quite honestly that had I seen it at a couturier's in Paris, I would not have thought it out of place."

Her hostess was momentarily incapable of speech. Her eyes filled with tears, and she pushed her clenched hands against her lips to hide their trembling. Finally she managed a whispered, "Thank you. Oh, thank you so very much."

Amanda came to her and put a hand briefly on her shoulder. "It's your dream, I know. I am so pleased to be able to assure you that you will be able to realize it." She laughed lightly, "Unless, of course, this is the only dress you have designed."

"Oh, no!" The tiny woman ran to a table across the room and returned with a book. "All of these, too. It is just that it takes so long to save enough money from the necessities to purchase fabric for making them."

"May I?" Amanda took the book and sat on the stiff horsehair sofa with its softening quantity of pillows. Opening the book she looked long and hard at each of the dresses sketched there and read all of the notes Mrs. Beame had made beside them about fabrics and colors.

David, finally, could stand it no longer. "Amanda. I think I shall call back in an hour or so, if you don't mind. Will that give you and Laura sufficient time?"

Amanda looked up rather vaguely. "Yes, dear. And if it doesn't, I can always send you away again." She was lost in the dress sketches before she'd finished her sentence. She didn't even hear her brother's slightly sarcastic, "Thank you so much."

"Merci du compliment, Papa?" Laura teased.

"Yes, indeed, infant." Grinning, David let himself out. Only Laura noticed his departure. His hostess was aware of nothing but his sister's attention to her designs.

"You like them? Oh, please tell me if you like them."

"Yes. Yes, I really do." Amanda looked up from the book in her lap. "You are really quite talented, Mrs. Beame."

Tears ran down Elvira Beame's cheeks. She hugged her arms around herself and rocked her slight body back and forth. "You just don't know. You *can't* know how much your praise means to me."

She turned eyes luminous with gratitude to Amanda and sought words with which to thank her. "When there is something that you want more than anything else in the world . . ." She swiped at her cheeks to remove the tears, swallowed hard and continued. "Ever since I knew that this was what I wanted, I have kept my sights set on my goal." She straightened, squaring her shoulders. "It has always seemed that the obstacles to my achieving recognition were insurmountable." She twisted her hands in her lap and leaned closer to Amanda. "But when you want something with all your heart . . . something good and true . . . when nothing else is as important to you . . . then you must go after it with all that is in you." Her expression begged for Amanda's understanding. "That is why I have skimped on food and wood for the fire and on clothing. . . ." She interrupted herself to thrust her tiny foot forward from under the threadbare hem of her gown to show her guest the sad condition of her footwear. "I've even skimped on my shoes, in order to purchase the fabric for the gown you've admired. To buy my paints and papers to design others and . . ." Her voice took a ring of triumph. "And now I have been told by someone who *knows,* who truly knows about fashions, that I have talent."

The tears started again. "You will never know how much you have done for me." She gulped back a sob, smiling. "I shall never mind doing without food or heat again." She lifted her chin, her eyes full of resolution. "Never!" The firmness left her voice and she was suddenly shy. "I don't know how to thank you."

Amanda sat still for a long moment. The tiny woman's words assaulted her spirit and sank deep into her very being. In her heart, she felt them take root and blossom. *When you want something with all your heart.* The words reverberated through her, filling her with purpose, setting her nerves tingling.

When you want something with all your heart. Tears of her own filled her eyes. With an effort she finally managed, "No, my dear." Her voice was husky. "It is I who am grateful to you."

Elvira Beame stared at Amanda, openmouthed. She saw the heightened color in her cheeks and the glow that started at the back of her eyes and grew to light them to brilliance.

She was filled with confusion and curiosity, wondering what she had done to cause such a reaction in the usually poised Englishwoman. An instant later, her speculation vanished in a flood of incredulous joy.

"I would like to set you up in your own establishment, if

you are willing." Amanda told her with a briskness she had to work to achieve. "You may, of course choose the place. I would suggest Philadelphia or New York, though Baltimore would do nicely, but it must be your choice." Amanda attempted to sound businesslike in spite of the dreaminess that tried to overwhelm her and added, "Of course there is San Francisco, as well."

Elvira looked at her in astonishment. Her emotions threatened to overwhelm her. She sprang up and began to pace the room. "How wonderful. I can't believe it. It is like a miracle. It *is* a miracle." She turned back to Amanda, stretching out her hands to her. "You have made all my dreams come true!"

Amanda smiled. "After you have chosen the city, you must give me a few months to arrange everything."

Mrs. Beame said softly, "Philadelphia, please." She seemed momentarily incapable of further speech.

Amanda was more affected than she cared to admit, too, for perhaps the little seamstress had inadvertently given her the key to making her own dreams come true.

David needed someplace to spend the time he knew Amanda would take over the dress designs. Fashion was one of her chief interests at home, and he was accustomed to long waits when she was with her London *modiste*. Of course, there he had his club in which to cool his heels.

He drove to the only place in English Bend that he could think of where a man could wait out a woman's dressmaking engagement. He pulled the gig up at the Golden Bough Saloon, flipped a coin to a tall youngster, and told him, "Take my horse somewhere in the shade, if you will. Please have the rig back in one hour."

The startled boy pocketed the coin and stepped forward to do as he was bid. David got down, crossed the boardwalk, and pushed through the swinging doors into the saloon.

170   Christina Cordaire

The place was sparsely occupied, he saw. The wives of English Bend had strong opinions about their men frequenting the saloon on a Sunday.

Webster was there, however, with Dawson and Sellers, the two men under his command that David liked the least. He'd noticed that Rivers seemed to make a point of avoiding them, too. It had given him a feeling of kinship for his most recently employed hand.

Not to join them would be insulting, he realized. With great reluctance he did so. "Good afternoon, men. Do you mind if I join you?

Dawson nodded but didn't speak.

Webster grinned and pushed out a chair with his foot.

"Good afternoon, Mr. Harcourt, sir." Sellers said.

The man's voice held a note David didn't like. Since Sellers never spoke without the slightly mocking quality, David had never called him on it, even though good leadership demanded that he challenge seeming insubordination. Since Sellers was uniformly unpleasant, he let it go.

He was well aware that the man had always seemed to resent him, however, and it made him just a little uneasy. Possibly Sellers resented being an American under a Britisher in the Confederate army.

David didn't give a damn. Soon they'd all be returning east, and he'd be rid of these two. It looked as though the Yanks were going to lay siege to Petersburg and General Lee needed every man.

David knew the rest of the men serving under him were content. Or at least they had been. Before . . .

"Won't you join us?" Webster held up the half-empty bottle of very good whiskey that they were drinking.

David smiled and used the phrase he'd heard so often since coming to this country, "Don't mind if I do."

Webster called out to the barkeep. "Hey, Mullins. We need another glass here."

"Sure thing." He bustled over with the glass. "How do, Mr. Harcourt?"

"Fine, thank you, Mr. Mullins."

Mullins went back to the bar with a grin. It wasn't every day a man got to be treated like a gent by a genuine English lord.

"Dave." Webster hunched forward over elbows propped on the table. "I got me a little problem."

David found to his surprise that, while he usually had no objection to Webster's calling him by his first name, it irritated him considerably to have him do it in front of Dawson and Sellers. He answered with a quirk of an eyebrow.

"It's having a man around that isn't one of our own."

David took a sip of his whiskey and steadily regarded Pete Webster. "I take it you're referring to Rivers?"

Webster flushed and went on. "We don't know him, Dave."

"We didn't know each other at first, either."

"That's not the same thing. Besides, there's too much at stake now."

David frowned. The ranch was only running cattle now. The shameful debacle of the attack on the Union payroll detail was soon going to be three months behind them. What was Webster getting at?

"He just makes me nervous, that's all." Webster squirmed under David's steady regard.

"Watch him, then."

Webster took a deep breath and expelled it. He wasn't satisfied, but he saw it was as good as he was going to get. "Okay. That might be a good idea."

Dawson and Sellers exchanged a look.

David wished he'd simply driven out into the countryside for half an hour and then driven back instead of coming to the Golden Bough. Now he'd have to take a walk to find his rig.

"Thanks for the drink." He rose and touched the brim of his hat.

As he walked to the door of the saloon, he could feel three pair of eyes boring into his back.

"Strange duck," he heard Dawson say.

"Shhh." Two hisses. Sellers and Webster.

Interesting. Suddenly he needed fresh air.

He started out, walking through the town to see if he could locate his gig. He had the devil of a time finding it.

The boy had taken it home and put it in his barn, but he was on the lookout for Harcourt. When he saw David walking, he called, "Hey, Mr. Harcourt, you still want your rig in an hour?"

David crossed the dusty street to him. "Now will be fine."

The boy pelted to the barn and led Pickwick out of the commodious center aisle, hay hanging from the corner of the gelding's mouth.

"Well done." David praised him. "Pickwick looks as if he's had a pleasant half hour."

"Thank you, sir." The boy blushed with pleasure. "Any time."

David climbed into the gig and frowned. "Don't I know you?"

"Well, you haven't seen me much, sir." The boy grinned. "I'm Ben. From Endicott's Mercantile."

"Ah, yes. You're my daughter's friend."

Ben stood stock-still. That Mr. Harcourt would trouble to remember him was more than he'd ever expected. That he'd condescended to call him Laura's friend was overwhelming.

He couldn't have spoken around the lump of pride in his throat if his life had been at stake, but his grin widened until it nearly split his face.

David smiled back at him and said as he drove away, "I'll keep you in mind."

Reese was having the devil's own time trying to keep his mind on what he was doing. Visions of Amanda, her face soft with love, her lips bruised from his kisses, kept intruding on his thoughts.

"Dammit, Rivers," he snarled at himself. "You'd better pull yourself together, or you're going to fall flat on your face."

He'd never accomplish his mission if he didn't succeed in putting aside every feeling he had for Amanda Harcourt. He had to trample, mentally, the affection he had for the woman's niece, as well.

His honor demanded it. Coming to Coronet had been like coming to his own private hunting preserve, having it turn into his own private heaven—only to have it turn again into his own private hell.

Now, tearing at a heart he thought he'd learned to live without, there was Laura . . . and, God help him, there was Amanda.

Because of who he was and what he'd come to do, his honor commanded that he ruthlessly close his mind and heart to the feelings he had for them both. In doing so, Reese Rivers condemned himself to live in an agony of spirit.

Having fought to survive with his honor intact all his young life, he'd learned to separate everything. Keeping everything in its own tight little compartment in his mind—forbidding one issue to run over to color the next—was all that kept him going. He fell back on the habit now.

Today, with Webster off to town, he'd decided to use his Sunday to search the high range for stray cattle, and report the count as an excuse if anybody noticed.

He had to get out to the line shacks and see what he could find this time. Amanda's accident had kept him from doing it in the storm.

Amanda. His gut twisted and he slammed the door to that compartment. He groaned aloud with the effort it took him to do it.

Webster. He'd think of Webster and the danger he knew the man represented.

If he kept asking him for the jobs that sent him out alone, Webster might catch on that he was up to something. Webster wasn't the brightest man he'd ever gone up against, but he had a suspicious nature. That could trip Reese up just as well as the wisdom of a Socrates. He wasn't going to make the mistake of underestimating the threat that Webster posed.

He'd selected Thor to ride today to give him the advantage of being able to cover a lot more ground. With Thor under him, he could do the tally of strays faster, leaving time for his investigations.

There were three line shacks. The one he thought of as the third shack was the one in which he'd spent those glorious, torturous hours alone with Amanda.

He knew he'd leave it for last. Even then it was going to be a tough assignment. The very thought of the place brought back memories that threatened to tear him apart.

Thor got him to the far range in record time. Once there, Reese rode him slowly through the area that was crisscrossed by draws in which cattle might be overlooked. That way, he cooled out the big horse while he made his count of the few cows he found there.

A quick scan of the open land with the field glasses he'd brought hidden in his saddlebags gave him his count in a tenth of the time it could have taken. With a grim smile of satisfaction, he headed for the first line shack.

The shack stood in a scraggly bunch of trees bordering a stream. The stream, thanks to the recent storm, now overflowed its banks to within twenty feet of the decrepit cabin. He frowned. That meant death to any hopes, however tenuous, that there might have been tracks to read.

Close to the shack, though, someone had built a rough shed over the hitching rack. He took care to halt Thor before he finished crossing the stream. That way, he'd neither spoil any clues left nearer the line shack nor leave any sign that he'd been there.

He dismounted with more than his usual haste. As he splashed his way toward it, he hardly dared to hope he'd find tracks there in that provident lean-to.

There were tracks there! About eight to ten different horses, judging by the varying shapes, sizes, and nail patterns of their shoes. Maybe more.

Staring down at the hoofprints he muttered, "Where the hell is a good scout when you need one?"

The marks left by this group of horses meant a lot less to him than they would have to a scout. Even to his less experienced eyes, though, it meant the one all-important thing. Many riders had been here.

They'd been here at about the right time, too, unless he missed his guess. All the manure was dry. Dry all the way through. The droppings were obviously well over a couple of months old.

An Indian scout could have told Reese within three days when the horses had been in this shed. Reese wasn't that good. Whether they'd been here before or after the attack on the payroll detail that had taken place less than five miles to the east, Reese didn't know.

One thing he did know, though. There was no reason for more than one, or two men at the most, to come to a line shack. There was no ranching reason for them to do so at any rate, and he didn't think they'd have met this far from Rosa's kitchen for a picnic.

His foolish sarcasm steadied him, and he straightened. Walking carefully toward the shack, he kept clear of the path to it. He searched that path as he went.

Nothing. Except for the hoofprints in the shed, every trace of human presence had been washed away by the storm.

He found he was holding his breath as he reached for the

latch. Shoving the door open he entered and stood just inside.

After a moment, his eyes adjusted to the dimness, and dusty emptiness met his gaze. Leaving the door standing wide open for light, he studied the accumulation of blown-in dust that covered the floorboards of the cabin.

There were marks from bootheels and scuffed footprints all over the surface. He felt his nostrils flare. They'd been here! He knew it down deep in his gut. Now if he could only find some proof that would link these prints with the payroll and with the men of Coronet, he could take action.

Eagerly he crossed to the window and opened the shutters. Then he began a systematic search of the cabin.

Nothing. There was no sign of even a single coin of the payroll. There was no carelessly abandoned piece of equipment that would tell him the men who had gathered here were men of Coronet.

Well, he hadn't expected to find anything. He'd just been hoping against hope that he'd be blessed with a miracle that would help him get this over with.

He wanted urgently to get it finished and get away from here. He had to get away from here—far away from here—to try to find some way to live with himself for the rest of his miserable life.

Savagely he forced all such thoughts from his mind. Fine lot of good he'd be to Jacob, the army, or anyone else if he let himself think of the consequences to his personal life that would come with the performance of his duty. There'd be time enough to regret his actions when he was an old and lonely man, with nothing but his precious honor to comfort him.

Quickly he moved to close the shutters. Now he had to get out of here pronto. Scuffing some of his prints so they wouldn't show too clearly that they'd been made long after the first confusion of footprints, he was gone.

Closing the door carefully, he walked beside the rain-cleaned path, stepping from rock to rock as he had on his way in. He made his way to where Thor stood just on the edge of the free-flowing stream.

Splashing in, he shoved his wet boot into his stirrup and mounted. One last glance around and he nodded. He was satisfied that he'd left no sign of his having been there.

Thor and he stayed in the stream until they reached the place they'd entered it. Then Reese backed Thor out of the stream bed.

To anyone curious enough to care, it would look as if two horses had entered the stream. This way, nobody would connect a single rider, possibly Reese Rivers, with the line shack. Not important, just a precaution, but Reese was used to taking precautions.

He legged Thor into an easy trot, then into a longer one, and on into a gallop. The stallion voluntarily flattened out into a dead run a minute later, and the fifteen miles to the next line shack started to fall behind them.

Reining the big horse down through the trot and finally to a walk every few miles, Reese forced him to take a breather. "Walk, you idiot." He patted the big stallion on the neck.

He walked Thor the last mile, in spite of his own impatience, to be sure he was thoroughly cooled out before he had to stand. As they walked, Reese located the second line shack and searched the area around it through his field glasses.

"There are some cows, boy. About twenty, one, two, four head. No draws." He added under his breath, "And no men around. I think we're home free."

When they arrived at the line shack, Reese experienced minor disappointment. This one had no convenient lean-to, nor any outcropping of rock to shelter horses under. There was no way there was going to be any sign of anything that might have happened around it any later than the day before yesterday.

He had to check it anyway. A quick scan of the area through his field glasses for any rider that might be nearby reassured him. He rode Thor over to where there was shade, dismounted, and dropped his reins.

With the same care he'd used at the last one, he approached this line shack. Inside, the floor was a lot cleaner than the other's had been. There were no telltale footprints to indicate that a group of men might have assembled here.

"In fact," he mused softly, "I don't think I've ever seen a line shack swept this clean." He grinned, guessing at the significance of the clear floor.

Opening the shutters to add light, he felt suppressed excitement rise in him. The cleanliness of the floor had definite significance in his mind.

His hunches had always served him well in the past. He wasn't about to ignore one now.

He surveyed the room as a matter of course, but it was the floor that held his answer, and he knew it. The walls were the same flimsy constructions that he'd seen in that other line shack the night of the storm. The night ... Amanda ...

With fierce determination, he wrenched his mind back to the task at hand. He concentrated on his hunch that the clue was the clean-swept floor.

Somebody had swept it to remove any trace of what they'd been up to.

Under the circumstances, he couldn't allow himself to entertain his strangely insistent thoughts of Amanda Harcourt. When they arose again, he forced himself to think, instead, of his last Christmas leave. The one he'd spent at Jacob's, with Jacob's wife and his two boys.

With Jacob Garner's widow and his two half-orphaned sons.

Thoughts of Jacob's sons and widow drove Amanda from his mind.

The floor. *Keep your mind on your work, Rivers,* he snarled at himself in his head.

He leaned back against one of the posts that held up the top bunk and puffed out his cheeks, letting the air escape his lips in a long burst that somehow eased him. As he did, his eye caught a tiny glint of metal just at the edge of the door sill. He hadn't seen it when he came in. He'd literally been standing over it.

He was on it now in a flash. Picking it up with infinite care, he wrapped it carefully in his handkerchief. Then he looked for anything else that might be there. There was nothing.

Elated by his single find, he got down on his hands and knees and began a minute inspection of the rough floorboards. Time slipped away as he looked carefully along the edge of every floorboard.

He found what he was looking for. Marks, probably from the blade of a knife, scarred one of the edges of a board. It was a short length ending at the wall just under the lower bunk. The marks were almost impossible to see, but he'd known what to look for.

He sat back on his heels and drew a deep, satisfied breath.

Rising quickly, he crossed to the doorway to take another good look out at the surrounding territory. It wouldn't do him a helluva lot of good to find what he was looking for if he was caught doing it.

All was as quiet as before. No living thing, except the few cows he'd ostensibly come to count, moved in the immediate landscape. He went back to the telltale floorboard.

He took care that his own knife blade rested only in the marks that were already there. Prying the floorboard up was the work of an instant. He lifted it away to stand it against the wall.

Taking a steadying breath, he bent close and looked into

the space below. The darkness under the opening made it difficult to see.

After a long moment, his eyes grew accustomed to the dimness in the recess under the floor. Reese made out the contents of the hole.

"Damn." The word was curiously flat, then followed by a string of foul curses.

There in the hole lay one of the sacks from the payroll. He reached out and touched a cautious finger to it, and memories assailed him. He saw the faces of the men who had died because they had been escorting it. Men he knew well. Friends. And Jacob, the best friend of all. Bitterness welled up in him.

He was supposed to feel elation, though, wasn't he? Shouldn't he be glad he'd found the proof that finally linked the men of Coronet to the massacre of the payroll detail? That was what he'd come to do, after all.

He couldn't let it matter that he'd come to admire quiet David Harcourt, the loquacious Mason, and a few of the others. Personalities couldn't be allowed to thwart justice.

He closed his eyes and locked his jaw. With tremendous effort he focused on the job he'd come to do.

He was agonizingly aware that his major problem was his own feelings for the Harcourts. He knew he had to get those feelings out of the way of his investigation. With a will that threatened to spin out of his control, he resolutely shut the family from his mind.

The space under the floorboard contained all the evidence he needed. Ghosts crowded around him as he stared down at it. Plain to read on the heavy leather dispatch sack was the emblem of the U.S. Army.

He knew better than to move it, and contented himself with feeling the contents through the side of the leather bag. It was enough to convict, he was certain.

Where the rest of the money had gone he would have to find out from the men he would soon place under arrest.

Right now his next move was to get in contact with the army.

He'd ask for men to watch the shack, too, while he was at it. Then he'd know who the scum was who had hidden this bag.

Only time would tell whether the man had done it with David Harcourt's consent . . . or, Reese grinned without mirth, whether his Lordship was being diddled by one of his men.

He replaced the floorboard carefully and made sure there was no sign of his ever having been there. Then he checked again to be sure there was no rider in the vicinity, and left the shack.

As Thor carried him back toward the big ranch house, Reese pulled out his handkerchief and inspected his find. It was easy to identify. It was part of the rowel of a spur.

Now he had only to identify the spur's owner. From the bit of hide and the gray hairs on it, he could easily deduce that it was somebody on a gray horse. Somebody who'd gotten mighty excited to spur hard enough to break a rowel.

His choices were narrow. There were only two men on Coronet who rode grays, David Harcourt and his second-in-command. Reese knew, without the slightest doubt, which of them would have spurred that hard. The cool Harcourt was too good a horseman to do so.

His next task would be to see if he could find the set of spurs that had lost this rowel. He'd have to search Webster's things and hope the man hadn't thrown the spurs away. The strength with which he hoped to find the damaged spur all but overwhelmed him. He knew then that he'd give anything, maybe even his own life, if he could somehow prove that Webster had pulled the payroll robbery without David Harcourt's knowledge.

"Keep dreaming, Rivers," he told himself in a desolate voice. "Just try not to let it interfere with your blasted investigation."

Thor flicked an ear back to listen to him. It seemed as if he didn't like the heavy sarcasm in his rider's voice. Rivers smiled a twisted smile.

God! What he wouldn't give if only Harcourt could be completely in the dark. If only Harcourt could be innocent of any involvement in this mess. Or, failing that, if only he'd learn that David Harcourt was not personally responsible for the killing of the men of the payroll detail.

Then he'd find a way to spare Amanda and Laura the heartache he was afraid he was about to cause them. He had no wish to push his bitter revenge past the bounds of establishable guilt.

In the back of his mind a quiet voice suggested that David Harcourt was not the sort of man to countenance the murder of an entire detail of men. God, his very soul cried out, if he could just prove that, there might be a chance for him with the woman he loved.

He'd give everything that he had for a chance like that. Even his life. But, with a sinking heart, he knew there was one thing he couldn't give. He would not give his honor. If Harcourt were guilty, Reese would see to it that he hanged.

And with Harcourt would die every chance Reese had of winning Amanda.

Chapter 18

David helped Amanda and Laura up into the gig, tipped his hat to the glowing Mrs. Beame, and lifted his hands. Pickwick obediently started forward, and at the flick of David's whip above his back, broke into a well-mannered trot.

David asked as he circled around the few houses on past Mrs. Beame's and headed back to Main Street, "Did you find she is capable of sewing your riding skirts?"

"Oh, yes, David." Amanda's blue eyes sparkled. "I want to ask Liz Sheriton to find a place for Mrs. Beame to set up shop in Philadelphia. Liz is a good friend, and she has the resources to do an excellent job until I can get there myself. I feel certain that Mrs. Beame will be a great success, so, of course, I'm going to finance her.

"Liz will help me launch her, I know. Now that she's married to her rich American, Liz never has enough to keep her busy." She frowned lightly. "Being rich in America must be tiresome. There are no tenants to look after, no church bazaars, harvest festivals and such to plan with the vicar and his wife. It has to be a dreadful bore."

"Oh, I dunno," David said without much hope he'd be heard, "I manage to stay pretty busy here."

Amanda did hear him. "You have a ranch to run and cattle to look after. It is not at all like being cooped up in a large city. Liz just has to be bored."

David decided to change the subject back to the matter at hand. "Obviously, then, you found Mrs. Beame capable of sewing your riding skirts," her brother said dryly.

"Oh, yes, David. And she is capable of *so* much more. She has designed several truly wonderful gowns. You should have seen her sketchbook."

"Spare me." He turned the gig into the main street. His conscience prodded him. Pursing his lips thoughtfully, he attempted to show interest in his sister's project. "I have to admit, though, that I thought that dress on the dressmaker's dummy in the corner was very pretty. . . ." His voice trailed away as they passed the Golden Bough.

Through the saloon's big front windows, he glimpsed Ralph Endicott talking earnestly to an intensely interested Webster. Dawson and Sellers were leaning forward hanging on the shop owner's every word, too.

Strange, he thought, *Webster isn't the kind of man to pay such attention to a shopkeeper. Nor, for that matter, is that dandified Endicott the sort to seek out a man like Pete Webster. What the devil's going on?*

David was well used to Webster's habit of pretending a gentility he didn't really possess. To bolster that image, he'd always looked down on Endicott. What had happened to make him now treat the shopkeeper like a friend?

". . . quite talented." Amanda looked at him sharply. "You're not hearing a word I'm saying."

"Hmmm? Sorry, Manda. Something momentarily distracted me." He smiled at her disarmingly and said, "You were saying that Mrs. Beame was a talented seamstress, weren't you? Please continue." He went right back to his own thoughts.

Amanda said, "Yes. She is quite talented." He didn't deceive her for an instant. She exchanged a meaningful look with her niece. "She has designed one gown to be made of armor plate like that on the ironclads that fought in Chesapeake Bay." She regarded him with a brightly inquiring look.

"That's nice, dear."

Amanda rolled her eyes at Laura, and Laura crossed her own in response.

"May I have one, too, Papa?"

"Have one, too?" He looked at them vaguely. "Oh, is your aunt getting one? If so, I'm certain it would be fine for you to have one as well."

"Thank you, Papa," Laura said demurely.

Amanda and she grinned at one another and lapsed into a conspiratorial silence. Now and again a giggle escaped Laura.

David didn't notice. He'd returned to wondering what the deuce Endicott had to say to Webster that was so bloody interesting.

Back home at the ranch, David, still solemn faced, disappeared into his study. Amanda and Laura went to change into more comfortable clothing.

Amanda put on a cool white muslin that was deceptively simple, and, she noted as she paused in front of her mirror, extremely flattering. After a dinner with Ralph Endicott, she felt her spirits deserved a lift.

Polly came bustling in. "Why, ye've changed!" Her voice made it sound as if Amanda had changed into a salamander at least, and not merely taken off the walking suit she'd worn to church and slipped into something more comfortable.

Ignoring her maid's outraged look, Amanda set about making her independence a little more acceptable to her. "Oh, there you are, Polly." She smiled at her radiantly. "I'm so glad you have come. I can't seem to find my wide-brimmed hat. Can you help me?"

Polly pulled a sour face to hide how much it pleased her to be necessary to her Lady Amanda. "Well, I shall try my best to help ye, of course, but it may take a minute, seeing the way ye've been tearing through your things without me all this time."

Amanda bit her tongue. It wouldn't do to let Polly know how much she enjoyed doing without her here on the ranch. Not for the world would she hurt her maid's feelings.

"Ahh. Here 'tis. Ye've just let it get to the back of things." She reached the broad-brimmed leghorn down and smoothed the brim before handing it to Amanda. "Ye're going to your dear sister-in-law's grave, aren't ye?"

Amanda felt her throat tighten as it always did whenever she had to speak of Faith. "Yes. There are some lovely flowers ready to cut in the garden. And it is Sunday." She turned away to the mirror to pretend that she was adjusting her hat.

"I know. I know." Polly patted her shoulder awkwardly, aware that her mistress was hiding tears. "Do ye want me to go with ye?"

Amanda turned and gave Polly a quick hug. "No, dear. I'd rather be there alone."

"I'll just go and see if Rosa needs me to help her a bit in the kitchen then."

Amanda only smiled.

In the study, Webster was telling David, "Endicott thinks he's seen Rivers somewhere before. Philadelphia, he thinks, and in a Union officer's uniform."

David was still annoyed at the condition of Webster's spent and lathered mount. He disliked having had to send for Mason to care for the big gray horse in the face of his second-in-command's neglect.

He answered Webster shortly, "Very well, have him watched and report back to me." He ordered tightly, "Dismissed."

Webster's face showed his surprise. David didn't order men around except on the battlefield.

David didn't give a damn. Ever since he'd regained consciousness at the site of the payroll robbery and found that Webster had killed the Federal troops to the last man, he'd been fighting antagonism toward him.

Today was Sunday. Sunday was the traditional day of rest. David had no intention of working so blasted hard at hiding the animosity he was feeling now toward Webster because of the condition the man had brought his horse home in.

Webster turned his hat around in his hands, looking for something to say. He wasn't happy with David's order.

David raised an eyebrow.

Webster left.

Amanda finished cutting her flowers and pushed them into the tall jar full of water she'd brought to hold them. The graveyard was at the top of a rise, and the wind on the hill had often blown over and broken the vases she had taken there.

One of them had been Faith's favorite, so now Amanda took only the jars. It was the flowers that Faith would love. She wouldn't have minded about the jars, and her daughter should one day have the rest of her flower vases. None of that had occurred to Amanda in the first throes of her grief.

Now, in the long shadows of late afternoon, she made her way up the gently sloping hill to the ranch's graveyard, and knelt beside Faith's grave, peaceful in the shade of the huge tree that sheltered the little cemetery.

Working her jar of flowers down through the grass until it was securely seated at the head of the grave, she settled herself comfortably beside it. She looked around the long vista that sprawled away into the distance, and smiled gently at the idea of giving the beloved departed a view.

Then she smiled at herself, come to report to the empty shell of a friend who was no doubt watching her from a glorious hereafter. She felt an obligation, though, to come and spend time at her friend's graveside, and if she took comfort in ordering her thoughts there, whose business was it but her own?

She'd hardly said all she'd come to share with her sister-in-law when a shadow deeper than that of the tree fell across the grave. Looking up with a faint surge of annoyance, she saw Webster.

"I thought I saw you come up here," his tone was hearty, as if he'd found her at a picnic. He stood too close over her, his hat in his hand and his blond hair gleaming.

Amanda scooted back a bit, irritated even more by being forced to retreat from him before she could rise. She regarded him stonily for a long moment.

Disconcerted by her silence, he tried to cover his uneasiness with a charming smile. "I so seldom have the opportunity to see you alone, Amanda."

"Oh?"

Stung by her indifference, he frowned. "You were happy enough to see me in Richmond."

Amanda's chin lifted. "Indeed, I was happy to see any man safely arrive in Richmond. The fighting took so many lives." Her tone was impersonal, her voice cool. "I don't recall giving you any indication that I was more glad to see you than any of the others." She was puzzled at his impatient expression and added, "Except, of course that you came with my brother."

"I know women, Amanda. I know that the look in your eyes said that you were interested in me as a man."

"I beg your pardon!" Amanda drew herself up to her full height. She didn't know which offended her the most—being told that he "knew women," or the implication that he had fit her neatly into that knowledge at a level that she found distinctly insulting.

Whatever the case, she heartily wished Pete Webster would take himself and his insulting overconfidence off. When he reached out a placating hand, she stepped back and gathered her skirt on the side nearest him as if she would prevent even her garment from touching him.

The gesture infuriated Webster. He snatched at her wrist and dragged her a step closer.

Reese Rivers had saddled Thor again after he'd rested from his morning exertions. He wanted to work him lightly to make sure the big horse didn't develop any stiffness. "A little sore, are you, boy? We'll work it off." He ran a comforting hand down the horse's long satiny neck. "Just a few minutes, and you'll be right as a trivet."

He rode the big black to the level space behind the big hill that served as the cemetery for the people of the ranch. Working the stallion in large circles at all three gaits, he soon had him relaxed and supple again.

"That should do it, Th—" His voice died as he caught the white flash of Amanda's dress up the hill at the little cemetery. *Who the devil was that with her and what the hell did he think he was doing!*

"Sorry, old boy." He turned the horse and raced him up the gentle slope to the graveyard. As he rode, he saw Amanda attempting to free her wrist from Webster's grip. All the while, she was struggling to maintain her cool dignity.

Fury exploded in him. If he'd been near enough at that instant to get his hands on Webster, he'd have killed him.

By the time he reached the couple, however, he recognized the force of his anger as that of a jealous man and got his temper back under control. The effort left his jaw locked.

He thought he'd disintegrate with the effort it took to appear casual when he heard Webster's snarled, ". . . think you're too almighty good for everybody, Amanda Harcourt."

Keeping his grip on the fury that filled him only because he knew Amanda would detest witnessing a brawl, he managed through clenched teeth, "Good day." He made the words sound like pistol shots.

Webster released Amanda and whirled to see a grim-faced Reese, murder in his eyes. Webster's glare promised to pay Reese back for this interruption.

Reese smiled.

Amanda, so caught up in her indignation at Webster that she forgot, momentarily, the embarrassment she would normally feel, gasped, "Good afternoon, Mr. Rivers."

Her eyes widened at the sheer evil of the smile he directed at Webster.

Rivers turned his head lazily and smiled a different smile down at her, his arms crossed and resting negligently on his saddle horn. " 'Afternoon, Miss Harcourt."

He drank in the sight of her, careful to keep the expression on his face noncommittal. He was even more careful to keep hidden the awful longing that surged through him.

She was still a little pale with her anger at Webster, her fine eyes still flashing blue ire. Dear Lord, she was beautiful.

Wryly, he decided he'd been damn smart not to fight the foreman. He'd have had a fine chance against the beefier man with his very bones turning to jelly because Amanda Harcourt was looking at him like he was some sort of hero.

She was so magnificent, standing there watching him, calm and clear eyed. Savagely he suppressed the flaming rush of possessiveness that shot through him. Then the sense of loss at knowing she never could be his followed hard on his passion and nearly overwhelmed him.

He was actually thankful that Webster was there to kindle his anger. He had need of his anger. Anger served as an anchor for his emotions, holding him firmly against the tide of his wild yearning for Amanda.

Ignoring Webster's hostility, Reese dismounted and dropped Thor's reins. "Anything I can help you with, Miss Harcourt?"

LOVING HONOR 191

His gaze was directed at her, but Amanda could feel that he was electrically aware of Webster. She answered as quietly as her racing pulse allowed, "No, thank you. Now that I've placed my flowers on my sister-in-law's grave," she threw a scathing look toward Webster, "I'm going back to the house."

Webster made a sound that indicated he objected to her leaving. Rivers stiffened and fixed him with a narrow-eyed glance.

He turned to Amanda. "I'll just walk you to the house, ma'am." He threw a challenging look over his shoulder at Webster as he took her elbow. "Now it's getting on for dark, you'd be surprised how many varmints come around."

Webster grunted as if he'd been hit and started for Rivers.

A look from his intended victim halted him, however, and Amanda found herself efficiently escorted from the tiny cemetery.

She heard Rivers say, "Thor, go home." In her head, though, she heard, *When you want something . . . something good and true . . . more than anything else in the world . . .*

She was almost giddy with the touch of his hand on her. She *wanted* something from this man. What *was* it she wanted?

Was it physical passion that drew her to the silent man at her side? Surely, even in her besotted state, she couldn't be planning to be the wife of a man she knew nothing about?

She'd never been so confused about her own feelings. She had no idea what it was that she suddenly knew she couldn't live without, but whatever it was, it was inextricably bound up with Reese Rivers. Somehow, no matter what the risk involved, she intended to find out what it was.

To that end, she told him, "Thank you, Mr. Rivers, I'd truly appreciate your company back to the house." With that she tucked her hand into the crook of his arm. She heard his breath hiss through his teeth as she touched him, and was glad that the tingle of awareness she was experiencing wasn't hers alone.

Leaning lightly on his arm over the uneven spots, she proceeded to descend the hill. Every now and again, shocked at her own boldness, she allowed the side of her breast to brush his arm.

She was stirred by the contact herself, but denied her body's reaction to the touch. She was making herself the huntress, and the light touch of her breast to her quarry's arm was but one arrow from her quiver. She was determined to find others.

Reese didn't know whether it was his surprise at her acceptance of his arm, or the proximity of Amanda herself that all but took away his wits. Whatever the cause, he moved in such a daze that he didn't even glance back at the sullen foreman.

If he had, he might have been somewhat mildly disturbed by the utter hatred on the man's face.

Instead, he was lost in enchantment. Once more—perhaps for the last time—he was privileged to be near *her*.

He refused to be reminded that tomorrow he planned to go to the town east of English Bend to send his telegram. The fatal telegram would summon the army investigators. The arrival of the investigators would put an end to any chance he might have ever to be near Amanda Harcourt again.

So, for just this shining moment, he would drink in with all his being the wonder of her presence here beside him in the approaching twilight. For just this last time he would allow himself to experience the joy of her.

When her body brushed against his arm, the blood rushed through his veins so fiercely he was light-headed. Knowing she was forever denied him, he prayed for another rough spot in their path. His whole being hoped against hope her firm young breast might again brush his arm.

The trip down the long hill and across the meadow toward the yard around the big house was magical. Birds called softly as they sought their nests, and the cicadas took up their evening song.

Between them, there was only the whisper of the hem of her skirt gliding over the tall grass of the meadow and the soft sound of her breathing. With his eye, Reese measured the short distance to the house and despaired. In too short a time they would reach it, and Amanda would say her quiet good-bye and walk out of his life forever.

Then she spoke and granted him reprieve. "I would like to walk down to the river. Would you accompany me there?"

He wanted to say "Of course," but he didn't trust himself to speak. Nodding, he turned toward the riverbank, careful to match her stride with his own, reluctant to break the spell—afraid to break the spell.

Amanda wondered what was going on in his mind. Was he surprised at her boldness in asking him to accompany her to the river? He was unusually quiet. If she hadn't been deliberately tantalizing him, she'd wonder about that, too.

As they left the meadow and approached the river, the last light of the sun faded softly away and the landscape around them was silvered by twilight. The sound of the river came to them, rushing between its banks. It was still swollen by the heavy rains from the storm.

She clung more tightly to his arm as she chose the way she wanted to take him. Twice she deliberately pressed her whole body down the length of his side when they reached places too narrow for them to walk through beside one another.

She felt like a wanton, but she didn't care. She was too elated by his obvious response to her.

Once he tried gently to disengage her hand from his arm as if he could better help her over a difficult spot, but she held to him all the harder. Wickedly she asked, "Isn't it lovely?"

His eyes seemed a little unfocused as his gaze went to the river, and she rejoiced at the shortness of his reply when he said, "Yes."

Without mercy, she led him to her favorite spot on the river. The little point of land pressed gently out into the river, held there safely by the roots of the grove of trees that made it a grassy bower, secure here where the river widened and ran more quietly.

She released him then, and was absurdly pleased to see that the deep breath he drew at being set free was ragged. He looked as if he were a man under torture.

A perverse sense of triumph filled her. After what he had done to her the night of the storm, he deserved all she intended to do to him.

She walked to the water's edge, drawing him onto the lush grass of the little point of land. "This has always been one of my favorite places. Do you have a favorite place somewhere, Mr. Rivers?"

"No."

"Oh." She looked back at him over her shoulder and caught the hunger in his eyes. A little thrill ran up her spine. He looked a very dangerous man to toy with, with that black scowl on a face filled with eyes that devoured her.

Well, she didn't care that she was treading on dangerous ground. Something wild and warm stirred deep in her heart, and she knew she was going to walk that ground, yes, and even stamp upon it if that was what it took to make Reese Rivers lose his rigid control.

More than anything just now she wanted to cause him to lose the fight he was waging. She wanted him to fail to hold in check whatever it was that was even now searing her with his steady regard. She smiled at him, her eyes challenging the heat in his eyes.

"I'm a little tired from our walk," she spoke softly, so that he'd have to come nearer to hear her words over the gentle babble of the water. When he was close enough, she reached out and took his hand, tugging on it as she sank gracefully to her knees on the grass.

Rather than resist her, he dropped to one knee beside her. She sat then, spreading her white muslin skirts around her with studied care.

When he didn't join her, but rested there on one knee with his weight against his heel and a wary expression on his face, she decided that wariness was not the expression she wanted to see on Mr. Too-Controlled Rivers's face.

With a conscious abandonment of the safety his control meant for her, Amanda threw herself back on the soft grass. She stretched and straightened her legs, causing her gown to rise a little. It was now high enough for him to see her white silk stockings as she crossed her feet delicately at the ankles.

She was pleased to see that he wanted to protest her lying there before him in the lavender twilight. She saw a muscle in his jaw jump. The hand that she had held a moment ago clenched into a fist.

Amanda racked her brains for her next move. All her life she'd been trained to propriety. How was she to know how to entice a man to the sort of madness she desired of Reese Rivers?

She writhed in frustration. Instantly he reacted. She heard the whistle of his indrawn breath, saw the way his gaze traveled the length of her body and returned to stop at her chest.

Good! If that unconscious movement had aroused something in him, what would some intentional ones do to this man who had so humiliated her?

He seemed fascinated by her chest. She cast back in her mind to her days in the schoolroom and the instructions of her embarrassed governess about things a lady *simply did not do in the presence of a gentleman.*

Instantly she used one. She took and held a deep breath, and watched a tic develop beside his eye. Pushing him further, she murmured, "It's so warm," and opened several buttons at the neck of her gown until the soft swell of the top of her breast was uncovered to his gaze.

Sweat broke out on his forehead.

Stretching her arms above her head she moved her body sinuously, as if stretching in the privacy of her own bed. She remembered another of her governess's taboos, and lifted her arms above her head, drawing the fabric of her bodice tight over her suddenly sensitive breasts as she thus presented them for Reese's inspection.

She had gone too far. With a groan, Reese lunged for her.

Before she had time to think, he had snatched her up to him, shaken her, then dropped back down on the grass with her, his body crushing her own.

As his mouth ground down on hers, plundering, demanding, she had time for only one flash of triumph before she was wildly answering him, kiss for kiss.

When they were desperate for air, he pulled his mouth away and snarled down at her, "Damn you, Amanda. What the hell do you think you're playing at?"

She answered him with a calm she was far from feeling, "I'm not playing, I assure you."

His answer was another groan, then his mouth captured hers again and she felt as if someone had plunged her into a volcano. Every nerve in her body responded to the wild urgency of his kisses.

Far from being frightened or shamed by the storm of passion she'd aroused in him, she was soaring on the elation that came with knowing that she had deliberately brought him to the brink of this delicious madness.

Then he pulled away, and she felt every muscle in his

body tremble with the effort it took for him to do so. "Amanda." His voice was so hoarse with emotion that she barely recognized it as his. "Amanda. Why the hell are you torturing me like this?"

She looked up into his eyes and read the hunger there, and suddenly she didn't think she was punishing him for his rejection of her in the line shack. Suddenly she knew that she was trying to push him past whatever had stopped him from making love to her then—whatever was stopping him now.

She no longer had *any* purpose but to push him past his strange restraint and make him surrender to her. She intended to make him hers. Completely hers.

The blood of a score of conquering kings rose in tumult in her veins as she looked straight into his eyes and drew his head inexorably down until his lips were touching her own.

He jerked his head back as if her lips had been burning coals. In a voice harsh with agony he gasped, "Oh, God, Amanda. Why are you doing this to me? I'm not made of iron!" He fairly shouted the last words.

She smiled and half rose on one elbow to whisper against his mouth, "I'm so very glad to hear it."

His reaction was all that she had ever dreamed in her wildest dreams. He fell on her like a ravening wolf.

Her wanton behavior had unleashed all that she'd sought to free. His hands plundered her body, driving her to heights of emotion she had never known existed. When he pinned her to the grass with his full weight, and his hand ran down her hip and thigh to the hem of her gown, she thought she would . . .

Suddenly he pulled away from her. Her senses rioted as he yanked her to her feet and shoved her to stand against a tree near the water's edge.

With passion-bewildered eyes she saw him lean himself against a boulder across the little clearing. Then she heard it, too. Rocks skittering along the path down from the meadow as someone made their way toward them.

Quickly she fumbled the buttons of her gown closed and smoothed her hair. Proudly she lifted her chin and stared levelly at Reese, letting him know that she was not ashamed of all that had just passed between them, no matter who was coming down the path.

Laura popped into the clearing. When she saw them, a grin split her face. "Hi, Reese. Webster told me you-all had headed down this way."

She looked from Rivers to her aunt. "Papa said to come to dinner, Aunt Amanda. It's getting cold."

Amanda gave Reese one last look that told him more than he could bear to know and walked regally and gracefully out of his sight with the child.

A long few moments slid by. Finally Reese moaned, "I'm glad something around here is getting cold."

Rising, he ripped off his boots and his clothes and dove out into the river.

Chapter 19

Reese rose well before dawn and headed for the barn. His fitful attempts at sleep had left him dry eyed and tense. Amanda Harcourt had denied him rest as surely as if she had been there in his bed beside him, tormenting him as she had on the riverbank.

Her extremely unlikely behavior haunted him. For the life of him he could find no reason for it. As surely as he knew himself, he knew she wasn't the sort of woman who'd go after revenge at the cost of her reputation.

Knowing that she wasn't getting back at him for his inexcusable behavior at the line shack, he was stumped. What could have caused her to tantalize him so?

Was she so innocent that she didn't understand the risk she was taking to arouse a man as she had him? *My God,* he thought, *I was within inches of . . .*

"No," he snarled cutting off that thought as he reached the barn. "She'd have to be worse than innocent. She'd have to be downright stupid!"

Thor whickered sharply at his voice. Then the big horse lunged up from his bedding at the string of epithets that followed Reese's first remark and stood wide-eyed, and blinking with his head hanging over the stall door.

Reese muttered and cursed as he saddled Thor. Amanda filled his mind and assaulted his senses. The memories of her that had sent sleep flying stubbornly refused to be dismissed.

Reese led Thor out into the cool predawn. "Easy, boy." He swung up into the saddle and walked the stallion out to the wagon tracks that led to the road to town.

Dawn was just breaking when he rode through English Bend. A faint golden light stained the sky's base at the eastern horizon.

Reese noticed every detail as he walked Thor to cool and rest him as well as pass through town without drawing notice to himself. Nothing new except the shingle the newly arrived sawbones had hung out just past Endicott's Mercantile.

On Main Street, nothing stirred but one lone dog, hunting for a cool space to nap away the day. From the way the dog's tongue lolled out of the side of his mouth, Reese guessed he'd been chasing rabbits all night.

Once he reached the last of the houses, he let the big horse choose his own pace again. Without his volition, his thoughts returned to Amanda. He was so ensnared in memories that he was lacking his usual awareness.

Behind him a good ways, Pete Webster followed. He wasn't happy to be riding this early, but he was elated to think he might be on the verge of trapping Rivers at whatever he was up to.

It had been Sellers's watch, so he'd been the one to wake Webster to tell him Rivers was on the move. Webster had cursed Sellers for his trouble, but still the man had offered to ride after the stranger with Webster.

"No, you and Dawson trail me. I'll want you there to help me bring him back if he's up to something, but I wanna be all by my lonesome when I catch that polecat at whatever he's up to."

"And if he ain't up to nothing?"

Webster had stared at him hard. "Then I think he's probably gonna meet with an accident. I'm gettin' mighty tired of havin' him around Coronet."

Sellers had assessed the look in his boss's eye and nodded. The smile that had dawned slowly on his face never reached his eyes. He'd nodded again and gone to wake up Dawson, leaving Webster yanking up his pants and stuffing his shirttail into them.

As usual, Webster hadn't been concerned with his big gray horse's comfort. He'd made short work of tacking him up, and had been on Rivers's trail in plenty of time to keep him in sight from a safe distance. Now his only worry was that the man ahead of him might sense his presence before he caught him at whatever he was up to.

Webster needn't have worried. Reese was anything but his usually alert self. Even after he'd put considerable distance between himself and the spot where Amanda Harcourt lay warm and sleeping, he was in no way free of her.

At no point in his ride was he able to get her out of his mind. He had ridden hard the last few miles to the telegraph office in the next town, in an effort to distract his thoughts from her, but she had been with him every step of the way.

Why? Why? That was what he couldn't get out of his mind. Why had Amanda tried to seduce him?

Dammit, that *was* what she had done. It had taken most of his trip to admit it, but that was exactly what she'd done. "Yes, done!" He surprised Thor with his vehemence. "If it hadn't been for Laura . . ."

His mind tortured him as badly as Amanda had done. "Why did she do it? Why?"

He walked Thor the last mile into town and dismounted at the telegraph office. The sun was well up now, almost directly above, and the town was about its business. Still, he hadn't a single answer to his question.

Shoving it out of his mind with an effort, he walked into the small building that served as telegraph office. He felt like a man going to his own execution.

The telegrapher was a young man in spectacles and eyeshade. He smiled tentatively at Reese as he approached.

Reese, realizing he probably looked grim enough to make the slight youth uneasy, managed a "Good afternoon."

The man relaxed and shoved a form over the counter toward Rivers. Reese nodded his thanks and picked up the stub of a pencil from the counter in front of him with a reluctant hand.

With a leaden heart he wrote out the telegram and passed it to the telegrapher. The telegram would bring the army. They'd arrest David Harcourt, and he, Reese Rivers, would become a man with nothing left but his honor to give meaning to his life.

"What are the charges?"

The slender young man counted the fatal words Reese had printed and told him what the wire would cost to send. Behind his round, gold-framed spectacles, his eyes were grave with the awesome seriousness of the telegram. Accepting the money Reese proffered, he stared at the man across the counter. Now he understood why he'd thought him dangerous when he'd first walked in.

"Send that right away, please," Reese said through wooden lips. Then he saw the telegrapher's eyes widen at something behind him and saw his mouth begin to drop open in a startled "Oh!" Reese whirled.

"Get 'em up, Rivers." Webster poked his .45 into Reese's stomach, hard. His grin was evil. To the young man he said, "Hand me that telegram."

"I can't." He gulped hard and tried to keep his hands from shaking, he seemed to shrink behind his long, dark apron. "It'd be against the law."

Reese said in a deep, calm voice, "It's okay, son. Don't get yourself shot over it." He watched Webster carefully as he leaned over the counter and snatched the paper from the telegrapher's hand. Swiftly he planned. When Webster's eyes went to the paper . . .

Just then, there was a clatter of hooves outside, and Sellers and Dawson entered in a rush. Reese's action-tensed muscles relaxed as he saw any chance of escape disappear.

Webster read the telegram and crushed it in his fist. "You dirty dog. You were sending for the army." Cursing, he slashed his pistol across Reese's face.

Reese regarded him steadily. Blood dripped down his chin from his torn cheek.

Webster lifted the gun to strike again. Dawson caught his arm. "Better not if you plan on taking him back to the captain."

Webster shot him a venomous look, then shook his head to clear it. Finally his eyes cooled. "You're right, Dawson. Let's get him outta here."

The telegrapher watched them rush the tall, dark man out to his horse, bind his hands to his saddle horn, and gesture for him to mount. The man did so with an air of fatalistic acceptance.

From his seat atop the magnificent black stallion he threw one look back into the tiny telegraph office. The young man ran his trembling hands down his apron, lifted his eyeshade, and nodded imperceptibly.

Then one of the men grabbed the reins of the tall man's horse. It reared and screamed, and they were gone in a cloud of dust and clatter of hooves.

The telegrapher reached a shaking hand out to his sending key. After a moment, he took a deep, quivering breath and began to send the words, as well as he could remember them, that the tall, dark man had given him.

Reese was only a little more battered when they reached ranch headquarters. They hadn't wanted to stop long when they'd had to rest their mounts, so they hadn't wasted much time beating him. As it was, night was falling fast.

David came out of the house as they approached, his features grim. "Larkin told me what was going on. I've sent the women to visit the Lattimores. Bring him into the study." He turned to lead the way, his shoulders stiff.

Reese was hauled off his horse before he could dismount, and his bonds were sliced free of the saddle horn. The carelessly wielded knife sliced the top of his hand as well. With Webster's gun mining for a kidney, he was shoved into the house after Harcourt.

David Harcourt stood, white faced in the lamplight, behind a handsome desk. When he saw the blood running over the back of Rivers's hand, he dug out his handkerchief and came around the desk. "I don't want to see any more of this, Webster." His voice was tight.

Webster snorted. "Maybe you'll wanna see a helluva lot more when you get a gander at this!" He slapped Reese's telegram down on the tooled-leather desktop.

Harcourt finished tying his handkerchief around Reese's hand before he turned almost casually and read the damning paper. Slowly he raised his eyes to Reese's. "Are you an army spy?"

"No."

David just kept looking at him.

"The man who led the payroll detail took that duty in my place. He was my best friend."

David sighed heavily. "I see." A long moment passed in which Webster's face became steadily more suffused with color. Finally David said, "I'm sorry."

Webster exploded. "Sorry! You're *sorry*, are you? Sorry a lot of dirty Yankees got killed?" His face twisted in a snarl. "You're sorry, all right! You're such a sorry son of a—"

"Webster!" Harcourt's voice was a whiplash.

Webster ignored him. Teeth bared, he released long-pent-up frustration. "You're one sorry soldier, Harcourt. Why, if you hadn't been knocked cold by that bullet that creased your head, we'd have just said a polite thank-you for the money and ridden off leaving all those witnesses alive!"

David shouted at him. "My God, Webster!" He was appalled. "It was an act of war, not a robbery!" His expression was incredulous, his voice outraged. "Are you trying to tell me they didn't respect the fact that we had them under our guns? Are you telling me they took up their arms again?"

"Hell, no, *Captain*." Webster used the rank like an insult. "I *ordered* the men to finish the job. I'm telling you that Sellers and Dawson and I killed those blasted Yanks off. And we did it while Mason and the rest of your gutless pet men stood around yelling 'no' and 'stop' like the bunch of yellowbellies that they are!"

"Good God!" All the blood drained from David Harcourt's face as he took in the enormity of Webster's crime. He stood frozen in his place.

Reese stood as still. His relief at learning David Harcourt was innocent of the massacre riveted him to the spot. Harcourt was innocent.

Webster spun to face Reese. He shoved his gun barrel into Rivers's stomach. With eyes that glittered with malice, he told him, "And I saved your friend for last." He thrust his jaw forward and informed Reese with obvious relish, "I had to shoot him twice to shut him up, he was so set on getting out what he thought of me."

An enraged shout of anger was the only warning Webster got. Reese slashed the gun aside with a blow from his hand and threw himself on him. With a crash that shook the room, Reese pinned him to the floor.

His hands closed around the writhing Webster's throat. If he died for it, he was going to have the satisfaction of choking the life out of this man.

Webster bucked under him, frantically striving to dislodge the man whose iron hands were stopping his breath.

Reese held fast, increasing the pressure, intending to crush Webster's windpipe.

Sellers rushed in. Raising his gun hand high, he tried to smash his gun butt down on the back of Reese's head.

Reese saw it coming and turned a shoulder instead. Even so, the numbing blow cost him. The hand on that arm slackened at Webster's throat, and Webster croaked, "Shoot him!"

Sellers stepped back from the struggling men on the floor and took careful aim at Reese's back.

David sprang forward, seized his wrist, and bore the gun down.

Sellers fired anyway in a last effort to do for the Yankee strangling Webster.

With a curse, David drove his fist into the man's jaw.

Sellers dropped like a rock.

David snatched up the unconscious man's gun and motioned for Dawson to drop his. Implacable purpose filled his face.

Instead of dropping his gun, Dawson took one look at where the Yankee and Webster fought sprawled on the floor and turned tail. He exited the room in such haste that he slammed into the doorjamb on his way out.

David watched as Reese Rivers rose unsteadily. His hand was pressed to the deep, bleeding gash Sellers's bullet had left across the top of his arm where it joined his shoulder. Already, blood ran freely down Rivers's arm and dripped from his fingers. David reached out to steady him.

Both of them turned to look down at Webster.

He lay where Reese had felled him. As the two men stared down at him, a dark stain spread ominously over the center of his shirt front.

Reese dropped to one knee and felt for a pulse in the wounded man's neck.

There was none.

Satisfied, he rose. Jacob was avenged.

LOVING HONOR

Reese stood there as the weight of his pledge to avenge his best friend's death lifted from him. He felt as if a thousand chains had dropped away.

Webster himself had killed Jacob. For that, he wished Sellers's bullet hadn't just grazed his own arm to go on and put an end to Webster. It would have been worth taking a bullet in the shoulder to have saved Webster for the hangman's noose.

It was done, however. Though Webster had met a kinder fate than he'd deserved, he'd paid with his life for the massacre of the payroll detail.

Now all that was left to do was to hunt down and bring back Dawson, and it would be finished. When the army men he'd sent for arrived, he'd hand over to them Webster's body, and Sellers. And, of course, Dawson—in whatever condition he insisted on attaining when Reese went after him.

He took a deep breath. It felt like the first lung-filling breath he'd had in months.

Then he turned, slowly, and looked at David.

Chapter 20

"I'm sorry," Amanda stood abruptly, "but I must go home."

Laura, from where she was playing checkers with the Lattimores' oldest boy, looked up at her aunt in surprise. "But we were to stay another day!"

"I know." Amanda spread her hands in a helpless gesture. "I can't help it, and I do apologize to all of you." She glanced around the homey parlor at the concerned faces of her hosts. "But I simply must go home."

Mrs. Lattimore put her knitting aside and rose from her chair. "What is it, dear?" She frowned slightly as she studied Amanda's stricken face in the lamplight. "What's the matter, Amanda? Are you experiencing some sort of premonition?"

That was exactly the case, but now that she heard the fact voiced by her friend, Amanda felt foolish. Nevertheless, she knew that something was not right at Coronet.

Restlessness assailed her as it had never before. She felt as if something momentous and horrible were going on at home, as if someone she loved were in grave danger. The strength of her feelings left her in confusion.

Her confusion was heightened to a point past bearing by the knowledge that she was no longer certain that her concern was for David. Always, until now, she'd known that her closeness with her best-loved brother had enabled her

LOVING HONOR

to sense those times when he was in peril. Now she was terribly torn. Now she felt as great—or dare she admit it, even greater—a concern for the enigmatic Reese Rivers.

She thought she'd go out of her mind trying to appear normal when her intuition was screaming that one, or both of them, nearest her heart might be in serious trouble.

She twisted her hands and turned troubled eyes to her host. "Will you send word to Mason that we must leave?"

Lattimore took one look at the strain on her lovely face and said, "It's going to be dark in less than an hour, Amanda. I'll alert Mason that you want to leave first thing in the morning." He patted her awkwardly on the shoulder as he went by her on his way to find Mason.

Laura jumped up from her prone position in front of the checker board. "Shall I go pack, Aunt Amanda?"

"No, dear. You just finish your game. I'll pack for us." Her voice gave away her nervousness. "I need to be busy."

Billie Jo Lattimore nodded and slipped an arm around her. "I'll just go along to help you, dear."

Together they went upstairs to the guest bedroom. Amanda was glad for her friend's company. It made it easier to cope with the awful feeling she had that something had gone dreadfully wrong on Coronet.

Mason was up and ready before dawn broke. He drove to the edge of the Lattimores' front porch, and sat there behind the team, patiently watching the first fingers of sunlight rise over the eastern horizon.

He'd been uneasy ever since Mr. Lattimore had brought Miss Amanda's message to the barn last evening. That Amanda wanted to leave before her visit to this family was scheduled to end left him with a bad feeling he'd been unable to shake. As a result of it, he'd spent a restless night, and was eager to get back to the ranch.

He wasn't sorry that he'd been the one to drive the women, since he knew that he'd take better care of them even than the excellent care several others of the crew would have taken. He was, however, sorry he couldn't be in two places at once. He was mighty anxious to know what had set Miss Amanda off and made her want to go home early.

If Miss Amanda was restless to go home, it had to be that she was worrying about the Captain. The Lattimores were wonderful people, and even if they hadn't been, Miss Amanda could get along with the devil himself, and she would, too, before she'd insult anybody's hospitality like this. He shook his head. Good thing the Lattimores were understanding people.

His stoic reverie was broken as the screen door jumped open and Laura ran out to him. " 'Mornin', Mason."

" 'Mornin', Miss Laura."

Laura swarmed up beside him. "Aunt Amanda's in a state, so we have to go home early." Her tone of voice was nicely balanced between disgust and inquiry.

Mason tilted the scales for her. "From what I heared your papa tell round a couple a' campfires about Miss Amanda's fits of intuition, I'd guess it's a good idea to mosey home and check on things."

Laura was quiet then, her eyes troubled, and Mason was sorry he'd spoken. He muttered, not for the first time, "Danged ole fool. When ya gonna learn to mind your flappin' tongue?"

He was spared the task of putting the girl's mind at ease by the appearance of her aunt. The Lattimores accompanied her out to the rig, still saying their good-byes.

Mr. Lattimore lifted Amanda up to the seat, his face full of concern. "You send word back to us that all is well, you hear? I don't want to stew for the next week because you got a fool notion to go home early, Amanda Harcourt."

Amanda leaned down and touched his cheek. "I promise to send word." She smiled at him sweetly, not for a moment fooled by his gruffness.

LOVING HONOR 211

Mason lifted his hat to them as he flapped the reins against the rumps of his team. Once they were far enough away not to put dust all over the Lattimores, he urged them to a spanking trot and headed them for home.

They reached the ranch by late afternoon. Amanda, staring as far in front of them as she could see, was the first to realize that the yard was full of horses. It was full of horses wearing the saddle blankets of the United States Army!

Her grip on Laura's hand tightened convulsively.

Mason said in a grim voice, "Stand easy, Miss Amanda. We don' know what's goin' on yet."

Amanda tried to see what was happening through the crowd of men and horses in front of the house. Failing to make out what was going on from where she sat, she told Mason, "Stop here, I want to get down, please."

Mason pulled the team to a halt and handed the reins to Laura. "Hold 'em, Miss Laura." With that, he jumped down and came around to be sure Amanda got down safely.

The minute her feet hit the ground, Amanda rushed to the house. "David!" Her voice held an edge of panic. There was panic in her heart for another, as well, but she *would* not let herself cry out his name.

And then he was there, standing straight and tall before her. Reese Rivers. But what a changed Reese Rivers!

She stopped in her tracks and put a hand to her mouth to stifle her gasp. Her eyes widened as they took in the sight of him.

His hair was neatly combed, his face freshly shaven, and he was elegantly garbed in a fresh and neatly pressed uniform. The fit of it could only be explained by custom tailoring. It was *his* uniform beyond the merest hint of a doubt. But it was the uniform of a captain in the army of the United States!

What did it mean? Yankees were the enemy. Reese

couldn't be one of the enemy! Her mind staggered at the thought.

Suddenly, in the midst of her bewilderment, her heart went still. David! Where was David?

Just then a broad shouldered man in a colonel's uniform walked between them. Over the mutter and movement of the men around her, Amanda heard him say, "Well done, Captain Rivers. I trust that these are the men responsible for the payroll robbery."

Amanda saw Dawson and Sellers, their hands manacled, marched out of the house to mount waiting horses. Her mind numb with shock at this invasion of her home, she looked around her, seeking an explanation.

Then she saw Pete Webster. Still with the stillness of death, he was lying in the bed of an army wagon just beyond the two men she'd been watching.

Her blood ran cold. What in heaven's name had occurred in her absence?

In an instant she took it all in, even as she heard Reese Rivers respond to his colonel, "Yes, sir." Dazed, she merely stood listening to the interchange between the two Union officers.

"This is the lot?"

"Yes, sir. The other men on the ranch are innocent of the massacre. They had nothing to do with it."

"Hell, Rivers, if you'd told me there were only three, I wouldn't have brought half the blasted fort with me. Any trace of the payroll?"

"There was nothing left except for the bag I gave to your sergeant. That was stolen from the Rebel Cause by the dead man. I recovered it from one of the line shacks."

"And the rest of it?"

"Gone to buy medicines for the South, sir."

"No arms or ammunition?"

"I believe not, Colonel."

"Well, I suppose it could have been worse." He turned

and looked at the two bound men. "And which is the leader, Captain?"

"The leader has been taken care of, sir. He's where he'll never bother us again."

"Well done." He stuffed his cigar in his mouth and walked away.

Amanda was certain she would faint. The men and horses she stood among whirled giddily around her. David! Her beloved brother David had been the leader of the men on Coronet. She swayed and clutched at the arm of the nearest Union soldier to steady herself.

He looked at her with concern plain on his youthful face. "Are you all right, ma'am? Can I help you?"

"No. Yes, thank you." She pulled herself together with a superhuman effort. "I'm quite all right. I just want to see Captain Rivers."

The private steadied her with both hands on her arms as he looked up at the men on the porch. Obviously he wasn't convinced that she was all right.

The Colonel seemed to have finished whatever he'd had to say to the Captain. He supposed it was all right to sing out, "Hey. Cap'n Rivers, sir. This lady says she wants to see you."

Reese turned to look and saw her. "Amanda." His heart stopped at the sight of her standing there in the melee of men and horses, a stricken expression on her face.

Recognition of the place she occupied in it set his heart pounding. There was hope for them now. Every obstacle to their love had been removed. At last, they could be one for the rest of their lives.

He had to get her aside and tell her that all was well, that it was over. "Sir! Permission to be excused," he called after his commanding officer.

The Colonel looked a little startled, then followed the direction of Reese's gaze. He smiled and said with forced gruffness, "Dismissed, Captain." Then he shouted, "Sergeant. Mount 'em up."

Reese plunged from the porch and pushed through the general scramble to reach Amanda. It was all he could do not to shove men aside as if they had no right to be there, because they didn't. No one had the right to stand between them anymore.

Amanda watched as Reese moved purposefully toward her, managing the long cavalry saber at his side adroitly through the crowd of men and horses. She struggled with the emotions that threatened to consume her. Inside she was burning fury one moment and deadly ice the next. How could he face her?

Then he was there. He was so close that his well-polished boots were all but hidden in the fullness of her skirts as they stood gazing into each other's eyes.

It took a moment for her expression to pierce the shining shield of his love. When it did, he backed away a step, shocked. It was as if she had hit him.

"Amanda. What is it? What's the matter?"

Whirling, she ran away from him, away from the staring horde of enemy soldiers that stood behind him. The effort not to weep almost overwhelmed her as she fought to sort out and control her feelings.

Reese caught her in three strides. "Dammit, Amanda, what's gotten into you?" He grabbed her wrist. A glance back at the grinning troopers, and he dragged her toward the barn.

In its shadowed recess, he looked down at her. His eyes were alight with his love for her.

One look at her tear-drenched eyes and he was lost. "Amanda." His voice was husky with emotion that put a world of longing into the simple utterance of her name. His gaze devoured her.

She looked up at him wildly. She couldn't even speak, she was so horrified by what he'd done.

Her mind was spinning with the enormity of what Reese had done to David. Did he think he could announce in one breath that he'd killed her brother and make love to her with his next?

Abhorrence surged through her. Hatred blossomed in her heart.

"How could you!" Her voice was filled with loathing. Tears streamed.

When he reached out for her, she threw up a hand to ward him off. "Don't you touch me," she spat. "Don't you dare to touch me!"

"But, Amanda—"

"Leave me alone!" She backed away from him until her back was against one of the horse stalls. "Murderer!"

Understanding exploded in his brain like a cannon shell. She thought that he . . . She believed he'd . . . His mind spun and tumbled for a moment in its effort to refuse to grasp her meaning.

Then fury flamed in him. His breath hissed into his lungs through clenched teeth. How could she? How the bloody hell *could* she?

How could Amanda believe he would sink so low that he could have killed her brother? What sort of monster did she think him?

What sort of perverted animal could kill a brother and then seek to take the sister in his arms? The idea was hideous.

Rage that she might even *briefly consider* him such an aberration filled him. Where was her faith in him?

Did she truly think that a man who'd twice tried, with all his strength, to protect her from his—and her own—passion would prove so bereft of any sensibility that he could do away with her nearest kin without a qualm?

He backed away from her. He felt as if his soul were draining out of him.

Outside, where there was still a sun in the sky, he heard the order, "Mount, ho-oh!"

In Reese's life the sun had ceased to exist.

The pleading hand he'd held out to Amanda dropped to his side. He gave his head a little shake. If that was what she thought of him, she could, obviously, want no part of him.

Savagely he slammed the door of his mind on all his hopes and dreams. Just as savagely he closed his lips against the words that would have made everything right between them.

If she chose to believe him a monster, then so be it. By keeping his silence, he would make it so.

From out of the dusty brightness behind him, the cry came, "Forward, ho!" The creaking, jingling sound of a cavalry column on the move filled the air.

His heart pained him with the bitterness of a thousand wounds. He cast one final look her way.

Where was the goddess whose glance as she'd left the clearing by the river had proclaimed her proud love for him? Where was his Amanda?

This Amanda averted her face.

Even as he died inside, rage rose again in him and gave him the strength to turn on his heel and stalk from the barn. Behind him, unseen, he trailed his shattered dreams.

Outside, striding to his horse, it was moments before he realized he was hearing his name being called. When it finally penetrated his anguish-born anger, he turned to see Laura running after him.

"Reese! Reese, wait." She arrived out of breath from the speed with which she'd run from where she'd been waiting in the buggy to see her aunt and Reese emerge from the barn.

She'd truly expected to see something quite different than an infuriated Reese stalking with angry strides to where a private held his horse for him. Disappointment fell heavy on her heart.

Something awful must have happened! Whatever it was, though, she had no intention of losing her friend. "Reese, what is it? What's the matter?"

He threw her a thunderous glance. "You'll find out soon enough from your aunt." His voice grated.

"Reese," she flatly stated what she knew to be the truth, "you're leaving, aren't you? *Really leaving!*"

Her face began to crumple. "I don't want to lose you, Reese." She gulped back a sob, fighting to keep her voice steady, trying to be grown up. "How . . . how can I get in touch with you?"

Gathering his reins, he swung himself up on Thor.

Laura was sure he was just going to ride away. Tears streamed down her face.

His deep affection for the child defeated him.

At the last instant, when the rest of the Yankees were riding down the lane to the road to English Bend, he reached inside his tunic and drew out an envelope. Tearing off the return address, he flung it in her direction.

"Good-bye, Laura." There was a finality in his voice that frightened her.

She knew with a dreadful certainty that he had no intention of ever seeing her again. That knowledge released more tears. Through a flood of them, she watched him turn Thor and send him cantering to his place at the head of the cavalry column.

Laura could hardly see, she was crying so hard. Without the slightest hesitation, she got down and felt with her hands in the dust for the scrap of envelope he had thrown at her.

The dust was warm under her fingers. It felt good to them, for they had gone icy with dread in the last few minutes.

Shaken by sobs, blinded by tears, it took her several minutes to find the small piece of paper.

Chapter 21

Amanda's life had become unbearable. Mason had questioned every one of the men left at the ranch, and no one knew what had happened to David. There was only the faintest hope, born of the fact that his horse was missing.

Amanda couldn't take refuge in that hope. She had heard Reese tell his colonel that he had taken care of the leader of the men who had robbed the army payroll, and she knew he meant David.

When she finally told Laura, the child lost all control. "I don't care what you think!" Laura shouted at her between sobs. "Reese Rivers didn't hurt my Papa."

She pulled out of her aunt's embrace, balled her hands into tight little fists, then shook one at her aunt. "Reese would never do such a thing. I don't care what you say!"

Laura ran, sobbing, out of the room. She left an anguished Amanda staring helplessly after her.

In the privacy of the kitchen, Polly conferred with Rosa. "What's to be done, do ye think? I've never seen her ladyship so glum."

"Aiyee, chihuahua. That is a question. She is saddened by the loss of Señor David, I have no doubt." Rosa wiped flour from her hands on her apron and turned to point a finger at her friend. "But you mark my words. She is very much in love with that handsome Yankee soldier."

"No! I don't believe that. She couldn't possibly be. Why, that man probably took his lordship out somewhere and shot him, the snake. He as good as said so to that colonel of his."

Rosa went back to rolling out her biscuit dough. After a time, she stopped and cocked her head to think for a moment. Finally she said softly, "The little señorita does not think so."

"Ye don't mean to tell me ye're basing your thoughts on those of a child?"

"She is the daughter of the *Patrón*. Surely she would feel a great loss if her *padre* were dead. I do not see that in her."

"No." Polly swelled up with indignation. "All you see is her making *my* Lady Amanda miserable by insisting that that awful man couldn't have done anything wrong!"

"Sometimes *los niños* have the right of things when their elders are too tangled up to realize they may be worth listening to."

"Tangled up! That's a good word, that is." Polly's voice rose to a wail. "Never in me life have I seen me lovely Lady Amanda so *tangled up*." She buried her face in her hands and cried like a child.

"Madre mía!" Rosa dropped her rolling pin and went to pat flour into the shoulder of her friend's dress in helpless sympathy.

Ralph Endicott was feeling very much in need of sympathy as he walked around his store. His sensibilities were outraged. The very idea! Someone must be playing a bad joke. And he didn't like it. He didn't like it one bit.

Things weren't going his way lately, and he was completely out of sorts. Wasn't it bad enough that he was losing the best clerk he'd had in years? Elvira Beame had given notice that she would be leaving to set up her own dressmaking establishment in Philadelphia—so she said—in two weeks. Wasn't that annoying enough without all these other complications?

David Harcourt's disappearance had turned Amanda Harcourt into a virtual recluse. She never came in to town to his store now. And when he'd attempted to see her at the ranch, he'd been told she was "not at home" by that snooty maid of hers. He'd fumed all the way back to town.

How he was going to persuade her to marry him—a hope Harcourt's disappearance had revived in him—he didn't know. And now this! He glared down at it.

"Mrs. Beame! Come here, if you please."

Elvira Beame exchanged a quick look with Ben. He smiled tightly. Both of them knew she'd better get herself over there whether or not she pleased.

She got across the store as quickly as she could and still maintain her dignity. "Yes, Mr. Endicott?"

"Look at this." He shoved a letter into her face.

She drew in her chin and moved her head back a few inches in an effort to get enough distance from the missive to be able to make out the address.

Endicott saved her the trouble. "It's addressed to Mrs. Amanda Rivers. Can you believe that? Mrs. Amanda Rivers!" He was working himself up into a state. He snorted, then said, "As if Lady Amanda would lower herself to marry that lethal-looking lout!"

Elvira's stomach tightened and she kept her face carefully straight. She didn't think any woman alive would mind having the chance to marry Reese Rivers, herself, but she knew she'd better not to say so. Instead she said, "I have no knowledge of Miss Amanda marrying anyone. I feel certain we would have heard."

"Yes. You're right." If he hadn't been so angry, her words might have cheered him. Instead, though, he wanted to vent his righteous indignation on the perpetrator of this hoax. "There is, therefore, no such person as Mrs. Amanda Rivers. Am I correct?"

LOVING HONOR 221

Elvira Beame nodded cautiously.

"And so the letter is undeliverable."

Elvira started to protest that they all knew whom the letter was meant to reach, but a warning look from Ben silenced her. She merely watched while Endicott stormed across the store to the postal section of which he was so proud and proceeded to scatter little wooden block stamps in all directions until he found the one he was looking for. "There!" He inked it and slammed the stamper down on the front of Amanda's letter.

"Now. It can be returned to England." He hesitated a moment, his eyes narrowing in thought. No. If he sent it back to the sender, they would know Amanda hadn't received it. They might write again. He decided it was better she not hear one word from someone who believed she might be *Mrs. Amanda Rivers*!

With a furtive glance in the direction of his employees, he slipped the letter into the trash basket. Grimly satisfied, he washed his hands in the air and got back to the business of running his store.

After a self-satisfied visual survey of the establishment, Endicott went into the storage room. The minute he did, Elvira and Ben put their heads together.

"Did you see what he did?" Their whispers were in unison.

Both nodded vigorously. Ben slinked around the far edge of the shop until he was in easy reach of the wastebasket there by English Bend's official post office. Gingerly, he fished out the letter.

Quiet as a mouse, he crept back to Elvira where she stood, her gaze still fastened on the doorway through which Endicott might emerge at any second. He told her, "This here letter is sure addressed to Miss Harcourt, no matter what *he* says. I aim to see that she gets it."

"What shall we do if he remembers it and decides to look at it again?" Elvira's voice was vibrant with concern.

"I'll take the trash out to the burn barrel right this minute."

"Good idea. I'll get the wastepaper basket from the front." She scurried off as furtively as Ben had, and was back in less than a minute, handing the boy the woven rattan basket. "Here," she said breathlessly.

"Thanks." Ben rushed soundlessly off to collect the other basket. He'd barely done so when Endicott came out of the storeroom.

"Perhaps," Endicott announced, "it would save everybody a great deal of trouble if I simply destroyed that letter. What do you think, Miss Beame?"

Safe in the knowledge that she would be instrumental in saving the letter if she delayed him, and not his accomplice in interfering with the mails, she answered, "I am not quite sure."

"Not sure of what? The matter is absurdly simple. The letter would be returning to a postmaster in England. It hasn't even a proper return address."

"Yes, but we . . ." She could afford to include herself in his scheme. She knew it was already thwarted. ". . . would be interfering with the U.S. Mail, wouldn't we?"

"Certainly not," Endicott blustered. "We'd simply be saving everybody trouble."

Elvira saw the reflection of flames from the burn barrel through the back door. Relief flooded her. Now she and Ben would be safe in pretending the letter had been burned.

Endicott said, "I fear the letter has dropped off the postal counter into the wastebasket. I'll just go retrieve it and dispose of it."

"Oh, dear," Elvira Beame said in mock distress.

"What is it?"

"I fear that we have already saved everybody all that trouble."

"Whatever do you mean?" He stood scowling at her.

"I fear Ben and I picked up the wastebaskets a moment ago, and I'm afraid he's already burning the trash."

LOVING HONOR   223

A long minute passed before he spoke. "Really." He struggled to hide his smile. "Then I suppose there is nothing more to be done about Lady Amanda's letter." He lost his battle to hide the smile. "Pity."

That evening when they got off work, Elvira and Ben met behind the store to discuss their problem.

"How will we get the letter to her, Ben?"

"We could give it to somebody heading out that way."

"Nobody goes in that direction except the hands from Coronet."

"Well, we could ask somebody to ride out there and tell her she has a letter." He corrected himself even as Elvira opened her mouth to do so. "Nope. Too dangerous. Endicott would murder me if whoever we told spilled the beans."

"Maybe she'll come into town soon."

"Not likely. Things are pretty mixed up out there after all that's happened."

"Then what shall we do?"

Ben thought hard. A grin split his face. "I know! I'll borrow Pauley Whitfield's horse. He always drinks himself into a stupor and sleeps it off until they clean up the saloon in the morning. He'll never know it's gone."

"Ben!" Elvira pressed a nervous hand to her breast. "They hang horse thieves."

Ben forgot his school English. "I ain' gonna steal it, for Pete's sake. I'm only gonna borrow it."

Elvira regarded him levelly, her lips prim. "I hope the sheriff will be willing to see the difference."

Ben grinned at her. "If he don't, you can sweet-talk him for me. He thinks you're somethin' special."

Elvira rolled her eyes. "You just get back here before anyone misses that horse. I don't want to have to say anything to the sheriff, thank you."

"Okay. I'll let you know how it goes."

It was well past midnight when Ben rode into the yard of the big ranch house on Coronet. He hadn't any idea what to do now that he'd gotten here. He guessed he'd just have to knock on the front door and hope nobody shot him.

Walking up the steps as boldly as he could, he raised his hand, curled it into a fist, gulped once, and knocked. Nothing happened.

A minute later he knocked again, and this time, he could hear someone running down the stairs to open the door. He hadn't known till then how nervous he was.

When Laura swung the door wide and said, "Golly, Ben, what are you doing here?"

"I brought this." He reached into his jacket for the letter.

Amanda Harcourt appeared behind her niece. "Ben. Whatever in the world are you doing out here in the middle of the night, dear?"

Ben gaped at her. He'd never seen a beautiful lady wrapped from her head to her toes in a froth of lace and pretty ribbons. He was sure his eyes were popping right out of his head. She looked like the prettiest Christmas package he'd ever seen, only better. He was momentarily struck dumb.

Laura lost all patience with him. "Aw, come on, Ben. Whaddya want?"

Mutely, he held out the letter.

Laura took it, looked at the address, and looked again.

Amanda held out her hand. "May I see it, please?"

Reluctantly, unsure of both the meaning of the strange address and of how her aunt would receive it, Laura surrendered the letter.

Neither she nor her aunt heard Ben clatter across the porch saying, "I gotta get this horse back."

As he cantered out of the yard, he called, "Good night."

Belatedly, Laura thrust her head out the door and shouted, "Thanks, Ben!"

A light sprang up in the bunkhouse.
Amanda called out, "Everything's all right, men. Thank you."
The lamp in the bunkhouse was extinguished.

❧ ❧ ❧ ❧ ❧ ❧ ❧ ❧

Chapter 22

Amanda stared at the letter. Her mind went numb. Her intellect refused to accept the evidence of her own eyes.

A long moment passed before Laura prompted, "Aunt Amanda?"

Amanda looked up at her with a dazed expression. "It's from your Papa. I recognize his handwriting."

"Well, aren't you going to open it?" Laura had to struggle to keep the impatience out of her voice.

Finally with shaking hands Amanda tore open the heavy vellum envelope. Still incredulous, she flipped up the first page of the letter it contained so that she could see the signature. David! It truly was from David.

She closed her eyes against the tide of relief that swept over her. Thank God. *Oh, thank you, God.* David was alive. He was alive! Her heart swelled till it felt as if it would burst from her chest. Her brother was alive.

She opened her eyes again and looked at Laura, searching for a way to break the news to her gently. "Laura, darling." She could hardly see the child's face through her joyous tears. She strove to speak calmly. "It's from your papa."

"Good," Laura responded matter of factly. "What does he say?"

Amanda turned and led the way into David's study. "Please light the lamp, pet. My hands are shaking too badly to manage it."

"Yes'm." She reached into the top drawer and pulled out the matchbox, struck a match, and lit the desk lamp.

Amanda sat in David's chair and spread the two sheets of his letter out in front of her.

"Dearest Amanda," she read in a voice choked with emotion. *"First, I send my love and best wishes to you and to my precious Laura."* She looked up to smile at her niece. *"And reassurances that Grandfather is well."* That was good news, and she was always glad to have it since Grandfather was well into his eighties now.

Her mind, however, was clamoring for an explanation of David's disappearance. It wasn't enough to know he was safe, now that she did. Now she needed, desperately needed, to know how he had gotten away to England.

"I hope that my sudden disappearance did not come as a shock to you." She stopped reading there and looked up at Laura with eyes that held both bewilderment and a wildness that would have boded ill for her brother had he been there in person.

She demanded of Laura, "How could he possibly think, even for one instant, that his disappearing off the face of the earth would fail to send us half insane with worry?"

Laura did nothing to sweeten her aunt's mood by saying sensibly, "Just be calm and read the letter, Aunt Amanda. Papa will no doubt tell us why he didn't leave us a message."

Amanda stifled the urge to reach out and give her niece a good pinch and went back to reading, *"But I take comfort in the knowledge that if it did, it was of short duration."*

Amanda looked up from those words to share a puzzled look with Laura. Short duration! The weeks since his disappearance seemed like years to Amanda.

"As you have seen from the direction that I used on the envelope, I am aware that by now you are Mrs. Reese Rivers." She gasped. Whatever possessed David? What

could have made him think... How could he believe that she and Reese were married?

How did David even know that anything had ever transpired between Reese Rivers and herself? Especially anything that might even hint of marriage?

Avidly reading the next sentence, she learned. *"Having come up against the determination of your Yankee, I have no doubt that he has wed you as he swore to (and sometimes at) me that he would."*

Wed her! "Wed her as he had sworn he would." Reese had told David that he was going to wed her? What did this mean? Reese had seemed always to try to maintain a safe distance from her, emotionally as well as physically. Especially since that fateful evening in the line shack when he had... when they had... when they had almost...

She seized her thoughts firmly. Then she faced her feelings honestly and without flinching. Unconsciously she lifted her chin as she told herself fiercely, *that evening in the line shack when Reese Rivers had almost made love to her in response to their mutual passion.* As she voiced that thought mentally, her knees went weak with the remembrance, and warmth flooded her body.

She admitted, too, that it was that evening in the line shack that had given birth to her own determination to force him to make love to her that Sunday evening on the riverbank.

But never, anywhere, except in her most intimate dreams, had the subject of marriage... She put her rampaging thoughts aside, determined to continue reading. *"He's quite a man, your Yankee."*

Again she lost her battle for reasonableness. A feeling as warm as summer sunshine permeated her being. *Her* Yankee. She wasn't sure she liked the way David had put it. She didn't think of Reese as a Yankee. So she just reveled in the thought that David considered him hers. Her Reese.

"Certainly, I owe him my life, as do Mason, Rogers,

Owens, Larkin, and Griffith." She didn't understand what David meant by that, but whatever he implied, she was overwhelmed with gratitude that David and the others were safe. For David was evidently saying that Mason and the rest of the men he named had nothing further to fear from the U.S. Army.

Laura made a little impatient sound, and Amanda read on. *"As he has no doubt told you, after Sellers's shot creased his shoulder and went on to kill Pete Webster, your husband put me through as intensive a session of questioning as I have ever been privileged to witness."* Her heart lurched. Someone had shot at Reese again, someone had... Then she remembered how vibrant with life he had been at their last meeting and went back to the all-important letter, *"Convinced at the end of it that I had nothing to do with the cowardly murder of his friends, he decided to dismiss the fact that I had planned the payroll theft. Acts of war don't call forth thoughts of retaliation in your Yankee, fortunately. Then, however, his problem became what to do with me. Actually, it was rather a splendid thing to watch him struggle to balance honor against duty without disservice to either.*

"His conviction that I would meet my fate at the end of a rope if I was still on Coronet when his colonel arrived decided the day." Amanda read the words in a garbled rush, almost mindless with impatience. How had Reese saved David? *"Though, confidentially, I strongly suspect that..."* Since her eyes outraced her tongue, she blushed but was able to keep the next words to herself, *the depth of his love for you and...* Fireworks exploded in her. She paused as she cherished the words, reading them silently a second time, *the depth of his love for you.*

Fearful, suddenly, that she might have damaged that love at their last meeting, she drew a deep breath and, refusing to consider that now, began reading aloud again, *"his obvious affection for Laura tipped the scales a bit in my favor."*

Laura interrupted her. "Let me see that. I can't believe my Papa was so stupid he didn't know that Reese was in love with you, and that was the most of what stopped him from letting Papa get hanged."

Amanda pushed Laura's hands away and raised both eyebrows at her in reprimand, *"At any rate,"* she read, *"he told me he had no intention of furthering England's sympathy for the Confederate cause by hanging one of the peers of her realm. He decided to exile me instead. (A very highhanded man, your Yankee!)"*

Laura laughed out loud at that, tickled at her father's humor. Amanda only smiled softly and mysteriously. Yes, she admitted to herself, Reese was as arrogant as a prince. And twice as prideful.

It was that pride that she feared. She had grievously wounded it when she'd believed him capable of harming her brother.

It was that pride that she was going to have to do battle against if she hoped to win him back. And Lady Amanda Harcourt had every intention of winning Reese Rivers back.

"Aunt Amanda! If you're not going to read it, give it to me."

"So here I am, pledged to stay put on our 'sceptered isle' for the next few years. (I am given to understand that your spouse will personally blow my brains out if I break my parole. A rather dangerous sort of chap, your Yank.)"

While Laura chuckled, Amanda's smile almost faded. Her heart stopped its regular beat to flutter painfully. Reese had risked everything to save David. She was sure the action had cost him greatly. Suppose the price had been too great?

Suppose he no longer thought her worth the cost, now that he'd found her faith in him shaken? Suppose, she felt dread rising in her . . . suppose he wasn't *hers* anymore?

That very quality of reckless danger in Reese to which

David referred might have caused him to cut his losses and to tear any love he might have had for her from his heart.

Struck motionless by the thought that she might have lost him, she sat staring straight ahead. Suddenly, remembering their last moments together, she was certain that he *was* lost to her. How else had he been able to leave her standing there in the barn, dying inside, and ride away?

It would have been such a simple thing for him to have whispered to her to trust him. To have told her he had sent David to safety.

He could have, at the very least, denied that it was he who had killed Pete Webster when she accused him of it—when she had called him a murderer. Instead Reese had let the situation test her, and she had failed the test.

Whatever she had had of Reese Rivers's heart she had lost there in the dusty yard the day she'd returned from the Lattimores'.

Reese Rivers was not *her* anything. Not anymore.

Her heart steadied and beat again with a slow sad rhythm. It came from a sorrow that she could only hope she would learn to live with.

She didn't know how she would do it, but she knew she had to finish the letter. Throwing her chin high and blinking repeatedly to clear her eyes of tears she read on. *"It is hardly a brotherly attitude on his part, of course, but, alas, there you have it."*

Laura clapped her hands with delight. "Papa thinks Reese is my uncle."

Amanda ignored the unintentional hurt the child's comment occasioned her and kept on to the end. *"Grandfather has agreed that we may give Mason charge of the ranch. I hope he will take it.*

"It was a little more difficult to persuade him to accept your marriage to 'a common colonial soldier.' Finally, however, he agreed that you were a fair price to pay for the safe return of his heir. I joke, of course.

"*Grandfather is, however, disappointed he can't marry you off to Lord Dunsmith and thus acquire the estate next to Kennerley, but he feels Reese will, beyond a doubt, make a more interesting grandson-in-law.*"

Amanda's voice was becoming so choked that she was afraid she would be unable to finish reading aloud. Valiantly she struggled on.

The impish delight died in Laura's eyes with the awareness that her aunt was suffering. Of course she knew why. She remembered with a heart that plummeted like a stone how Reese had left Coronet.

"*I wish you joy in your marriage.*" Amanda's voice broke and she fumbled the closing words out through trembling lips. "*With your Yankee, I can assure you it will never be dull.*" She gasped for her next breath. "*I am relieved that you have at last found a man worthy of you, my dear.*"

Her brother's fond good wishes were more than she could bear. Amanda pushed the letter to Laura and covered her face with her hands. Her body shook with her effort to control her sobs.

She had made such a mess of everything! There was no way it could ever come right.

Laura took the letter up and finished reading it for Amanda in a tiny, awed voice. "*My very best wishes to your husband.*" She shot a look at her aunt to see how she took that, and sighed. Not well. "*I look forward to getting to know him better when this war of Northern aggression has come to its inevitable, sad conclusion and he brings you and Laura to England as he promised.*

Laura's heart gave a hopeful little bound as she read that, but she contained it for her aunt's sake. "*I send all of my love to Laura and to you. Until we are together again, your devoted brother, David.*"

Laura finished quietly and looked up at her aunt. Silently she vowed she would give anything she had to ease her distress. "Aunt Amanda." She tried for lightness in her tone, but her voice came out thin and reedy instead of jovial.

She sighed and tried again with a little more success. "Here's a good one on Mr. Oily Endicott."

Amanda sat up straighter and took her hands away from her tear-streaked face.

"Listen," Laura read, *"Post Scriptum, I addressed you as Amanda Rivers because I should hate any confusion arising in our postmaster's mind as to whom to deliver this rather lengthy missive. Your ob. ser., etc., D."*

Laura tried a chuckle, but it didn't make it. Her effort brought a weak smile from her aunt, however, and Laura felt rewarded. She reached out and touched her aunt's hand.

Immediately Amanda took it in her own. Her voice was husky as she said, "Isn't it wonderful to know that your Papa is safe at home in England? That Captain Rivers didn't harm him after all?"

Laura didn't answer because she knew Amanda didn't expect her to. Besides, how could she say anything when the only words that came to her mind were "I told you so"?

Chapter 23

Laura didn't know what to do about her aunt. She felt a great responsibility because she still had the address that Reese had thrown down at her that fateful day.

Should she tell her aunt? Or might getting her in touch with Reese Rivers just serve to deepen her hurt?

In all her days, she'd never been in such a quandary. If only she could talk about it with somebody.

Mason might have been a good choice, but now he was too glum because of the war news. He'd cheered up a little when Aunt Amanda had called the men together and read them the fragment of the letter that told them they'd all been exonerated and David was safe. But Mason really believed in the right of states to govern themselves, and now that cause looked hopeless.

There wasn't much point in talking to her pony. Warbonnet couldn't talk back. And she really needed somebody's besides her own opinion on this.

She'd ask Polly what to do, because she knew Polly loved Aunt Amanda more than anything, but Polly *hated* Reese Rivers. And she put a fair amount of passion into it, too. His name had only come up once between them, but Polly had gone on so, that Laura couldn't figure out which she hated about him most, the fact that he was a common colonial who had upset her Lady Amanda by daring to en-

LOVING HONOR

gage her affections, or because she firmly believed Reese Rivers had done away with *her* Papa.

Laura sighed and grumbled, "You'd think that Papa's letter would have made everything all right. It sure did for me and the men."

It just set Polly off, though, to know Reese had sent David away. Didn't seem to matter to her that he'd saved her Papa's life by doing it.

Polly hung on to the belief that, if Reese hadn't come, David's life would never have been in danger in the first place. Didn't she know that if it hadn't been Reese, the U.S. Army would still have sent somebody, and *that* somebody might have just hanged every man jack of them?

She choked up a little at that last thought. If it hadn't been for Reese! And now Aunt Amanda had sent him off hurting so bad that his eyes showed it. Laura wasn't sure she deserved to know where he lived, even if her eyes were the ones looking pretty miserable these days.

Except it was mighty hard just to stand by and see how her aunt was suffering. Laura blew out her cheeks, then let the air out in an explosive sigh. "I need some help!"

She put her thinking cap on. "So, who does that leave for me to talk to?"

She slouched out on to the front porch and thumped down the steps. "I need a rock." She grimaced down at the neatly polished toes of her boots, said, "Too bad," and looked around for a rock to kick.

A few minutes later the appearance of her boot toes had gone down, but her spirits had gone up just a little. That little was enough for her to start thinking clearly again, instead of just wallowing in her problems, getting nowhere, paying no heed to what went on around her.

As she pursued the rock she'd sent flying toward the back of the house, the soft sounds of an old Spanish song caught her attention. "Rosa! Why didn't I think of Rosa?"

She started toward the kitchen, skidded to a stop, and

said a quick prayer that Polly would be upstairs getting Aunt Amanda dressed. Aunt Amanda had let Polly take a lot more care of her lately.

"And I consider that a *very* bad sign," Laura muttered as she went on tiptoe to peer into the kitchen.

"Good. The coast is clear." Pulling open the back door, she called, " 'Morning, Rosa."

She went straight to the high stool next to the big kitchen table on which Rosa did almost everything but the cooking. There, she climbed up and sat.

Rosa turned from poking up the fire in the big black iron stove and looked at her a long moment. "Hmmmm. So now, at last, you remember your old friend Rosa?"

Laura blushed fiercely. "I've been busy making my aunt feel at home, Rosa."

"Your aunt always feels at home here, *muchacha*."

Laura squirmed. "All right. *I* was getting used to my aunt."

"*Sí*, that I can understand." Rosa's voice fairly creaked under the load of sarcasm she put on it. "Your aunt, she is so difficult that she takes a great deal of getting used to, that one."

"Aw, Rosa. Have a heart. I wanted to get to know her. You saw a lot of her when she used to come here before and when I was a baby, but I didn't. All I did was eat and sleep the last time she came."

"That is so." Rosa relented. "And now? What is it that troubles you now?"

Laura's sigh of relief shook her slight frame. "I don't know what to do, Rosa."

"Ahhhh?"

"No. It's true." Laura scowled her sincerity. "You see, I know that she and Reese Rivers love each other . . ."

"*Verdad.*"

"Yes, it is true." She saw the sparkle in the housekeeper's eye. "You knew it all along, didn't you?"

Rosa shrugged.

"Well, anyway. She mopes around like she's gonna die for missing him and for the *terrible injustice* she's done Reese."

She liked the sound of that "terrible injustice." She'd have said it again, but Rosa turned and fixed her with a dark stare.

"Well, it was!" Laura defended her position hotly. "He did save my Papa when nobody else could have, and Aunt Amanda called him names, I know she did."

Rosa took one of her hands off her hip to shake a finger at the girl. "And of course, Mr. Captain Reese Rivers, he silenced her bitter words of upset with a comforting *beso* . . . a comforting kiss, did he not? And, too, he quickly followed his kiss with gentle words of explanation that put her worrying mind at ease?" Sarcasm dripped from every word. "Yes?" Her eyebrows drew down in a thunderous frown. "No!"

"No! It wasn't like that." Laura rose to Reese's defense. "He got on his horse and rode away, he was so shocked and hurt."

"Ahhhh?"

"Rosa, you're not being fair."

"That is a possible thing. But no matter. I don't think your *amigo* Reese Rivers did a fair thing either. He should have thought how the señorita would feel to come home to a yard overflowing . . . that is the right word?"

"If you mean all the Yankees all over the place, it'll do. Teeming might be better, though."

"*Gracias* . . . teeming with enemy soldiers, and there was Pete Webster dead right in front of her in that wagon. Maybe she don' like him very much, but he is a man who sat across the table from her for many meals. And he was *dead*!

"Then the *señorita* sees her true love. And what is it that he wears?" She threw both hands up toward the ceiling.

"He is wearing the uniform of those men she has thought of as enemies." Down came her hands to shake both index fingers accusingly.

Rosa's *s*'s sounded more like hisses to Laura now.

"And, to make her day even better," Rosa threw up her hands again and flung them in a wide circle, "there isss no sign of the brother she loves? Aiyee, *chihuahua*!" She glared hard at Laura, her teeth clenched and her eyes narrowed.

Very quietly, Laura said, "Guess when you put it that way . . ." She gnawed her bottom lip.

"Good! Now you see what is how your aunt feels. It is good that somebody sees what your aunt feels!" She turned away to poke savagely at the fire under one of the round, heavy cooking surfaces of her stove. Satisfied that it was hot enough, she plopped her kettle of soup on it, stirred once vigorously and turned her full attention back to the child.

"Then," she spoke straight at Laura, her eyes locked with the girl's, "this brute of a man, thinking only of his own wounded feelings, rides off and leaves *Señorita* Amanda there alone to wonder what has become of her beloved brother. Hah!"

"Golly. I never thought of it that way. I just thought that Aunt Amanda was being unfair not to know that Reese could never hurt her or anybody she loved."

"Ah, *muchachita*. You have much to learn of being an adult. Things are not so . . . how you say? . . . black and white when you are older. You will see.

"It is sometimes that one lover hurts another. That is the path that love takes. How is it you *Anglos* say it? 'The course of a true love does not run so smoothly'? . . ."

" 'The course of true love never runs smooth.' "

"Hokay. So that is the way it is said. The problem is that the course of what was never really love don' run so smooth, too. And also the course of deceitful love ... or of one-sided love."

She threw up her hands, scattering drops of soup from her stirring spoon. "So who is to know, when they are hurt and bewildered ... that is the right word, bewildered?" At Laura's nod, she continued. "... bewildered, which it is that she finds herself in?"

Laura sat frowning while she sorted all that out. When she had it straight, she looked up at Rosa, bewildered herself. "Then, Rosa, what shall I do?"

"What do you mean, little one?" Rosa's anger melted to tenderness.

Laura said in a very small voice, "I am the only one around here who knows where he is, or," she made her statement absolutely truthful, "at least I have an address he gave me."

"Ahhhh." Rosa's expression became thoughtful. Slowly she closed the distance between them. She lowered her bulk into a chair next to Laura.

With a heavy sigh she told the child, "We must think, *muchachita*. We must think of this thing very carefully."

Laura sat regarding her with round eyes full of relief. She was glad to have shifted her burden to Rosa's well-padded shoulders.

Fifteen hundred miles away in Philadelphia, Reese Rivers stood surrounded by a black-clad group of business associates at his father's graveside.

He'd spent the two months since leaving Coronet in a frantic rush to his ailing father's bedside and an exhausting attempt to absorb all that the dying man wanted him to know before death forced him to relinquish his kingdom to his prodigal son.

A phase of Reese's life was over. He acknowledged it with reluctance.

Looking around at the men present at the funeral, he

wondered if they were mourning his father's passing. Two months ago, he would not have been able to, himself. In the time since his arrival, however, he had gained an insight into his father's driven personality that left him with the ability to mourn the man.

His face betrayed nothing of his thoughts as he stood in the light drizzle of the gray Pennsylvania day accepting the condolences of those around him. Deep inside, however, he was expressing to a merciful God his profound gratitude for the admiration and reluctant affection that had grown between his estranged father and himself.

Stepping forward, he shoveled the first dirt onto the coffin. Then he turned away to enter the next phase of his life. A phase he vowed would include Amanda Harcourt.

Not far away, in the best section of downtown Philadelphia, Elvira Beame stood staring around her at the beautifully appointed shop that Amanda Harcourt had procured for her. In her arms, tightly clasped to her chest, she held her book of designs.

The sketchbook was her most cherished possession, and she had hardly let go of it since she'd left English Bend, Texas. It had been the sketchbook that had caused Miss Harcourt to offer her this wildly wonderful chance to realize her dreams.

She looked at the seven assistants waiting for her orders. They looked a little apprehensive. Almost as apprehensive as she felt.

She removed her bonnet with hands that trembled with eager anticipation. Placing the book of designs on a table, she opened it to the first page.

She looked solemnly at the seamstresses who were to be her staff. Then she said, "Come and see."

The rush with which the seamstresses came to look was most gratifying. Elvira took a deep, happy breath and began to explain what she hoped to accomplish.

LOVING HONOR

When she had finished showing them the last sketch, there were no further doubts. The apprehension had fled. The women were chatting softly about fabrics and colors.

And all eight of them were smiling.

Amanda smiled over at Laura. "I'm so very proud of you, dear. You look as if you had been riding sidesaddle since birth."

Laura was glad she'd finally mastered the darned sidesaddle. She was happy, too, that she'd pleased her aunt.

She'd wouldn't be really happy, though, until she could see her aunt Amanda smile without that hint of sadness that lurked in her eyes nowadays.

"Thanks, Aunt Amanda. I hope Papa will be pleased, too."

"I'm sure he will be delighted."

"When are we going to England?" Instantly she regretted bringing that up. Clearly the subject was painful for her aunt.

She wondered if it was because Papa had said that Reese Rivers was planning to bring them to him in England and now that wasn't going to happen. Or was it because going to England would put so many miles between her aunt and Reese?

Puzzling it all out was such a chore. It would have been so much simpler if she could just ask her aunt what it was Amanda wanted.

Rosa had told her, though, that grown-ups were very complicated, and that they were strange about their innermost thoughts. Furthermore, Rosa had forbidden her to question her aunt, assuring Laura that she'd just make a muddle of things.

It sure was hard, though, not to talk about Reese to Aunt Amanda. If Rosa didn't come up with a plan soon, she might have to take matters into her own hands and devil take the hindmost.

Inspiration came in a brilliant flash. Laura turned to her aunt eagerly. "Aunt Amanda? Can we ride down to the river?"

She saw her aunt hesitate. Amanda's face paled, and her eyes grew dreamy with remembrance for an instant. Then the sadness that Laura hated so was there again, dulling her aunt's lovely blue eyes.

Suddenly Laura was filled with certainty. She didn't have to wait for Rosa any longer. She knew her own plan was going to work.

She saw her aunt take a deep breath and lift her chin, a sure sign that she was preparing for the worst. Turning her head so that her aunt couldn't see, Laura smiled to herself.

Surely a plan that came so suddenly and clearly just had to work. Laura mentally crossed her fingers and said a quick prayer. It didn't hurt to cover all bases.

"Why, yes, dear. We can ride down to the river if you would like to."

Calmly Laura turned Warbonnet toward the river. Amanda, all unsuspecting, followed on Evening Star.

Triumph blazed through Laura like summer lightning.

Chapter 24

Laura led the way. She rode just far enough in front of her aunt so that Amanda couldn't influence the direction they took.

"Ooops!" was all Laura said when her haste caused her horse to stumble in the rocks. If she'd fallen on her nose, it would have been worth it for what she had planned.

"Say," she marvelled to her mount, distracted by her near tumble, "this darn saddle is sure hard to fall out of." She flexed the leg she'd just tightened around the horn on which it rested. "Might not be so bad to have to ride this way in England, after all."

She heard Amanda call, "Not that way, Laura. Let's go further *up*stream."

Laura heard the faint note of panic in her aunt's voice, and, pretending not to hear, ignored it. She hardened her heart. If she were going to force her aunt to agree to her plan, then it had to be at the particular place on the river's bank to which she was headed.

"Here we are!" she sang out cheerfully, and guided her horse into the clearing where she'd found her aunt and Reese Rivers that Sunday night.

Mercilessly she called back to her. "This is a pretty spot. Let's get down for a while." She unhooked her right leg and slipped from her saddle.

Looking to where her aunt was about to enter the clearing, she saw her face was pale and tense. A little twinge of conscience had to be squelched before Laura could say, "My leg's a little tired. You don't mind if we rest here a minute, do you?"

Amanda, strain clear on her face, said faintly, "Of course not, dear." She rode her horse the rest of the way into the clearing with as much enthusiasm as if she rode into a prairie fire.

Evening Star, sensing her rider's reluctance, came to a halt immediately. Amanda dismounted without her usual grace.

Laura pretended she noticed nothing unusual, and sat down on a large flat rock. She patted it in an invitation for her aunt to join her.

When Amanda had sat—as if she were sitting on a hot stove—Laura began her campaign.

"Isn't this a lovely clearing?"

"Yes, it is."

"Have you ever come here before?"

Amanda's voice sounded a little choked. "Yes. It used to be my favorite place."

"But it's not anymore? Why?" Laura filled her voice with incredulous surprise.

Amanda seemed unable to answer, and Laura plowed on. "Why did it stop being your favorite place?"

Amanda just shook her head and averted her face.

Laura saw the quick tears her aunt sought to hide, and for just an instant, she wavered. Then she remembered Reese's smoldering eyes as he'd ridden away, hurt showing in every line of his rigidly erect body, and she pressed on.

"Oh." She let the word carry a world of meaning. Then she added, "I remember. Of course you've been here before." She hoped she was sounding natural. "This is where I found you and Reese Rivers that evening Papa sent me to call you in for supper."

Amanda was silent.

"Did Reese do something to upset you here? Is that why it isn't your favorite place anymore?"

Amanda shot to her feet. "I'd like to go now, if you're rested."

"Golly, no. My leg still feels like a limp noodle."

Amanda moved to the edge of the river, and broke a long twig off a willow there. Absently she began plucking the leaves.

Laura refused to let up. "Did Reese really do something dreadful to you, Aunt Amanda?"

Amanda pretended she hadn't heard Laura's question over the soft slide of the gurgling river.

Taking a deep breath, Laura raised her voice. She framed a sentence she knew would get a reaction from Amanda. She spoke it hesitantly. "Is that why your dress was all. . . ?"

"Please!" Amanda whirled to face her. Tears she could no longer hide spilled over and ran down her cheeks.

She fought for calm. She could hardly let her niece think that Reese Rivers, Laura's cherished friend, had . . . What? She had no idea how much the child knew about . . . what she might be thinking.

And what could she tell her? That she, the child's aunt, had deliberately sought to drive Reese Rivers over the edge of passion? That she had *tried to force him* to lose his iron control and make love to her here in this very clearing?

Even in her tormented state, with her emotions tumbling beyond her ability to manage them, Amanda experienced a swell of triumph as she remembered how she had driven him. How she had won! If Laura had not arrived just when she had . . .

"No!" The sharpness in the single word was as much a protest at the loss of the glorious heights to which she and Reese had been rushing before Laura's appearance as it was a denial of any wrong Reese had done her.

Giddy with the remembrance of his kisses, she wrenched

her thoughts from that magic moment and brought them back to the here and now, to her niece. "No," Amanda repeated more calmly, "Mr. Rivers did nothing to offend me that evening, Laura, truly."

And he hadn't offended her. It had been she who had gambled and risked giving offense. For, if he'd turned away from her in disgust at her wanton behavior, she would have quietly died.

"Really? He looked so . . . so uncomfortable. Usually he looks glad to see me."

Amanda took a deep breath and said in a shaky voice, "We'd been . . . He'd been . . ." Dearest Lord, what could she tell a child?

"Oh." Laura felt the need to help. "You'd been kissing. Why didn't you say so?"

Amanda's breath left her in a flood of relief. "Yes," she grabbed at the reprieve. "Yes, we'd been kissing."

Her sense of fair play caused her to confess, "I made him kiss me." There, that was as close to the truth as she could come with a young girl, but it soothed her conscience to at least get that close.

She added for good measure, a sop to her clamoring conscience, "I deliberately set out to make him kiss me."

"So you really like him, then?" Hope soared in Laura. It looked as though she might get the two of them together, after all. The idea of Reese as her uncle strongly appealed to her.

"Yes." Amanda's voice was husky. "Yes." She fought the tears that threatened to start again. "I really like him."

Laura approached her next question very carefully, her voice very soft. "Do you love him?"

Sobs burst from Amanda. No power she possessed could have held them back. She plopped down on the grass, the same grass she had so wantonly pulled Reese down to with her that wonderful evening, covered her face with her

LOVING HONOR

hands, and cried as if her heart had not already broken into a thousand aching pieces.

Laura's eyes widened. Contrition overwhelmed her. She flung herself off the rock and rushed to her aunt.

What had she done? Why had she done it? She was simply not up to handling the grief she had so cruelly provoked in her aunt.

"Oh, Aunt Amanda! I'm sorry. I'm so sorry!" She wished that she had left well enough alone. How could she have been so hateful as to cause such anguish in her aunt? Oh, *how* could she have done this?

Amanda sobbed for another full minute. Laura sat helplessly patting her back and feeling lower than a snake's belly.

When Amanda's sobs began to subside, Laura dug her handkerchief out of the skirt pocket of her riding habit and proffered it.

"Thank you." Amanda blew her nose twice, then looked up at Laura with swimming eyes. "Thank you, dear. I'm sorry if I upset you."

With the cessation of her aunt's tears, resolution returned to Laura. She felt like a mangy cur, but that wasn't feeling bad enough to let her aunt go on without the man she so obviously loved.

Even mangy curs did good sometimes. This one was determined to. "You love him. Don't you, Aunt Amanda?"

Very simply, with no attempt to spare her own pride, Amanda said, "With all my heart."

Laura brightened with relief. "Then what's the matter, Auntie?"

"Oh, darling." Her voice was full of pain. "I have no idea where he is. Those Yankees at the fort who wouldn't sell us medicines for your dying mama surely won't tell anybody in this family how to find one of their officers." She shook her head sadly, her eyes defeated. "No. There is no way I can reach him. And we both know he is too full of injured pride to come back for me."

Laura could hardly bear the sorrow in Amanda's eyes.

Amanda went on, "I have driven him away, Laura. Driven him away by my lack of faith in him."

She reached out for Laura's hand and held it. "You see, in my fear, I truly believed he had harmed your papa when he told his colonel that he'd 'taken care of the leader.'"

Laura's eyes misted over in sympathy. She might so easily have felt exactly the same way if she'd heard Reese's own voice say that.

Amanda went on miserably, "I just knew he had to be talking about Dav . . . your Papa."

She let go of Laura's hand and twisted the handkerchief into a hard knot. "I just knew Reese was saying he'd killed him." She lifted anguished eyes to her niece. "Never in my wildest dreams did I think of England."

"Of course you didn't!"

"Then I saw Webster's body, and I knew that Reese had killed him, too." She ducked her head and gulped a breath. "And of course, I had no way of knowing, but to me there was nothing else to think, nothing else to believe.

"I was filled with such shock and sorrow that I seemed to lose all thought of Reese and what he was and what he meant to me. For just those few moments, despite all my feelings for him, he became a monster."

Laura patted her aunt's shoulder.

Amanda placed a hand over Laura's and smiled up at her tremulously. "Sit beside me?"

Laura dropped to the ground like a pine cone, snuggling close to Amanda.

For a long moment, Amanda simply sat and held her niece's hand.

"What happened in the barn?" Laura was amazed at her own temerity.

Amanda didn't even seem to notice. She smiled in remembrance. "He dragged me in there and demanded"—she lowered her tone of voice as if she would sound like Reese—" 'What's gotten into you, Amanda?' in the angriest of tones."

"Even angrier than when he was in bed with his bullet wound? I thought he sounded like an angry bear roaring then."

Amanda sniffed. "No. Not like that. This was worse, because . . ." She took a deep breath to steady her voice. "This was worse because he was bewildered and confused by my awful, traitorous attitude."

"That was stupid, Auntie. Reese should have known that just seeing him in a Yankee uniform would have upset you."

"Well, dear. Remember, he had a lot on his mind." Could she really be sitting here justifying Reese Rivers's dreadful desertion to her niece?

She scowled. Evidently, because she kept on, her brow clearing. "Remember, he had to convince his colonel that he'd eliminated the leader somehow. And he had to do it without having the colonel demand a body as proof, or Sellers or Dawson giving your Papa away if they knew Reese *hadn't* killed him."

She frowned thoughtfully, feeling her way to understanding as much for her own sake as Laura's. "Maybe Reese and your Papa arranged it so that Dawson and Sellers *believed* Reese had killed him. I don't know."

Laura thought, *You'd know if you'd asked him,* but she didn't think it was a polite thing to say just at this moment.

Amanda came to that conclusion herself, anyway. "Oh, if only I'd gotten a grip on myself and *asked* him, instead of jumping to obvious conclusions!" She turned a face full of entreaty to her niece. "You do understand?"

Laura lied. "Of course." Secretly, she thought her aunt had acted as dumb as dirt. Heaven forbid that she, Laura, should ever go to pieces and chase off somebody anywhere near as great as Reese who might love *her* sometime in the future.

Her aunt was saying, "And, of course, now it is all too late. No matter what I really believe about Reese, no matter how much I love him, he is gone." As she finished speaking, she rose and dusted at her skirt.

Managing a brisk tone for the sake of the child, Amanda announced, "Life goes on." She offered the travesty of a smile. "And if we don't hurry, we shall be late for lunch."

"Auntie." Laura didn't move from where she sat.

Amanda looked inquiringly back at her.

"If you made him kiss you here in this clearing . . ." She hesitated, feeling her way again. "If you could make a man like Reese kiss you, than I'll just bet you could make him do a whole lot more."

Amanda's breath left her body. Did her niece have any idea how much more she had forced Reese to do there in the twilit clearing that long-ago Sunday?

No. Surely not. The child had no idea of what she had interrupted. Amanda sat recovering from her momentary shock.

Her niece found the words to go on. "I mean if you could make Reese kiss you when he didn't want to because he felt he was about to hang Papa . . ."

As Laura paused a second time, her words tore through Amanda. Of course! Reese had spared her the betrayal she would have felt toward David if she had let him make love to her!

Reese had ignored the intoxicating clamor of his own body to keep from letting her dishonor hers. The knowledge of what he had done left her weak with love for him. She barely heard Laura's next words.

"Then why couldn't you try a little harder and make him want to marry you?"

Hysterical laughter bubbled up in Amanda. She put her

hands over her mouth to stop its escape. *Reese! Oh, darling Reese. You were saving me from myself!*

Poor, beautiful, wonderful, valiant Reese. If she'd known that, she would never have tormented him so.

She sat up straight as another thought hit her. That would have been a shame, because if she hadn't set out deliberately to torment him past resistance, then she wouldn't have known that she could win. And she still had every intention of winning Reese Rivers as her own.

If ever she found him again. Her heart plummeted. *If* she ever found him again.

Laura reached out and touched her aunt's shoulder. How she hated to see the light die out of her face. Very quietly she asked, "Would it help any if I told you I had Reese's address back at the house?"

Chapter 25

Laura's head was still spinning. Aunt Amanda's sudden total disregard about whether or not they would be late for lunch while she closely questioned her niece about Reese's address had confused her.

That inquisition had been followed by a headlong dash to the ranch house that could have endangered their lives. The rush up the stairs to pack had been the finishing touch.

Laura grumbled, "I could have done very nicely with lunch, you know."

"No time," Amanda snapped, "Go pack. You say he's in Philadelphia, so pack for a city. Enough for a week. We'll buy more when we get there."

Laura stomped into her room. "Golly. Aunt Amanda gives orders sharper than that Yankee colonel did."

Suddenly Mason shouted from the yard, "Whaddya mean bringing these horses in and leaving them loose like this, you two?" Mason didn't show respect to anybody who abused a horse.

Laura was glad she was safe in the house. Finally Mason gave up and led the horses to the barn. She could hear him grumbling all the way.

A minute later, Rosa and Polly came charging up the stairs. Polly rushed into Amanda's room with Rosa right behind her. "What is it? What's happened?"

LOVING HONOR

Amanda whirled to face her, "Oh, Polly. Good! Pack for a week in Philadelphia."

Rosa mumbled, "No lunch yet. *Madre mía.*" She headed back downstairs to find a way to keep the food warm without ruining it all. Her curiosity could wait until her job was done.

Polly smiled widely at her employer, "Ah, good it is. I'm that glad ye've decided to get away to civilization at last. But wouldn't ye like me to pack for a little longer stay?"

She sounded so wistful it brought a smile to Amanda's face. *I wonder if you would be so happy to pack if you knew that I fully intend to throw myself at Reese Rivers, Polly Grimes.*

Polly asked, "Philadelphia? Isn't that where ye were trying to set up the little clerk from Endicott's as a dressmaker? Is it her ye're planning to visit?"

Amanda remembered Elvira Beame then. Her mind and heart had been so full of thoughts of Reese that she'd never thought beyond *him* since that awful moment when he'd turned on his heel and left her standing, dying inside, there in the shadowed quiet of the barn.

Little Mrs. Beame *was* in Philadelphia. She'd not given the poor woman a thought after setting everything up for her through Liz Sheriton and Liz's husband's secretary.

And she would have to have gowns made by Elvira once she had arrived. Elvira would fashion gowns that would set Philadelphia agog. And Amanda would wear them in pursuit of Reese Rivers.

Amanda's dear friend, Liz Sheriton, who'd helped her a few months ago by getting her husband's secretary to find a shop and assistants for Elvira, would no doubt be happy to help her now. She should enjoy helping.

Liz had pursued her husband, John, mercilessly and with great skill until the poor man had finally given up and caught her. Liz would be a willing participant in Amanda's determined pursuit of Reese Rivers, Amanda was sure.

Amanda looked into her mirror and smiled. She had ruthlessly gone after Reese there on the riverbank she had just bathed in her tears. She had every intention of going after him in Philadelphia with as little mercy as before.

She told her reflection, "And this time, I'll have some help in setting my traps for him."

Polly reared up from her packing. "Did ye say ye wanted traps, milady?" She frowned. It wasn't like Lady Amanda to interfere with her arrangements for her clothing. Her tone was a little stiff as she said, "I thought a single trunk would do best for a sea voyage."

Amanda grinned like an urchin. She hadn't meant luggage when she'd mentioned traps. She'd been speaking of something far more exciting, something that would change her life. Something that was going to put back the zest and happiness that she thought had gone from her forever.

She laughed a little breathlessly. "No, Polly, a trunk will be fine."

Her spirits lifted. Her plans began to take shape. She could make Elvira the excuse for going to Philadelphia if she should need one. She knew the tiny designer wouldn't mind. Not after all she and Ben had risked to get her letter from David to her. And it would serve to save Amanda's pride.

Not that she had any pride when it came to Reese Rivers. She remembered the evening she had offered herself to him during the thunderstorm.

A faint blush stole over her face. He'd rejected her then, and she'd thought she would die of shame.

Then, in speaking of her own dreams, little Elvira Beame had given her words to live by. *If you want something with all your heart . . . Something good and true . . .* That had been all that Amanda needed to put her fierce pride in her pocket and set about breaking Reese Rivers's iron will.

She'd done it, too. And the game had been worth the candle! She'd sacrificed all the lonely pride in the world to bring him to his knees—to make him bend to her and break under the force of his own longing for her.

She, Lady Amanda Harcourt, had acted like anything but a lady to accomplish it, but she had conquered him. She'd made him completely hers . . . because he belonged in her life. Or would have if Laura hadn't come at just that moment.

So now, she was ready to stuff her pride in her pocket again. And it was so much easier, now that she realized that he'd resisted her so staunchly for her own sake.

She was determined to go hunt her quarry down in his home in Philadelphia. Philadelphia! The address!

She flew from the room leaving Polly openmouthed. What if Laura had misplaced it? Panic filled her.

She forced herself to stop before she charged into her niece's room. There was no need to panic, after all.

Thanks to Laura, she knew what city to look for him in. If necessary, she could hire one of the new Pinkerton men to trace him. Liz's husband's secretary could find one for her.

Holding herself in check, she rapped lightly on the doorjamb. "Laura, dear?"

Laura looked up from the pile of clothes she'd amassed on her bed. "Yes, Auntie?"

"Do you have that address?"

Laura suppressed a smile at the overly casual tone of her aunt's voice. Suddenly she felt a little devilish, and said, "I think so."

Then she heard her aunt's quickly indrawn breath and saw the stark expression her words brought to Amanda's beautiful face. Instantly contrite, she ran across the room to the little square jewelry box her father had given her to keep her mother's single strand of pearls in.

"Ohhh." She almost wanted to cry, she felt so awful. Why had she had to do that? "Yes, Auntie. Of course, I have it."

She turned earnest eyes to her aunt. "I wouldn't lose it. I

couldn't let anything happen to it. It would be like throwing away a friend." She knew that she was babbling, she was so ashamed of her moment of deviltry.

Standing in the doorway, Amanda forced herself to reach out her hand slowly. She had never wanted to snatch anything so much in her life. "May I see it, please?"

"Of course." Laura went over and put it in her hand. "You may keep it."

Amanda looked down at the scrap of paper. Nothing she owned was as precious to her as that tiny fragment of parchment. This was her lifeline, her passport back into the world of people who allowed themselves emotions, who allowed themselves to feel.

Waves of relief swept over and over her. She had not lost him. She could find him again.

She might have driven him away, but now she could go and find him again. It took a mighty effort on her part not to clench her fist shut on the wonderful scrap of paper.

One glance down at it, and the address was forever emblazoned on her brain. She could do what she knew good manners dictated that she do. She gave the paper back to its owner, her fingers clinging a little to this last tangible proof of Reese's presence in her life. "Thank you, dear," she said in a husky voice. "Thank you very much."

Laura watched her aunt go back to her own room. She was glad to see that her Aunt Amanda's step had regained its former buoyancy.

When she heard her call out to Polly, "Don't pack too many things for me. Laura and I can share a trunk. We'll be getting whole new wardrobes in Philadelphia," she knew her aunt was all right again.

She was so happy that she ran across her own room and bounced on her bed. Clothes slipped from the pile she'd made onto the floor. She didn't care, she was so relieved to have her wonderful, vibrant aunt back!

* * *

The cruise to Philadelphia was uneventful. They only ran into one storm, a brief summer squall that tossed them about, wet them thoroughly, and passed on.

It didn't pass on soon enough for Polly. "I don't care if it was *only a little squall,* milady," she informed Amanda with stiff dignity. "When I get back to England," she announced firmly, "I am never, never going to get on another thing that puts out to sea." Polly sniffed sharply in reproach, for all the world as if the brief summer storm had been Amanda's idea, then her voice became a wail. "If ye should do, ye will have to take young Wiggins as yer maid, for *I'll* not go, and that is that!"

Amanda only smiled at her. She had enjoyed the squall.

She had gloried in it. She felt as if it were a perfect prelude to the stormy time she foresaw with Reese at their next meeting.

She wasn't far off.

Liz Sheriton breezed into the sumptuous suite she'd assigned Amanda. "Here, look!" Expensive vellum and parchment envelopes of all shades of white and every suitable size for formal correspondence spilled out of her hands as she rushed across the private sitting room to her friend.

Her husband's secretary, on loan to Liz for yet another of her projects, hurried along behind her, stooping every other step to retrieve those she dropped.

Amanda turned from where she'd been watching the steady stream of activity in the two luxurious gardens behind the Sheritons' mansion, both theirs and their back-door neighbors', and smiled at her friend. "Good afternoon, Liz. Sorry I hadn't gotten back downstairs to you after I changed. I became absorbed in watching all the activity next door. Good afternoon, Mr. Anson."

Mr. Anson looked up at her shyly, then responded as he

rose from the floor, his hands full of fallen invitation "Good afternoon, my lady."

Liz Sheriton looked momentarily distracted by Amanda's interest in her new neighbor. "Hmmmm, yes. That house has only recently sold." She added as if it were forced from her, "Since you wrote to tell me you were coming, in fact."

Her husband's secretary seemed to get something caught in his throat just then. He fell into a fit of coughing that precluded conversation for a moment.

Liz frowned and waved an elegant, well-manicured hand. "Shoo, Mr. Anson. And thank you so much for picking up all that I spilled. I don't know what I would do without you."

"I'll get you a box, Mrs. Sheriton."

"A box? We aren't scheduled for the opera, are we?" She peered at him, frowning again.

"No, ma'am. You already have a box for the opera season. I meant a box for you to carry the responses to your invitations in." When she continued to frown at him, he added gently, "So that you don't drop them when I have gone and there is no one to pick them up."

"Oh, Anson. You are such a jewel." She turned to Amanda and waited until he was out of earshot to say, "Such a worrier, too. The maids will pick them up if I drop them."

"Perhaps Mr. Anson is worried that you will not know who has accepted."

"Oh, but I have already checked them off on the list. All the invitations I sent out for the ball in your honor have been accepted. Isn't that marvelous?" She paused, her eyes troubled. "Except for the one I sent to Reese Rivers."

Amanda's heart thumped heavily with disappointment. Reese was not coming.

She'd been so looking forward to the ball. Liz had spared

no effort to make it the gala affair of the season, and she had been so sure...

Liz tried to distract her friend. "I declare, that man has always been such a puzzle. Can you imagine the son of one of the richest men in this country running away to join the army when he was nineteen and staying all these years?

"Why, he probably wouldn't be back yet if his father hadn't sent for him when he was dying. Stiff-necked, you know. And his father even worse. Paid no more attention to Reese as a boy than his wife did, and she told all Philadelphia that she never wanted a child. Imagine. Everyone says it took approaching death to make Mr. Rivers send for Reese. Some say it was only concern for his business enterprises that made him do it even then."

Amanda felt pain cramp in her chest. Actual physical pain assaulted her in waves. It came in sympathy for a lonely boy who'd grown up with parents who didn't want him, hadn't cared for him.

And on top of it all was her horrible denunciation of all that they had had between them. There was that dreadful moment in the barn when she had accused him of the murder of her brother.

How her lack of faith in him had wounded him! Knowing that had been bad enough for her to bear. Now there was this. Amanda hadn't known Reese had had a personal tragedy. Her heart quailed to realize he'd had to face it all alone.

He'd had to face it without her, and worse, he'd had to face it with the fresh scar of her betrayal on his heart. Her face showed her distress.

"No need to feel so sympathetic, Amanda. They didn't get along at all. The father was as bad as the mother, a cold old thing who didn't ever have any feeling for Reese as a boy either, I hear."

As Amanda looked even more stricken, Liz added hastily, "But I did hear, too, that they made their peace before old Mr. Rivers passed on, though Reese refuses to mourn him."

Shrugging away thoughts of death, Liz tapped one of the handsome vellum squares against her chin. "Now, I just wonder why that nasty old Reese hasn't accepted my invitation?"

Amanda couldn't even begin to guess. She refused to think he simply might not want to see her again—not when she felt as if every minute was an hour long as she endured the creeping passage of time until the ball.

If she was so desperately looking forward to seeing his dear face again then he must long to see her as well, mustn't he? Surely he cared as much as she did. Surely he did.

A hollow feeling developed in her middle.

Didn't he?

❦ ❦ ❦ ❦ ❦ ❦ ❦ ❦

Chapter 26

The night of the ball was bright and clear, with the stars so near that they seemed close enough to touch from the rooftops. After Polly had left her, they seemed to taunt Amanda.

Still, she pulled herself away from watching them out her tall balcony door reluctantly. Reluctantly, too, she admitted that the stars reminded her of those on the night of the thunderstorm.

She went weak with longing as she remembered the evening that the storm had trapped her in the line shack on Coronet. Trapped her with Reese Rivers.

She gave herself an impatient little shake. Every storm and all the stars reminded her of that night when he'd first held her in his arms. She wondered if she would ever see stars or storms again without her thoughts returning to Reese.

That night the stars had been unusually close, too. With all her heart, she wished that she could think of these that spangled tonight's Pennsylvania sky as an omen, a portent telling her all would be well.

But Reese hadn't even responded to his invitation. He had not even bothered to decline. Her heart was heavy with that knowledge.

How Liz had fumed over Reese's lack of response! She'd behaved most peculiarly, with much more vigor than she usually displayed.

Liz had sputtered that even if Reese was rag-mannered, certainly his secretary was not. "Tandal, the secretary Reese inherited from his father, is the soul of propriety," she'd told Amanda. Reese's lack of response must have a dire meaning.

She'd said she had no idea what Reese was up to. Not these days, he'd been behaving so strangely lately.

Amanda had asked, "What do you mean? How has he been behaving strangely?" *And how do you know?*

Liz hadn't replied. She'd just gone on with her own lament.

First, she'd worried that Reese hadn't received his invitation, but Anson had assured her that he'd seen to it himself, knowing it was of special significance.

So why hadn't Reese responded?

Amanda could hardly bear to admit how much she'd looked forward to seeing him tonight after the interminable months since she had. Now she would not. In her disappointment, she forgot Liz's almost guilty behavior.

She went to the long pier glass in her dressing room. Elvira had taken such pains with her gown. She'd been as eager to create something that would captivate Reese Rivers as she had been to create a gown that would make her name as a dressmaker.

The result was exquisite in its simplicity. There was only the fabulous gossamer fabric, tucked and draped intricately to fit her closely through the bodice, then floating free like golden mist . . . and Amanda.

The second dream would be realized, beyond a doubt. Elvira would become a very popular dressmaker after tonight. But the first? Amanda's dream?

For Reese wasn't coming. . . . Amanda cast a despairing glance outside. Moonlight had silvered the magnificent house behind Liz's and was just beginning to steal across the garden. It deepened the shadows cast by the trees there, and dimmed the glorious stars as it became brighter.

Amanda sighed. She'd never thought of moonlight as sad before.

Then Liz was there in the doorway, lovely in a gown that exactly matched the heavy emerald necklace that had been a recent gift from her beloved, besotted husband. "I knocked, but you must not have heard."

She stopped short, "Oh, Amanda. You look marvelous."

"Thank you. You must have my dressmaker fashion some of your own gowns."

Liz ignored the sad note underlying her friend's comment. "Indeed I shall." Mentally, she promised herself that she would, right after she killed Reese Rivers.

She beckoned imperiously. "Come on, Amanda." She smiled and held out her hand. "Your ladyship is needed in the reception line. After all, it is you that Philadelphia is coming to see. We Americans are very impressed by titles, you know."

Laughing together, Liz still pretending she didn't hear the note of sadness in her friend's laughter, they headed for the stairs. On her way down them, Liz plotted revenge against Reese Rivers for what his absence was doing to her friend.

"How lovely you both look," John Sheriton greeted them as they reached the foot of the long marble stairs. He kissed his wife lightly.

It was not the kiss, but the look that passed between them that filled Amanda with envy. What if Reese never looked at her like that? What if. . . ?

With an effort, she pushed Reese Rivers and her feelings for him to the back of her mind, and concentrated on her social duty. It wouldn't be the first time in her life that attendance to her duty had come to her rescue.

Donning a smile, she took her place in the receiving line just as the first guests arrived. She nodded and chatted and answered questions with her usual aplomb, forbidding her mind to return to the heartache of Reese's indifference.

Almost an hour later, her cheeks aching from her continuous smile, she was certain that she had, indeed, met all of Philadelphia. Her hosts and she were laughing their relief and turning to go join the multitude of guests assembled in the Sheritons' huge ballroom when there was a stir at the front door. Hesitating, they turned back to see.

Fridley, the Sheritons' butler, looked as close to flustered as he had ever been in all his very dignified life. It took him a moment to decide what he must do.

In that moment, Amanda saw him. Reese Rivers had come. But what a different Reese Rivers! Gone was her rugged cowboy with his overlong hair and his suntanned face, and in his place was another Reese.

From the top of his well-barbered head to the tips of his patent leather dancing pumps, he was groomed as well as any man she had ever seen. He was the picture of civilized male perfection in the exquisitely tailored dark evening clothes he wore.

Only his eyes, lightly mocking, remained those of the Reese Rivers Amanda knew and loved.

Her heart skipped a beat as she registered the difference in him. What would that difference mean to them? To her? Would he still. . . ?

Fridley evidently made his decision. He reached out with all the authority accorded his position as chief servant in the Sheriton mansion and took Reese's hat. He looked as if he were certain that, whether on the list of those attending or not, Mr. Rivers would be very much a welcome guest.

Then Reese moved, and Amanda forgot Fridley's existence. Reese moved with the same unconscious grace Amanda remembered. He walked with the same powerful strides with which he'd crossed that distant yard full of Yankee soldiers, horses, and swirling dust on that day in Texas that, now, seemed so long ago. And as he moved, he took her breath away.

With eyes for no one but Amanda, he crossed the broad expanse from the door to her.

His eyes burned with a light that almost frightened her. Without removing his gaze from her eyes, he reached down and seized her wrist. Lifting it, he took her dangling dance card in his long fingers, opened it, and sent a shiver of shock through her as he tore a part of it away.

Startled, Amanda looked down at the mangled remains hanging from its twisted gold-and-silver cord. Then her gaze shot back to his eyes, demanding an explanation for his bizarre action.

When he spoke, his voice was the deep music she remembered. "That many dances, Amanda. That many and no more."

His blue eyes were dark with intensity. "The rest are all mine." He carried her hand to his lips. His gaze never left her own wide stare. Brushing the back of her gloved fingers with a kiss, he said in a voice too low for the others to hear. "I'll come for you."

Amanda's breath left her with a violence that told her she'd been holding it since he'd approached her. Her mind was spinning.

One part of it fumed, *What does he mean, behaving in such a fashion? This is Philadelphia! They are in what serves the fledgling republic as a civilized society. How does Reese Rivers think he can get away with such highhanded behavior?* But the other part just kept hearing, over and over, his voice saying "I'll come for you."

Reese smiled at her. It was a tight, eye-narrowing smile that was almost a threat, then he turned away.

In a daze, Amanda watched him walk to the ballroom doorway where Liz and her husband had paused to wait for her. As she was coming back to herself, she realized that she'd just behaved with all the poise of a certified ninny.

She heard Reese say, "Good evening, Mrs. Sheriton. John." He sounded for all the world as if he were one of the guests who had had the courtesy to respond to his hostess's invitation!

Amanda waited for him to make his excuses. She waited in vain.

Offering no word of explanation for his unexpected presence, Reese bowed gracefully to his hostess and host and walked into the ballroom with all the confidence of an honored guest. Immediately he was engulfed by a crowd.

Amanda watched from the broad hallway, aghast. Then she felt the faint stirrings of irritation as she saw the women all trying to engage Reese's interest.

Startled, she acknowledged that she was experiencing a flare of jealousy. Enough of this. It was beneath her.

Amanda drew herself up to her full height and sailed regally to the entrance into the ballroom. There, as she stopped, the gossamer material of her gown continued to drift and move as if it seethed with a life of its own, glittering in the candlelight.

With her host and hostess on either side of her, Amanda was well aware of the picture she made. Filled with perversity, she had every intention of using that picture to distract the guests' attention from Reese. She lifted her chin imperiously and surveyed the room without a smile.

It was the right touch. Every head turned to see a real English Lady. There was the faint rustle of a collective sigh as the assemblage weighed her and found her all that they had hoped she would be.

Amanda accepted their tribute with a gracious nod. Then slowly she lowered her chin, and just as slowly relinquished her chilling manner. She rewarded them with her most regal and radiant smile and stepped into the flower-bedecked ballroom.

Instantly she was surrounded by men clamoring for an introduction and a dance. John Sheriton presented them to her with some amusement.

The first gentleman to see her dance card exclaimed, "But there are only five lines here, my lady."

Amanda merely looked at the speaker, her blue eyes luminous.

He flushed and said, "You must have caught it on something and torn off the rest of it." His voice stronger as he recovered from the spell of her eyes, he proclaimed as he scrawled his name in the third space, "I shall get you another."

Before he'd finished his sentence, the other spaces were filled. There was a murmur of approval for his suggestion from the men who had been unable to place their names on her card, and he rushed off.

As the orchestra began to play, the first of her partners stepped forward to claim his dance. Amanda danced and smiled until finally she was dancing with the fifth and last man on her mutilated dance card. As she did, she saw Reese Rivers speak briefly to the leader of the orchestra.

The musician smiled and bowed.

Then Reese locked his gaze on her.

Again her breath caught. She missed a step, and her partner asked solicitously, "Are you fatigued? Would you prefer to sit out the rest of this dance?"

Amanda smiled at him vaguely and shook her head. Her mind was completely occupied with Reese Rivers. Just then, she couldn't have said anything coherent if her very life had depended upon it.

Reese started toward her so purposefully that Amanda's knees went weak. Had he been any other man in the world, she would have begun to flirt with her dance partner. But he wasn't any other man, he was Reese.

The music ended, and Amanda, murmuring the expected response to her partner's thanks, stood and watched Reese every step of his way across the ballroom. Her partner's voice trailed off as he realized she no longer heard a word he said.

Amanda was aware of no one but the man advancing on her with the strange expression in his eyes. Not even the blistering glares of the elegantly garbed, envious women around her touched her.

Just as Reese reached her, the brilliant opening strains of a waltz spilled forth joyously, filling the ballroom. Without a word Reese swept her into his arms.

There was a faint gasp from the many guests who watched them at the blatant possessiveness of his action. They were fascinated as the couple took the floor.

One by one the other dancers stopped and left the dance floor. The tall, dark Philadelphian and the golden woman in his arms both were blessed with more than their fair share of beauty, and the cream of the city's society stood and watched them with obvious pleasure and more than a little curiosity.

The floor left to him, Reese Rivers was seen to pull the lovely Lady Amanda closer still. Scandalously close he held her, their bodies firmly in contact as he increased the speed of the waltz now the floor was his alone.

The music picked up tempo to follow Reese as he turned faster and faster, leading Amanda breathlessly through the sweeping steps of the intoxicating dance. He held her, willing captive, so tightly to his side that they were not two entities, but one.

And then, as all the guests watched, Reese Rivers danced with Lady Amanda Harcourt through one of the many pairs of French doors standing open to the terrace, and they were gone.

The spell that had held the ballroom in thrall was broken.

With nervous laughter, men ashamed of having stared like schoolboys went and found their partners. Women who hoped no one had noticed the envious longing on their faces moved into the men's arms, and the Sheritons' guests danced to the slowing tempo of the waltz, as bemused as if they had just witnessed magic.

Chapter 27

Outside the ballroom in the moonlight, Reese stopped. Still he held Amanda.

She could feel her heart racing from their dancing . . . and something more. Close as he held her, she could feel his heartbeat, too, strong and steady, and only a little fast.

She couldn't resist. She moved her gloved hand from his shoulder to the nape of his neck. Through her fine kid glove she could feel the warmth of his skin and the crispness of his hair as it curled against his collar.

Suddenly she remembered when he'd touched her there to see if she were dry after the soaking rains of the thunderstorm on Coronet. As she remembered, she moved the hand he'd held for their dance to his chest. Under her palm, she felt his heartbeat race.

"No, Amanda." Passion flared in his eyes as he told her, "There will be nothing between us when we touch." Gently, he took her hands and removed her gloves. Then he stripped off his own. He tossed both pairs on a nearby marble bench.

His eyes were shadowed, and Amanda was unable to read his expression. She knew he stood with his back to the light from the ballroom deliberately, not by chance.

How she wished she could see his face, could read his purpose. It didn't matter, though. He had come for her. It was a declaration. In her heart, she knew Reese loved her still.

She had no way of knowing if he had forgiven her betrayal. Cruelly, perhaps, she didn't care.

She had paid for whatever pain she'd caused Reese a thousand times over in the hell of these few months in which she had been so sure she'd lost him.

She held her head high. Her eyes issued him a challenge.

Reese answered by grasping her wrist firmly and pulling her with him down the broad steps of the terrace to the lawn.

Amanda threw a single glance behind her. Startled, she saw Laura standing at an upstairs window.

The child was watching them, for all the world as if she had known they would be there. She was grinning from ear to ear. That was all Amanda had time to see.

A silent Reese led her swiftly through the Sheritons' garden to a gate in the back wall that stood ajar. Once they were through it, he locked it behind them.

Still without a word, he led her along the perfect paths of the house beyond the Sheriton gardens. He led her to the house she had idly watched and had wondered about.

She followed him across the terrace and through open French doors without question. Inside, in a moonlight-flooded room, they faced one another.

She sensed that he had brought her here so that they would not be disturbed. Here, she knew, they had time. Time to settle things between them.

She studied the planes and angles of his face. It was a luxury she'd not had since he'd lain wounded and helpless at Coronet, and she lost herself in it now.

She told herself that her memory of the tiny details of his face had grown dim to the point of needing refreshing. That was a lie, of course, and she knew it. If she'd never seen him again after that awful scene in the barn, she would still remember his face until her dying day. It was only an excuse to stand and drink in the sight of his beloved features.

He stood easily, calm and confident under her regard, watching her in return. After a while, he asked, "Would you care to sit?" He indicated a pair of wing chairs, the only two pieces of furniture in the room.

She shook her head. She felt as if she could stand like this forever, with only moonlight separating them. She asked, "This house is yours?"

"It belongs to me now, yes."

Amanda suddenly remembered Liz's strange behavior and Anson's strategic fit of coughing. "Liz knew!"

"Yes. She was kind enough to tell me you were coming."

"And you bought this house? . . ."

"So that we could converse without fear of interruption." He was becoming impatient. "Enough." He frowned. "It is time, Amanda."

His comment roused her from her attempt to understand all that had been happening without her knowledge. The edge on his voice warned and steadied her.

"Time for what, Reese?" She was glad to hear her own voice was firm. She refused to be put on the defensive. There were certainly things she felt it was time for, yes, and past time.

There were things that she had to know before anything could be put right between them. She had no intention of going without answers—or perhaps apologies—any longer. So she asked, "Is it time for you to tell me why you let me believe you had murdered my brother?"

"It's time to ask you how you could have believed I would do so."

She didn't respond to that. She stood proud and straight in the moonlight and waited for him to go on.

"How could you think I would do anything to hurt you, Amanda? Where was your faith in me?" There was the barest hint of pain in his voice.

Amanda ignored it. Whatever he might feel he could easily have remedied by coming to her at any time.

She had been the one powerless to rectify anything between them. Until Laura had told her where to find him, there had been nothing she could do. Her feeling of helplessness had almost killed her.

Remembering, she could feel anger rising in her. "Where was your mercy, Reese?" She felt as if her eyes must burn a hole in him. Her voice grew husky. "I came home to Coronet and found the yard full of enemy soldiers. A friend was lying dead in an army wagon. My *brother* was *missing*."

"Amanda." He took a half step toward her.

She stopped him with a gesture, her eyes accusing. "Then I heard the man I loved and trusted assure his colonel that David was where the army would never have to worry about him again."

Her anger blazed hot in her now. It was born of the outrage she still felt at his desertion of her that fateful day. "And you. You were there in the uniform of an enemy, giving the lie to all that I had thought you."

"Amanda," he said again. His voice was rough with regret, low with compassion. He closed the distance between them.

Was that pity she heard in his voice? How dare he pity her? Frustration and resentment exploded in her. She slapped him with all the strength she could summon to the task. "How *could* you? How could you leave me to suffer so?"

"Damn you, Amanda!" Reese grabbed her by her shoulders and snatched her to him.

There were no words to express his rage. He shook her until her hairpins fell out and her glorious hair tumbled like molten gold down her back to her waist, pale in the moonlight.

She pushed her hands against his chest to free herself. It was futile, his grasp was merciless.

"Damn you, Amanda," he repeated, but the words were full of agony this time, and trailed away to a whisper. He sighed and it shook his frame.

In a stronger voice and a tone of resignation he said, "I love you, Amanda."

Slowly he pulled her closer, lifting her until she was standing on the tips of her toes, her weight between his two hands. "I love you, blast you," he murmured against her lips.

His gaze bored down into her own. "I love you more than life, Amanda Harcourt. I love you so much that I risked my honor to save your brother. I love you so much that I lied to the army."

He gave her a little shake. "That army was my entire life before there was you. I resigned my commission because of that lie. Everything I ever valued I threw away for you. To save your brother for *you*."

He gave her another little shake, but there was no harshness left in him. "Blast you, Amanda." But his voice was gentle.

Her heart soared. Her senses exploded with the joyous knowledge that he loved her.

If he had not held her so strongly, she was certain that she would have been able to fly around the room, borne aloft on the power of this love she now knew they had for one another.

That he loved her enough to imperil his precious honor humbled her. It was an awesome feeling.

But humility didn't come easily to a Harcourt.

"Put me down, please," she said in her quietest voice.

It was as if she had stabbed him to the heart. His face ravished by regret, he lowered her until she stood on her own two feet.

That was the way she wanted it. The blood of those nagging kings required it of her. She had to face him as an equal, not as some rag doll caught up helpless in his grasp.

She let him suffer an instant longer. It was the least she could do to make up for her awful months of desperation since he had left her alone in the barn on Coronet.

Then she told him just as quietly, "I love you, too, Reese Rivers."

His face filled with astonishment. Gone was the polished Philadelphian. Reese was her beloved rough cowboy once more. Amanda's heart could barely contain her joy.

Reese read the expression on her face. As acceptance dawned, it was echoed on his own.

A groan escaped him. He snatched her back against his chest, and crushed her to him with a hunger that Amanda found quite satisfying.

His kisses rained down on her with all the passion she could wish for, all the love she'd feared she had lost. They were balm to the wounds in her spirit—the wounds her innermost being had sustained when he'd ridden away with the cavalry.

As she stood in the moonlight in the circle of his arms, she knew the terrible days of longing were over. There were so many things she wanted explanations for, but they could all wait. None of them were of the slightest importance just now.

Nothing mattered now. Nothing in life mattered so much as her love for this man who held her in his arms—that sacred love and the boundless love with which he loved her in return.

As his lips claimed her own, she felt as if they were ascending to the very stars. Suddenly she discovered the greatest treasure a woman could possess. She knew with glorious certainty that she and Reese Rivers had been granted the precious gift of a wondrous love.

He was hers, completely hers, and she was just as surely his very own. She drew a deep, contented breath and snuggled deeper into his embrace. They would never be apart again.

Epilogue

They stood in the prow of the ship, the spray bursting up around them, rainbowed by the afternoon sunlight. Amanda leaned back against Reese, locked in his arms, and watched the white sails billowing above them, their straining canvas rushing them toward England.

Reese bent his head and spoke into her ear. "Warm enough?"

She turned her head to look up over her shoulder at him and smiled. "I'm fine."

"Can't wait to see David and your grandfather?"

"Hmmmmm." She touched her forehead to his chin, and he kissed it. She felt as if she radiated contentment. His perceptive question added immeasurably to the wonderful warmth of the feeling.

"Laura is anxious to be with her father again, too." She turned in his arms to find him toying with a tendril of her long, windblown hair and smiled. "Are you looking forward to again meeting the man you exiled?"

He looked at her, winding the length of hair around his forefinger, teasing amusement alight in his eyes. "Of course I shall enjoy seeing your brother again." He kissed the gleaming strand wound round his finger before he loosed it. "The man owes me his life."

Amanda was saved answering that by the precipitous arrival of her niece. "Aunt Amanda, Uncle Reese! Did you know that there is a little platform up there on one of the masts?" She leaned over nearly backward to point high above them. "It's called a crow's nest."

Amanda and Reese looked at one another. By their silent agreement, Reese was the one to speak. "On no pretext are you to attempt to climb the rigging to the crow's nest, niece of mine."

Laura frowned at him. "I didn't say I was going to."

"Such a declaration was unnecessary, niece." Reese's voice was stern.

Laura couldn't stand it. "But there's nothing to do!"

"Your cabin is full of books and games, dear," Amanda told her. "And the first mate is eager to engage you in a game of chess."

Laura surrendered. "Oh, very well." She started to walk back across the gently rolling deck, her steps dragging, her eyes turned longingly upward.

"We shall have to watch her carefully."

"I shall demand her promise to forgo a dash up the rigging."

"Thank you, dearest." She looked up at him tenderly, her eyes full of love.

His eyes darkened, and he stepped closer. "It is almost time to dress for dinner, Mrs. Rivers."

Her lips parted as her breath quickened. She found it impossible to mistake the intention in his gaze. "Yes," she breathed so softly that the wind carried the sound away before it could be heard.

His gaze locked with hers, he lifted her hand. Watching her, he placed a long kiss in its palm.

Amanda's eyes went soft and dazed.

Reese folded her fingers around the warmth left by his kiss, and tucked her hand securely into the crook of his arm.

Amanda shivered with the thrill that shot through her

Her knees lost their strength, and she wondered if she would be able to walk across the gently pitching deck.

Her hand firmly caught against his side, Reese started for their cabin. When they arrived at the door, he turned her to face him and leaned down. In a quiet, husky voice full of meaning, he informed her, "I find I do not share my new niece's opinion that there is nothing to do aboard ship, Mrs. Rivers."

The wind did nothing to disturb Amanda's answer this time, for it was only a blush.

ROMANCE FROM THE HEART OF AMERICA
Homespun Romance

Homespun novels are touching, captivating romances from the heartland of America that combine the laughter and tears of family life with the tender warmth of true love.

__ANNA'S TREASURE 0-7865-0069-7/$4.99
  by Dorothy Howell
__SOMETHING BORROWED 0-7865-0073-5/$4.99
  by Rebecca Hagan Lee
__HEART'S SONG 0-7865-0081-6/$4.99
  by Deborah Wood
__FAMILY RECIPE 0-515-11589-4/$4.99
  by Pamela Quint Chambers
__MAKE BELIEVE 0-515-11610-6/$4.99
  by Teresa Warfield
__HOMEWARD BOUND 0-515-11637-8/$4.99
  by Linda Shertzer
__SUMMER LIGHTNING 0-515-11657-2/$4.99
  by Lydia Browne
__LOVING HONOR 0-515-11684-X/$4.99
  by Christina Cordaire
__TEA TIME 0-515-11721-8/$4.99
  by Dorothy Howell (September)

Payable in U.S. funds. No cash orders accepted. Postage & handling: $1.75 for one book, 75¢ for each additional. Maximum postage $5.50. Prices, postage and handling charges may change without notice. Visa, Amex, MasterCard call 1-800-788-6262, ext. 1, refer to ad # 411

Or, check above books and send this order form to: The Berkley Publishing Group 390 Murray Hill Pkwy., Dept. B East Rutherford, NJ 07073 Please allow 6 weeks for delivery.	Bill my: ☐ Visa ☐ MasterCard ☐ Amex _____ (expires) Card#_____ ($15 minimum) Signature_____ Or enclosed is my: ☐ check ☐ money order
Name_____	Book Total $_____
Address_____	Postage & Handling $_____
City_____	Applicable Sales Tax $_____ (NY, NJ, PA, CA, GST Can.)
State/ZIP_____	Total Amount Due $_____

Recipes from the heartland of America

THE HOMESPUN ✥ COOKBOOK ✥

Tamara Dubin Brown

Arranged by courses, this collection of wholesome family recipes includes tasty appetizers, sauces, and relishes, hearty main courses, and scrumptious desserts—all created from the popular *Homespun* series.

Features delicious easy-to-prepare dishes, such as:

Curried Crab and Shrimp en Casserole

- 1 large can crabmeat
- 1 can shrimp
- 2 tablespoons flour
- ½ teaspoon salt
- 1 tablespoon chopped green pepper
- 1 pint milk
- 2 tablespoons butter
- 1 teaspoon curry powder
- 1 tablespoon chopped onion

Cream the butter and flour. Add milk. Cook over slow fire, stirring constantly until slightly thickened. Add salt and curry powder. Stir until smooth and remove from fire. Put onion and pepper into cream sauce and mix well. Shred crabmeat and clean the shrimp. Spread a layer of crabmeat in casserole and cover with a layer of cream sauce. Repeat with shrimp and cream sauce. Repeat this until all is in the casserole. Bake at 300 degrees for 30 minutes before serving.

A Berkley paperback coming February 1996

If you enjoyed this book, take advantage of this special offer. Subscribe now and get a

FREE
Historical Romance

No Obligation (a $4.50 value)

Each month the editors of True Value select the four *very best* novels from America's leading publishers of romantic fiction. Preview them in your home *Free* for 10 days. With the first four books you receive, we'll send you a FREE book as our introductory gift. No Obligation!

If for any reason you decide not to keep them, just return them and owe nothing. If you like them as much as we think you will, you'll pay just $4.00 each and save at *least* $.50 each off the cover price. (Your savings are *guaranteed* to be at least $2.00 each month.) There is NO postage and handling – or other hidden charges. There are no minimum number of books to buy and you may cancel at any time.

Send in the Coupon Below

To get your FREE historical romance fill out the coupon below and mail it today. As soon as we receive it we'll send you your FREE Book along with your first month's selections.

Mail To: **True Value Home Subscription Services, Inc., P.O. Box 5235
120 Brighton Road, Clifton, New Jersey 07015-5235**

YES! I want to start previewing the very best historical romances being published today. Send me my FREE book along with the first month's selections. I understand that I may look them over FREE for 10 days. If I'm not absolutely delighted I may return them and owe nothing. Otherwise I will pay the low price of just $4.00 each: a total $16.00 (at least an $18.00 value) and save at least $2.00. Then each month I will receive four brand new novels to preview as soon as they are published for the same low price. I can always return a shipment and I may cancel this subscription at any time with no obligation to buy even a single book. In any event the FREE book is mine to keep regardless.

Name _____

Street Address _____ Apt. No. _____

City _____ State _____ Zip _____

Telephone _____

Signature _____
(if under 18 parent or guardian must sign)

Terms and prices subject to change. Orders subject to acceptance by True Value Home Subscription Services, Inc.

11684-X